"Do you know what I'd like to do right now?"

Faith shook her head in response to Ben's question. Her teeth closed on her lower lip, betraying nerves.

"I want to take you home with me and tuck you into my bed for a nap. I want to lie there next to you." Ben wouldn't even have to be touching her. He'd be satisfied to watch her sleep.

Color touched her cheeks and he thought he saw yearning in her eyes before they shied from his. "That's just weird."

He smiled at her. "Maybe. Of course, that's not all I want, but it would be a start. Just... knowing you were sleeping soundly, right there next to me."

"I don't understand you," Faith whispered.

His own voice low and husky, Ben said, "I'm willing to give you a chance to, any time you're ready."

Dear Reader,

The relationship between twins is a fascinating one often explored in fiction. The extremely close bond that sometimes exists, especially between identical twins, is hard for those of us not born a twin to understand. I, of course, like to focus on relationships that have gone bad. It intrigued me to imagine twin sisters with completely different needs. One craves the closeness born in the womb. The other is, almost from birth, horrified to see this other person who is a reflection of her. How can they help but hurt each other, no matter how much they also love each other?

And what's going to happen to these two women, whose ability to love each other has been damaged, when later they fall in love with the heroes? Wonderful questions I loved exploring.

Because Charlotte's and Faith's lives are so entangled, their stories had to be as well. I'm just glad the two books are coming out in back-to-back months! The first THE RUSSELL TWINS story, *Charlotte's Homecoming,* was released in July 2010, and now you have Faith's story.

Enjoy!

Janice Kay Johnson

P.S. If you want to write, please do so c/o Harlequin Books, 225 Duncan Mill Road, Toronto, ON M3B 3K9, Canada.

Through the Sheriff's Eyes
Janice Kay Johnson

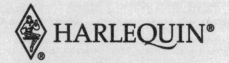

HARLEQUIN®

TORONTO • NEW YORK • LONDON
AMSTERDAM • PARIS • SYDNEY • HAMBURG
STOCKHOLM • ATHENS • TOKYO • MILAN • MADRID
PRAGUE • WARSAW • BUDAPEST • AUCKLAND

Recycling programs
for this product may
not exist in your area.

ISBN-13: 978-0-373-71650-0

THROUGH THE SHERIFF'S EYES

ABOUT THE AUTHOR

The author of more than sixty books for children and adults, Janice Kay Johnson writes Harlequin Superromance novels about love and family—about the way generations connect and the power our earliest experiences have on us throughout life. Her 2007 novel *Snowbound* won a RITA® Award from Romance Writers of America for Best Contemporary Series Romance. A former librarian, Janice raised two daughters in a small rural town north of Seattle, Washington. She loves to read and is an active volunteer and board member for Purrfect Pals, a no-kill cat shelter.

CHAPTER ONE

BEN WHEELER HATED TO fail at anything.

He hadn't made a habit of it in his seventeen-year career in law enforcement. Oh, there'd been screwups, sure. Like the one that had landed him in the ICU for a week with a bullet hole in his gut. But that time, he'd taken down the guy who shot him and a second one who'd been *about* to shoot him, so he couldn't exactly call it a failure. He'd lived, they'd died. And naturally, there were cases—particularly in Homicide—that had gone cold, which he hated.

But failing to find an ordinary guy... Not a professional hit man or anything like that, not someone who knew how to disappear as a career skill. Nope, just a sleaze who'd abused his wife and, now that she'd left him, wanted to teach her a vicious lesson. Ben couldn't think of an excuse in the world for his failure to locate Rory Hardesty and put the son of a bitch behind bars.

His fingers flexed on the steering wheel despite the brief glower he gave them. He wished like hell there was a different, logical route to take into West Fork—one that wouldn't add fifteen minutes or more to the drive.

One that wouldn't take him past the Russell Family Farm, coming up on the right once the highway rounded a curve that followed the river.

Every time he saw the damn farm, he was slapped in the face with the reminder that he'd failed.

Was still failing.

He should have been able to keep Faith and Charlotte Russell from being terrorized and hurt.

He'd spent this afternoon in Everett helping train volunteers for a program that kept first-time juvenile offenders out of the court system. He was giving his time generously because he believed in preventative law enforcement. Nip crime in the bud, so to speak. Make teenage offenders who'd surrendered to an impulse to shoplift or threaten someone face sober citizens from their own community who could assign real-life punishment while also offering the kind of attention and caring the court system couldn't. The kids who took the opportunity seriously wouldn't have the crime on their records. Ben liked the concept.

He'd keep his gaze straight ahead as he passed the farm, he told himself. Allow no more than a brief glance, to be sure there wasn't an ambulance or police car with flashing lights there to signal trouble. Not that there would be at this time of day—Hardesty liked the midnight hour.

Less than half a mile past the Russell farm, the highway led into the small town of West Fork in the foothills of Washington's Cascade Mountains.

Ben's town now, although he didn't know yet whether it would be permanent. He'd taken the job as police chief a year ago and still hadn't decided whether the decision had been good or lousy. Life was undeniably more peaceful here than it had been in Los Angeles. *Peaceful,* however, could be considered a euphemism for boring. He hadn't made up his mind which it was.

For a man who had worked his way up from a street officer in the LAPD to a lieutenant in Homicide via long stretches undercover in Vice, spending his days worrying about a chain saw stolen from a rental outfit or graffiti on the high-school gym wall felt unreal. Most of his officers were young and inexperienced, not toughened by ten years or more of urban crime like the homicide detectives who'd worked under him in Los Angeles had been. These days, the most dangerous place he stepped into was the city council chamber. He and the conservative, unimaginative idiots who made up the council did not see eye to eye on most issues. Unfortunately, he was dependent on them for his paycheck and continued employment.

Although Ben had been feeling satisfied with his afternoon's accomplishments, he'd been growing increasingly tense from the minute he'd left the courthouse in Everett. All because he'd have to pass the Russells' place, which made him think about Rory Hardesty, about Charlotte, and most of all about Charlotte's identical twin sister, Faith, who was Hardesty's ex. The two were twenty-nine, he knew; Faith had lived in West Fork her entire life except for the four years of college, while Charlotte had come home only recently to help Faith and their dad.

His squad car came abreast of the cornfield within which Faith had designed a maze that was a huge hit with area teenagers. Then he passed the handpainted signs strung along the highway, promising Antiques! Fresh Organic Produce! Plant Nursery! Local Arts & Crafts! Corn Maze! It was about the same time he'd moved to West Fork that the Russell Family Farm had been converted from real agriculture to primarily retail. Whether the farm/store/nursery amalgamation was doing well enough to keep the property from being sold off as neighboring ones had been, he had no idea.

Ben was startled to see that his turn signal was on and he was slowing. What in hell? He'd been avoiding the farm and Faith Russell in particular for weeks now. He had no new information to offer her.

But, damn it, here he was turning in anyway, pulling into the hard-packed dirt parking lot in front of the nearly one-hundred-year-old barn that housed the retail business.

Faith's Blazer was parked beside her father's battered pickup truck up by the two-story yellow farmhouse. It was late enough in the afternoon that she was home from the elementary school, where she taught kindergarten. He knew she came straight home every day, changed clothes, then went straight to work at the barn, taking over from the part-time employee who filled in days when Charlotte wasn't able to. Don Russell, the twins' father, had been injured in early August when the tractor had rolled on him. Now, in October, he was becoming more mobile, but was still on crutches and couldn't be of much help to his daughters in keeping the farm going. Ben had seen the strain on his face; Russell felt guilty as hell that his land, his farm, was still in the family only because Faith was willing—no, determined—to work herself to the bone to save it.

Russell wasn't the only one feeling guilty. If only Ben could find and arrest Faith's ex-husband, that would take a hell of a lot of pressure off her.

A van and a car were parked in front of the barn, which meant Faith had some business. He parked beside the car and, after a moment, got out.

Spiky purple asters bloomed in the narrow bed in front of the barn, as did a clump of sunflowers at the corner. A scarecrow sat atop a bale of straw right outside the barn doors. Sheaves of dried cornstalks and a couple of pumpkins added to the Halloween appeal. Between the corn maze, the pumpkin fields and the wagon rides, Halloween was big for the Russells.

Damn it, what was he *doing* here?

He knew the sight of him upset Faith. She probably wasn't any happier to see him than she would have been to see her ex-husband stroll in.

Her divorce had been final over a year ago. The marriage had lasted three years, and resulted in only one police report, after Hardesty had beaten Faith so viciously she'd have died if a neighbor hadn't called 911. He'd gone—too briefly—to jail, and she had left him. What little Ben knew of the marriage had come from Charlotte, who'd told him that the final beating had been the worst, but not the first. Hardesty had hurt his wife over and over again. Until that last time, she'd lied when she got medical treatment for broken bones and concussion. Forgiven him again and again. Intellectually, Ben knew how the dynamic of an abusive relationship worked and why the women often came to think they were at fault and deserved the punishment. Textbook info aside, he still didn't really get it.

Sometime this past summer, Hardesty had apparently gotten over any sense of shame and decided Faith should be ready to forgive him again and come back to him. When it became clear that wasn't happening, he'd gotten mad.

First, in August, came a middle-of-the-night arson fire that did some damage to the barn. That was when

Ben had met the Russell sisters. A week or so later, a cherry bomb was lobbed through the dining room window when both women were sitting at the table. Ben had arrived to find Faith white with shock, her silken skin bristling with shards of glass from the shattered window. She'd been virtually deaf for nearly a day after the explosion and was damn lucky her eardrums hadn't been permanently damaged.

Hardesty hadn't gone back to his apartment, hadn't shown up to work the next day. He'd vanished—until the night he broke into the farmhouse and attacked Charlotte, thinking she was Faith. Concussed and with an eight-inch-long gash from a knife, Charlotte had gone to the hospital.

"Rory wouldn't have hurt Charlotte on purpose," Faith had insisted. "Only me."

As if that made it all right. Ben hadn't quite managed to hide his rage, he knew, remembering the way her eyes had dilated when she'd seen his expression.

Ben muttered an obscenity under his breath and felt like a fool, standing here outside the barn, afraid to go in.

Only, he told himself, because he didn't want to upset Faith.

Too bad he knew a lie when he heard one, even when he was the one telling it.

Still asking himself what he was doing here, Ben stepped inside, then paused to let his eyes adjust to the dim light. Small windows let in some sunlight, and double doors thrown open on one side of the barn to allow customer access to the nursery area outside made a bright rectangle.

The space in here was divided by open shelving units

built of rough wood that sectioned off garden supplies from art and antiques from produce. In the middle of the barn, a large counter held displays of hand-canned jams and jellies as well as an old-fashioned cash register.

No one was behind the register. His eye was caught by a woman picking through a bin of Yukon Gold potatoes and filling a bag. He recognized her from the library, where she worked.

Ben nodded. "Ms. Taylor."

A potato in her hand, she looked up, momentarily apprehensive. "Chief Wheeler. Oh, dear. I hope you're not here because there's a problem?"

"No, I came to speak to Ms. Russell or her father. Whoever's handy." He smiled. "I might buy some of that raspberry jam while I'm here."

"It's divine, isn't it?" She laughed. "I think Faith is outside helping someone."

"Thanks."

He was halfway across the barn when Faith and a pair of women came in from the nursery area. Faith was pulling a flatbed cart with half a dozen large, potted shrubs on it. With her head turned away as she said something to the other women, she didn't see Ben immediately.

Oh, hell, he thought, frozen in place.

He never got over the shock of the first sight of her. She was so damn beautiful. More than that, she made him think about sunshine, golden roses in bloom and picket fences. Home, the kind he'd never had. She was grace and sweetness.

All good reasons for him to stay away from her. He wasn't the man for a woman like her, not after the life he'd led. Growing up first with a drug-addict mother, then in foster homes, going straight into the ugly world of inner-city law enforcement—these things didn't make for a man who could be domesticated enough to belong behind a picket fence.

But damn it, sometimes he just wanted to look at her. To drink in the sight of her corn-silk blond hair, worn most often in a braid that hung down her back or flopped over one slender shoulder. The delicate, beautifully sculpted lines of her face and her pretty mouth. Her eyes—God, her eyes, a blue richer than the sky. Her slim body, endless legs, long-fingered hands he could all too easily imagine touching the five-year-olds she taught every day as she gently guided them.

And yeah, he could imagine those hands touching him, too, although most of the time he didn't let himself.

This, of course, was why he'd stopped by today. To see her. Nothing else.

He'd gotten himself breathing again when her head abruptly turned and her startling eyes gazed right into his. They widened and darkened, and he'd have sworn color rose in her cheeks.

God, he thought. *She thinks I have news about Hardesty.*

He was deluding himself if he thought she was reacting to him sexually. Hell, no; he was fated only to be the bearer of tidings, good or ill, as far as Faith Russell was concerned.

It didn't help that he was wearing his uniform. That was another thing different for him here in West Fork. He'd been on one plainclothes assignment or another for his last ten years in L.A. There, the uniform got taken out of mothballs mainly when he had to attend funerals. Now he embodied the police department in this town, so he wore a uniform most days. It felt both constricting and conspicuous to him. Conspicuous, of course, was the point.

"Ms. Russell," he said in an easy voice. "Ladies. Looks like you're in for some fall planting."

"It's the best time to put in shrubs and trees," one of them told him. She studied him with interest. "You're Chief Wheeler, aren't you? I've been wanting to talk to you about the proposed skateboard park. I know there's some controversy about it…."

Smiling an apology at Faith, he drew the woman aside and, while her friend paid for the shrubs, let her say her piece. He recognized her name once she introduced herself. Sonja Benoit managed the video-rental store in town, while her husband owned a car dealership. They had two teenage sons, which might have been why Sonja had gotten involved in the grand plans to build the skateboard park on a vacant lot near the high school. It might also be, he speculated, that Guy Benoit was fed up with chasing skateboarders off the grounds of his dealership.

By the time Sonja was satisfied that her committee had his support, her friend was pulling the cart outside and Faith was ringing up the potatoes, corn and lettuce for Ms. Taylor, the library clerk. A moment later, he and Faith were alone. Dust, shimmering in the sunlight, billowed out front as the two vehicles reversed.

Faith turned to look at him as he walked toward her. Her face was nearly expressionless. "Do you have news, Chief Wheeler?"

Not Ben. She hadn't called him Ben in weeks.

"No," he said quietly. "I didn't mean to alarm you. I

only stopped by to be sure you're all right, and that you haven't heard from Hardesty."

A shadow passed over her eyes, as if a cloud had blocked the sun from a lake's surface. But after a moment she shook her head. "If I could tell you how to find him, don't you think I would?"

No, he wasn't sure at all. He was very much afraid that Faith still had mixed feelings about her ex-husband. Despite what that scum had done to her, she was the kind of woman who believed in redemption and who wanted to forgive.

Granted, ultimately she'd divorced him. But Ben had asked himself, what was to say she didn't still want to believe that the man she'd married—and presumably once loved—was really a decent guy, somewhere deep inside? Ben had seen a photo of her taken at the hospital after the brutal beating. The mere idea of Faith, battered and bloodied and bruised, made a tide of violence rise in him.

She would only withdraw further from him if she knew what he was thinking, though, so all Ben could do was say, "Yeah. That doesn't mean he hasn't left a message or sent you some kind of little reminder."

If he hadn't been looking closely, he might have missed seeing her flinch. She suppressed it quickly and managed to stare straight at him.

"I'll let you know if I hear from Rory."

God damn it. She did know something.

But he only nodded brusquely. "All right." He cleared his throat. "Are you still getting some time in at the gun range?"

"Yes, but not as much." She made a helpless gesture. "I'm…pretty busy."

Yeah, that was one way to put it. She was working full-time as a teacher and running a business, too. Not to mention caring for her father. She looked more worn down every time he saw her. Sooner or later, he was afraid, she'd break.

The thought made him feel sick and helpless, and roughened his voice. "Do you keep the gun with you?"

She nodded. "It's in my purse behind the counter."

He had mixed feelings about the idea of her owning a handgun at all. Like most cops, Ben would have been happiest if no civilians were armed. In Faith's case, he was far from convinced that she'd have what it took to shoot her ex-husband. On the other hand, twenty-four-hour-a-day protection for her wasn't an option, and if Ben knew one thing, it was that Hardesty would be back. His attacks had escalated. He wasn't done.

Ben frowned. "It would be better if you had it on you."

"I don't have enough cleavage to tuck it in my bra," Faith snapped. "Sorry."

No, she didn't have big breasts, but he liked what she had just fine. More than fine. She was long and limber and sexy.

He was very careful not to let his gaze drop to her body, although he was painfully aware of it and how little she wore. The summer heat wave had persisted into October, and it was too damn hot in here for her to wear an overshirt to conceal any kind of holster. The snug-fitting cropped chinos she wore with a cap-sleeved T-shirt that barely touched the waistband of her pants left nowhere to hide anything.

He thrummed with the effort it took *not* to look.

"Rory wouldn't dare attack me in here, anyway," she said, and Ben realized she was blushing. He wondered what she'd seen on his face.

"The time he walked in here and your sister ordered him off the property, she thought he'd have hit her if Gray hadn't come in."

Gray Van Dusen was another sore point for Ben. He was the mayor of West Fork who had hired Ben as a big-city cop to keep this small town safe. Gray had been enraged when Ben had failed to prevent Charlotte from being attacked and hurt—it so happened that Mayor Van Dusen was deeply in love with Charlotte Russell.

Ben didn't have many friends who weren't cops, but he'd thought Gray might be one. No chance of that anymore. The tension between them hadn't yet gotten in the way of their working relationship, but sooner or later it would if not resolved.

"I'm rarely alone for more than a few minutes," Faith said. "And I promise you, if I see Rory walk in I'll head straight to the counter and grab the gun."

"What do you do at night?"

"I put it under my extra pillow."

He hated the idea of her having to snuggle up in bed with a Colt .38. His voice had descended to a growl when he said, "I suppose you can't carry a handgun at school."

Faith looked shocked. "I hope you wouldn't seriously suggest that!"

He reached up and kneaded the taut muscles in his neck. "No. You should be safe there, anyway."

"You know, he might have given up. Or…shocked even himself, when he saw what he'd done to Charlotte. That's what—" She stopped so abruptly, his eyes narrowed.

"What?"

Her pupils dilated. "I was just going to say, that's what I think."

Uh-huh, sure she was. Damn it, had she talked to the scum and wasn't admitting it? Why?

"I saw the pictures that were taken the night you came into Emergency," he said flatly. "I've seen damn near everything, and those shocked me. Seems what he did to you didn't shock him. Don't kid yourself—all he's doing is lying low."

She stared at him for a stricken moment, then turned and walked away.

Swearing under his breath, Ben followed. "Faith…"

Radiating anger and pain, she spun to face him. "Why are you here?"

To see you. To know you're okay, if not happy.

"I'm doing my job."

"Scaring me? Trying to intimidate me? That's your job?"

He willed his expression to go blank. "I have never, and will never, try to intimidate you. Scare you, yes. Until you're willing to admit Hardesty is capable of really hurting you…"

A shudder ran through her, and then she was screaming at him, "I believe it! I saw what he did to Charlotte! I know what he did to me!" She swallowed. Ended in a whisper. "Do you think I wasn't there?"

He couldn't stand it. Ben reached out to pull her against him.

Faith backed away so fast she bumped against one of

the stools behind the counter. When he took another step toward her, she whipped behind the stool and gripped it with both hands as if she was prepared to brandish it like a lion tamer to hold him off. Her eyes were wild.

"I want you to leave."

"I didn't mean to…"

"Now."

God. Feeling as though his chest was being crushed— as if *he'd* been the one under the tractor, not Don Russell—Ben backed away.

"I'm sorry, Faith," he said, throat feeling raw.

She didn't say anything, only stared at him with that same angry ferocity. He'd been right; she didn't like him any better than she did her ex-husband.

No, Ben realized, as he made himself turn away and walk toward the open barn door, right now she hated him even more than she did Rory Hardesty. She still had a habit of softening sometimes where Hardesty was concerned. Pretty clearly, she'd be happiest never to see Police Chief Ben Wheeler ever again.

That, he thought grimly, was one thing he could do for her. Stay away.

Unless he could bring her the news that Hardesty was behind bars.

Or until a 911 call came in some night after Faith's ex-husband returned to make sure no one else could have what he couldn't.

Ben didn't look back. He got in his patrol unit and sat behind the wheel while he calmed himself enough to drive without killing someone.

He was scared in a way he didn't ever remember being before. Scared that the next time he saw Faith Russell, she'd be lying battered and bloody on a gurney—or dead, being fitted into a body bag.

It was a good five minutes before he could back out and drive away.

CHAPTER TWO

FAITH MADE IT THROUGH the day, and the next day, on sheer willpower alone. She didn't know why Ben Wheeler's visit had shaken her so badly, but it had.

He had.

From the minute she'd seen West Fork's new police chief, she'd tumbled hard. It would be silly to call what she'd felt love, but it was more than lust. Maybe it was most accurate to say she'd known right away that she *could* love him. The shocking thing was, she'd never felt anything so potent and next-thing-to-painful for Rory. Rory and she had dated for over a year before he'd asked her to marry him. She'd liked him, felt comfortable with him. He'd felt right, as if he fit into the life she wanted.

Ben, Faith had known from the first moment, could blast her life as she knew it to smithereens.

In fact, he'd hurt her right away by asking Charlotte, not her, out to dinner. For all the troubles that lay between Faith and her twin, jealousy over a man had never been an issue. That night, while her sister was out with Ben, Faith had sat at home and burned with envy.

She still didn't quite know what had happened between them, only that Char had said there weren't any sparks. She'd been convinced that Ben was really interested in Faith and not her. Sometimes, Faith thought that, too. The night when Rory had tossed the cherry bomb through the window, Ben had seemed to have eyes for no one but Faith. He'd cradled her on his lap while the medic plucked shards of glass out of her flesh, and he'd rushed her to the hospital himself. His tenderness had made her feel safe.

But it seemed as if every time he held her and comforted her, he regretted that he had. She'd never seen a face close down tight the way Ben's could.

Either he felt nothing for her, or he didn't like what he did feel and refused to act on it. Either way, seeing him *hurt.*

She might have told Ben about Rory's last phone call if only he wasn't always so irritated with her, so scornful. She knew he didn't understand any more than her own father and sister did why she had endured three years of marriage to a man who was abusing her. She despised herself enough, thank you; she didn't have to spend time with a man who believed she was so spineless, he had to bully her into defending herself from Rory.

That was why she'd bought the handgun, why she'd spent a total of thirty-six hours to date shooting at the range. She *would* defend herself, and Daddy and Char, too, if they were in Rory's way. Faith still felt queasy every time she picked up the Colt .38, but her hands were steady when she lifted it and aimed, and she could rip the heart out of the target.

Char was always the one who'd been adventurous, strong. Faith was the timid twin, the compliant one. The one easily wounded.

The perfect sucker for a man like Rory Hardesty, she knew now.

The worst thing about seeing Ben this time, she thought, was that she'd had to lie to him. Rory *had* called, a couple of weeks after he broke into the house and slashed Charlotte with the knife thinking she was Faith.

During the phone call, he'd sounded relieved to hear that Char had recovered. He claimed that he wouldn't be moving back to West Fork. He'd sounded truly sorry for scaring her, and for what he'd done to Char.

The only thing was…his tone had changed at the end of the conversation. He'd asked if he could come see her if he was back in West Fork visiting. She told him no, and to add weight to her refusal said she was in love with someone else. His voice had changed after that.

"What about your wedding vows?" he'd asked. "Do you ever think about what you promised?"

She'd clutched the phone, thinking about all the times she'd forgiven him. About how close she had come to dying at his hands, which would have released her from her vows in a final way. And she didn't say a word.

But he did. "I don't like the idea of you with anyone else, Faith," he'd told her, and she recognized the anger simmering in his voice.

She'd tried to convince herself it wasn't anger, that it was really grief for what he'd been foolish enough to throw away, but she hadn't quite succeeded. It had sounded like a threat to her.

Right after Rory called, Faith hadn't been able to bear even the idea of seeing Ben again, of having to submit to his questions, of having to remember the horrible years of her marriage. Of giving him even more grounds to pity poor Faith Russell, too weak to stand up to a bully. Anyway, what good would it do to tell him?

They already knew Rory was a threat. Ben, especially, was convinced he would be back.

So she hadn't told him about the call, and she wasn't going to now. There wasn't any point, and she had a right to defend herself against Ben as well as Rory.

But he'd known she was hiding something, which brought out the aggressor in him. Faith could tell he'd been determined to make her bare everything to him, every doubt, every fear, every weakness. She'd had no choice but to order him to leave and not come back, even though he meant well in his own way.

She could count only on herself, but that wasn't necessarily a bad thing. Faith had spent a lifetime trying to clutch her twin sister close—so close, she'd driven Char away. And once she had lost her identical twin, she'd grabbed for Rory instead, enduring too much because he was all she had.

Well, she wasn't the same woman now. She and Char had come close to healing their breach, and Faith was truly grateful for that. She wouldn't repeat the mistakes that had alienated them in the first place. Char was mostly living with Gray now, their wedding planned for November. Faith wouldn't let herself lean on her sister. And Daddy was still convalescent—the idea of him trying to protect her really frightened Faith.

Saturday, she decided, she'd see if Char could work for a few hours, freeing her to drive to Everett to get in some practice at the gun range. She hadn't been for nearly a week now, and to stay strong and confident she needed to shoot often. Handling the gun should become second nature.

Thinking about it, Faith picked up the phone and dialed her sister's cell-phone number.

"Sure, Saturday morning is fine," Char said, after being asked. "I was just thinking about you. Any chance you want to go swimming at the river tomorrow after you get home from school? Maybe Marsha could stay a couple of extra hours."

Faith hesitated; even the meager salary she was paying the nice woman who worked Tuesday through Friday at the farm ate into their inadequate profits. But it didn't seem as if she and Char ever had time to do fun things, only the two of them. Gray was such a big part of Char's life now, and Faith couldn't leave Daddy on his own for very long yet, either.

"I'd love to. It's supposed to be hot again tomorrow," she said. "You want to come by and get me?"

"Okay." There was a muffled voice in the background, which Faith assumed was Gray's. Char laughed, then said into the phone, "See you about four?"

"Four," Faith agreed.

THE SIGHT OF HER SISTER in a bikini shocked Charlotte. Faith had lost weight. Too much weight.

Since their late teens, Charlotte had been the skinny one. She'd always had more nervous energy and not much appetite. Later, she'd deliberately lost weight— part of her strategy along with dying her blond hair dark—to ensure that she and Faith couldn't be mistaken for each other. She had hated being an identical twin, having another person who looked so much like her. Some of her earliest memories were of throwing gigantic temper tantrums when their mother tried to dress them the same. Too much of her life had been consumed by her near-frantic need to separate herself from her sister.

When she'd come home almost two months ago, Charlotte had realized that next to her sister she looked bony. Urban angular, she'd convinced herself. But, darn it, the food was better here at home. Corn fresh from the field, real butter from a local dairy, bacon and eggs for breakfast instead of a hasty bowl of cereal. She'd been gaining weight ever since, while Faith, stressed almost past bearing, had been losing it.

Charlotte just hadn't realized how much, until now.

She had the sense not to say anything. Faith had reason to be scared. Reason, irrational though it would seem to most anyone else, to be driving herself so hard to try to save the family farm. With the fabric of her life so torn after Mom's death four years ago, the failure of her marriage and now Rory's cruel and terrifying attacks, Faith had to hold on to the one solid piece of her life that she could: home. The heritage they'd both grown up taking for granted.

Daddy, Charlotte believed, was ready to let the farm go. Neither of his daughters could imagine what he'd do if it was sold and carved up into a housing development, but Charlotte could tell he was uneasy with the theme-park kind of farm Faith had created and with the retail business that brought in most of the income. No matter what, Don Russell would never be a real farmer again. He was tired. Once he'd have bounced back quickly from the kind of injuries he'd suffered when the tractor had rolled on him. Fifty-nine years old now, he was struggling with the pain and the limited mobility and the indignity of having his daughters have to care for him like a baby in the first weeks.

Because she understood her sister, Charlotte was doing her best to help. She had accepted a job with an

Eastside software company in part because she could do a fair amount of the work from home. She was putting in several hours every evening so that she could fill in a few mornings a week at the farm. Gray didn't mind, overwhelmed as he was with his part-time mayor, part-time architect gigs, which he said felt more like full-time mayor, full-time architect. He often worked evenings, too.

Charlotte knew that she could help her sister and father only so much, but she should have noticed how Faith's weight was plummeting. Instead of just helping out at the farm, maybe she should have suggested more fun outings. Did Faith ever *have* fun anymore?

As always, they had made their way upriver, over a tumble of boulders and under the railroad bridge, to a favorite spot that was private and offered a pool deep enough to allow them to cannonball off a rock into the water. The river was running even lower than it had been the last time they'd been here, she noticed as they waded in. Winter had been unusually dry this year, so there wasn't much snowmelt to run off.

The water was cold enough to discourage any sane person from wanting to plunge in. Inch by inch, was her plan—one Faith ruined by splashing her. Of course she splashed back, and pretty soon they were both immersed to the neck and squealing as they waited for their bodies to grow numb.

"See? Isn't it better this way?" Faith finally claimed.

"Yeah, right."

Faith rolled onto her back to float. After a minute, sounding a little guilty, she said, "You still don't have a dress."

Charlotte steadfastly refused to go shopping for a wedding dress without her sister, but Faith never seemed to have a minute to spare.

"Not this weekend." Faith was still floating, her fat, wet braid drifting beside her like kelp. "But maybe next weekend."

"Okay," Charlotte said softly, knowing Faith probably couldn't hear her with her ears beneath the water.

The wedding she and Gray were planning would be simple. She had no intention of spending thousands of dollars on a dress, and she wasn't the type for flounces or pearl-encrusted fabric, anyway. How hard could it be to find something simple and ready-made? Not that she would dare say that aloud. Faith was more interested in the details of the occasion than Charlotte was. She had always enjoyed planning all the details of parties. Faith cared about things like flowers and a cake. Thank goodness she hadn't offered her own wedding dress, assuming she'd kept it. Charlotte found herself hoping Faith had trashed it, hateful symbol that it must seem to her.

Eventually they got out of the water and lay in the sun, talking idly. Faith told her sister about this year's crop of kindergarteners, which included the requisite couple of hellions, a few kids who, in her opinion, shouldn't have started for another year and two girls who were already reading at a first-grade level or beyond. Charlotte was still feeling her way around in her new job; she'd been working on computer-security projects before, but was now helping enhance already successful management software with on-demand customization capabilities. Mostly she told Faith about the personalities in the office.

Faith asked lazily, "Do you and Gray want to come to dinner this weekend? Sunday, maybe? Dad likes Gray, you know."

Charlotte laughed. "I know. But then, *everyone* likes Gray. How else do you think he got elected to office?"

Faith laughed, too. "You're right. *I* like Gray."

Actually, she and Gray had gone out a couple of times, some months before Charlotte had come home. They'd liked each other; there just wasn't anything else there. And yet, according to Gray, the minute he set eyes on Charlotte, he wanted her. Had maybe even fallen in love with her, although he hadn't called it love for a few weeks. He hadn't even realized Faith and Charlotte were identical twins, maybe because he'd seen through Charlotte's facade from the beginning to who she was beneath. She hadn't yet quit marveling at the knowledge that he loved her—she wasn't sure she'd ever be able to. It was a miracle that he did, and that she'd been able to let herself love him in return.

"Have you seen Ben lately?" Charlotte asked.

As if by chance, Faith turned her head away, pillowing it on her arms. "Um. He came by a couple days ago. No news. He seemed annoyed that I don't carry my gun in a holster at all times."

"Oh, sure." Charlotte eyed the back of her sister's head. "You don't have it with you now, do you?"

There was a moment of silence. "In my beach bag."

"You're kidding."

Faith rolled over then sat up, her gaze level. "Nope. I carry it everywhere. Except school, of course. Then I lock it in the car, in the glove compartment."

Charlotte looked at the lemon-yellow-and-white bag,

repelled at the idea of a handgun nestled inside it alongside the suntan lotion. "Wow. I didn't realize."

"We're all alone here," Faith said, her voice cool and expressionless. "What if Rory showed up right now? Even if we screamed, nobody could get to us in time to help."

Charlotte shifted uneasily and stole a look over her shoulder.

"I'm ready," her sister said with remarkable calm. "I told you that."

Charlotte looked back at her sister's face in awe and disquiet. Had Faith really changed so much? Or was the armor she wore no more than a thin crust disguising the vulnerability and fear beneath?

Anger surged through Charlotte. Why couldn't the police find Rory? Was it too much to ask that Faith be able to feel safe?

"Maybe I'll stay at the house tonight," she decided.

Faith only shook her head. "I'm ready," she repeated. "You couldn't do anything."

"I can keep the baseball bat next to the bed."

Faith's mouth curved faintly. She'd been the one ready to swing the bat at Rory's head last time, except that he'd run before she could. "We've changed the locks," Faith said, "and Dad should hear if Rory breaks a window." He was still sleeping downstairs, in the hospital bed they had rented when he came home after he was hurt. He could probably manage the stairs now with his crutches, but why should he?

"Maybe," Charlotte said doubtfully. "The way he snores, how *can* he hear anything else?"

They both giggled. As long as they could remember, Dad had been insisting that he didn't snore. Mom always said she'd tape him some night, but she never had, and somehow teasing him about it didn't feel right without Mom here. Some nights this past summer Charlotte had even taken comfort from the familiar sound drifting upstairs.

"Maybe you and Dad should come stay at Gray's, just until Ben finds Rory," she suggested. She'd tentatively talked to Gray and he was willing, even though the two of them loved the time they had together, without anyone else.

"I let him terrorize me for three years," Faith said, sounding completely inflexible. "I won't let him make me go into hiding, Char. Anyway... How long would we have to stay with you and Gray? Two weeks? Two months? What if Rory never comes back? Or if he waits until Daddy and I go home again? No. I appreciate the offer, but it's not necessary."

Charlotte found her eyes resting on the tote bag, with its sunny colors and a semiautomatic pistol tucked inside. Faith followed her gaze, as if understanding what she was thinking. Her expression stayed resolute, almost stony. It was as if her weight loss was a manifestation of what was happening to her—Faith's soft, gentle nature had hardened, as though baked in a kiln, the process altering her very substance.

Uneasily, Charlotte thought about how little it took to shatter kiln-fired stoneware.

Suppressing a shiver, she said, "If you change your mind, you're always welcome. Even in the middle of the night. Okay?"

Faith reached out and hugged Charlotte, pressing her cheek to her sister's. "Thank you," she whispered. "I love you, Char."

"And I love you," Charlotte whispered, too, thankful that the words came so readily these days, a balm to soothe the hurt of ten years of estrangement.

Cold prickles walked up her spine as she thought about how precious their restored bond was. She could lose her sister so quickly if Rory stole into the farmhouse some night and slipped into Faith's bedroom without waking her. A gun would do no good at all, if she didn't have time to reach for it.

FAITH SHOWERED before bedtime to cool down, even though she had been swimming in the river only a few short hours ago. The day's heat had risen in the house, found no escape. Despite the fan in her bedroom and the fact that she'd wrestled her sash window up, she was toying with the idea of taking a pillow and sheet downstairs and sleeping on the sofa in the living room with Dad.

If only he didn't snore…

She had always enjoyed hot weather; she'd even thought that if it weren't for Daddy and the farm she might have liked living in southern California or the Southwest. The idea was one she played with while waiting for sleep some nights. Starting anew where no one knew her both appalled and intrigued her. It would be so lonely, but also—she had thought a long time about the right word to describe the shimmer of excitement she felt, and settled on one—*liberating*. When she was younger, that kind of freedom had held no appeal. After the years of her marriage, though, she'd begun to imagine what it would be like to stand entirely, selfishly alone. To be the quintessential island.

It was only a fantasy, of course. She had a feeling she

would wither and die if she truly found herself plunked down in Phoenix, say, knowing no one, unfettered by any ties.

And yet, sometimes she was so very tired.

She had gradually turned the water temperature colder and colder, and now it rained down on her, nearly icy. With a sigh, Faith turned the shower off and stepped out shivering. She towel-dried, then brushed her hair and plaited it with practiced hands. She knew from experience it would still be damp come morning, and help keep her cool.

Momentarily, head tilted as she gazed at herself in the mirror, Faith wondered what she'd look like if she cut her hair boyishly short, like Char's. She laughed at herself. Silly—she'd look exactly like Char! Except different, really. She had become aware these past two months that they might be identical twins, but they didn't move alike or laugh alike or even make the same gestures. Passing as each other wouldn't be easy, as it had been when they were mischievous children.

Rory wouldn't like it if I cut my hair.

Faith went still, looking at herself in the steam-misted mirror. Her eyes had widened, the shade of blue deepening, as she did battle with the tight knot of fear that had ruled her for too long.

"I should cut it," she whispered. "Because."

No. She shouldn't do anything at all because Rory liked it or didn't. If she cut her hair in defiance of him, she would be giving him more weight than he deserved.

And *she* liked her hair long. She always had, resisting haircuts while Char had experimented with every length when they were teenagers.

Faith began to breathe again. She wouldn't give Rory any power at all. She'd think about him only as a threat, the reason she would be target shooting tomorrow again.

She went back to her bedroom and found it considerably cooler after the cold shower and with her hair wet and the braid heavy down her back.

Dad had long since fallen asleep. She'd heard the rumble of his snoring as she'd crossed the hall from the bathroom. A farmer his entire life, he rarely stayed awake much past nine o'clock, but he no longer awakened with dawn, and he napped in the afternoons, too. She worried a little about how much he was sleeping, although the doctor insisted that was normal, part of the healing process. She still thought some of it might be depression.

Faith turned off her light and stood for a minute looking out her bedroom window at the cornfield. She could see the highway from here, too, and on the other side of it a glint of river between stands of trees. The moon was nearly full and low in the sky, a buttery yellow that looked mystical but was probably, unromantically, caused by smog in the atmosphere. A month from now, on All Hallow's Eve, it would be a sullen orange, the harvest moon.

She left the curtains open and lay in bed, the covers pushed aside, enjoying the wash of air over her skin as the fan rotated. The faint hum was mesmerizing, a kind of white noise that soothed her. Faith fell asleep to the sound of it.

She never slept soundly anymore. Waking suddenly wasn't unusual. Old houses made noises, and sometimes Daddy got up at night to go to the bathroom. Faith thought it was a creak that she'd heard. She always left her door open now, in case her father needed her. The rectangle was dark, inpenetrable. She lay staring toward it, holding herself very still as she listened intently for the thump of his crutches, or the quiet groan of the hundred-year-old house settling.

Nothing. For the longest time, there was no repetition. Her instinctive tension eased. She began to relax, let the weight of her eyelids sink. She was always so tired....

This creak was closer. On the stairs, or in the hall. Faith went rigid. There was another whisper of sound— something brushing the wall, perhaps.

Her pulse raced and her blood seemed to roar in her ears. Was it Rory? How had he gotten into the house without her hearing glass break? The front and back doors both had dead-bolt locks now.

One hand crept for the cell phone on her bedside table. Before she could touch it, her eyes made out the deeper shadow within the dark rectangle that was the doorway.

It was too late for the phone. Faith eased her hand back, then shoved it beneath the pillow beside her and found the hard, textured grip of the gun.

I'm not ready for this.

She heard breathing now. Her own, but someone else's, too. He had stepped inside the bedroom, almost— but not quite—soundlessly. Not Daddy, no thump or scrape of crutches. The shape took form in moonlight. He was only a few steps from her bed.

Something snapped in Faith, and with a scream of terror and rage she lunged for the lamp switch even as she lifted the gun.

In the flood of light, he threw himself forward, his face contorted and a deadly knife lifted to stab.

Faith went cold. As if she were outside her body, she saw her second hand come up to brace the first, her thumb folding just as it ought to.

Rory was almost on top of her when she squeezed the trigger.

CHAPTER THREE

THE RING OF THE PHONE WOKE Ben with all the subtlety of a bucket of cold water dumped over his head. Cursing, he groped on his bedside table for the damn phone.

"Wheeler," he growled into it.

"Chief, this is Ron Meagher." One of his young officers, greener than baby peas fresh from the pod. "You said to let you know, day or night, if anything comes in about the Russells."

"Yes." He stifled an obscenity and swung his legs to the floor, then turned on the lamp, blinking painfully in the flood of light. "What's happened?"

"We just had a call from Faith Russell. She says she shot her ex-husband."

Damn it, damn it, *damn it*. Ben grabbed the jeans he'd left draped over a chair and yanked them on.

"Is he dead?"

"She seemed to think so. Dispatch said she sounded real cool."

Cool? Faith? Maybe, but beneath the surface she would be dissolving.

"I'm on my way." He dropped the phone and tugged yesterday's T-shirt over his head. Not bothering with socks, he shoved his feet into athletic shoes. Weapon at the small of his back, he snatched his wallet and keys up, then was out the door at a run.

He drove faster than was legal, faster than was safe. The moon was high and silver now, an improvement over the sickly yellow it had been earlier, hanging on the horizon.

Don't let the son of a bitch be dead, he prayed, with scant hope any prayer from him would be answered. He and God weren't on cordial terms. He tried anyway. *Faith can't handle it. Shouldn't have to handle it. Don't let him be dead.*

He didn't pass a single car on the city streets or the highway. Long before he reached the farm, he saw the multicolored, rotating lights of police cars and ambulance.

He tore into the farmyard, heedless of potholes, and came to a skidding stop behind Faith's SUV. The scene was nightmarishly similar to the other time he'd been called out here in the middle of the night, when Charlotte had been battered and slashed.

Please, not Faith, he thought. She was so fragile. Strong, too—more than he'd credited her with on first meeting. But gentle, not made for what she'd suffered.

If she'd really killed Rory Hardesty, that would be much worse for her than being hurt would have been.

Burgess was in the kitchen, along with two EMTs.

"Dead?" Ben asked, and got nods all around.

Burgess kept talking. Ben didn't hear. He walked straight through the dining room to the living room, where he heard voices.

Faith was there, sitting on the sofa beside her father. Meagher, looking about eighteen in his blue uniform, had just asked if she had a license for her gun.

"Yes," Ben said hoarsely. "She has a license."

She looked up at him, but not as if she were glad to

see him. Not as if she felt anything at all. He had seen eyes like that, too often in his years in law enforcement. Utterly and completely empty, as if tonight she had lost her soul. He wanted nothing so much as to sit down and cradle her in his arms, but he had a feeling that if he did he'd be holding a mannequin, not a living breathing woman.

Her father was watching her, his face drawn. He wasn't touching her, and Ben suspected she'd rejected his embrace. She sat with her back straight, her hands quiet on her lap, as if she were a guest not quite comfortable in this home but determined to hide it.

Brushing by his young officer, Ben laid his hand against her cheek, marble cool, and took an icy hand in his. He felt his lips pull back in a snarl. "She's in shock, damn it! Meagher, get her a cup of tea or cocoa or something hot. *Now.*" He turned and, not seeing an afghan, wrenched the comforter from the hospital bed. Her father reached for it and helped him settle it around her shoulders.

"I told you I'm all right," Faith said, words belied immediately when a shiver rattled her body.

"Sure you are," Ben said. He decided he didn't give a damn how stiff she would be in his embrace. He sat next to her and lifted her onto his lap, tucking the comforter around her.

She began to fight him.

"Don't," he said, and tightened his arms.

She struggled for another minute, then subsided when he simply held her close. She shivered again, and her teeth began to chatter. Her father looked on helplessly.

What the hell was Meagher doing? Ben wondered

in raw fury. *How long did it take to heat water in the microwave?*

Waiting, Ben pressed her face into his shoulder and pressed his cheek to her hair. It was damp, he realized, and when he groped under the comforter for her braid he found it to be wet. That wasn't helping. Cheek against the top of her head, he murmured, "I'm sorry, Faith. God, so sorry. You shouldn't have had to face this. I'm sorry, sweetheart."

She didn't say anything, only kept trembling against him, her nose buried in his throat as if she couldn't resist seeking the warmth of his skin.

Ben looked at her father. "Has anyone called Charlotte?"

He started. "No. I'll, uh, do that. I was too worried about Faith...."

Who probably needed her sister more than anyone else in the world. At any other time, Ben might not have liked knowing that, even though he had been very careful to avoid offering himself up as her rock. But right now, all he wanted was to give Faith whatever she needed.

Don Russell levered himself to his feet and, with the help of the single crutch that was within arm's reach, shuffled over to the bedside stand where his phone sat.

Ben could hear his side of the conversation, punctuated with pauses.

"Gray? It's Don. Hardesty got in the house tonight. No, don't know. Faith shot him. She's..." His sidelong survey of his daughter was uneasy. "If Char can come... Okay. Thanks."

He ended the call and met Ben's eyes. "They're on

their way," he said, unnecessarily. Despite a tension between the sisters that Ben had never understood, he sensed that either of them would have gone to Siberia or the Congo or, hell, Timbuktu, for the other without any hesitation. He, who had been essentially alone all of his life, even during his brief marriage, wondered what it would feel like to have someone love you like that.

It was unlikely he'd find out, and seemed even more so with his fortieth birthday looming up ahead.

His body heat seemed to be helping her. Faith's shivers came less often and she was warming up, nose, hands, cheeks. Meagher finally showed up with a mug of cocoa, flushing when he encountered his boss's glower.

Ben shifted Faith, bundled like a mummy in the comforter, to the sofa beside him and helped her grasp the mug. She sipped, and let out a sigh of relief as the hot liquid reached places he couldn't.

Ben stayed where he was, keeping her against his side and reminding her to drink, until a commotion at the back door announced the arrival of Char and Gray. Only then did he murmur in Faith's ear, "Your sister's here," and stand up.

She looked at him for a moment, as if she couldn't help herself. Her eyes were no longer blank, but rather filled with so much emotion, such horror, he almost wished he hadn't stirred her to life again.

Involuntarily he reached out, but the movement was abortive because Char flung herself across the living room and enveloped her sister in her arms.

"Faith. Oh, God. Faith, honey."

Ben backed away, leaving them to it. He had to do

his job. He just wished his chest wasn't so tight with anguish that every breath he drew hurt.

Turning to face Gray didn't help.

Like Ben, Gray Van Dusen was a tall man, over six feet and broad-shouldered. A few years younger—maybe thirty-four, thirty-five—Gray had brown hair streaked lighter by the sun, a pair of level gray eyes and an easy, relaxed style that could morph into hard-ass in an instant. Right now, his pitying gaze shifted from his fiancée's sister and went cold and hard when he looked at Ben.

"What the hell happened?"

"I don't know yet. When I got here, Faith was in shock. I didn't want to leave her until Charlotte could take over."

After a moment, Gray nodded in concession. Faith was more important to him, too, than any investigation.

"I've got to get on with it," Ben said abruptly to the room, and walked past Gray as if he weren't there.

In the kitchen, he determined that Meagher had, astonishingly enough, called for a crime-scene crew—borrowed from the county as the small city of West Fork didn't have much need for one of their own—and the medical examiner. Both were en route, the young officer reported.

Ben nodded and, reluctantly, started upstairs.

Before he'd taken over, West Fork police would have turned the case over to the sheriff's department because they had no officers experienced in homicide investigation. He might yet have to do that, if there seemed to be any doubt about tonight's events—he knew he was emotionally involved, whether he liked to admit it or not. If it turned out the dead man *wasn't* Hardesty, or

Hardesty hadn't been carrying a weapon, things could get messy.

A couple of the steps creaked under his weight. Had Faith's ex spent enough time at the house to know to avoid them? Or were those faint sounds what had woken her?

In the hall at the top of the stairs, the first room on the right was Don Russell's. Unsurprisingly, it had an air of disuse. On the left was Charlotte's, where Ben had talked to her when she was recuperating from Hardesty's last assault. Bathroom beyond, also on the left. And finally, Faith's bedroom.

The door was wide open. The overhead light wasn't on, but the bedside lamp was. Had Faith turned it on? If it was Meagher, if the idiot had done a thing in here but verify Hardesty was dead, Ben would string him up by his thumbs.

Ben pulled on the latex gloves he carried in his glove compartment, but didn't have to touch either knob or door.

The body lay sprawled beside the bed. In fact, the dead man had been so damn close to the bed when the bullet—bullets?—struck, he'd slid down the side of it, fountaining blood on the quilt. Shit, Ben thought; from the quantity of blood, she'd likely gotten him right in the heart.

He pictured her at the range, taking methodical shot after shot, never flinching, her hands steady. Had she been envisioning this moment when she pulled the trigger? Seen her ex-husband in the white paper target?

Reality, Ben had long since learned, was one hell of a lot more brutal than anything the imagination could conjure.

He eased into the room with a sideways step to avoid walking where the intruder had. Sticking to the perimeter, he circled to a position near the foot of the bed and squatted on his haunches so he could see the face.

Rory Hardesty, Ben saw with relief. No mistake there, except on Hardesty's part. He'd misjudged Faith, big-time.

At first Ben couldn't see any weapon, which worried him. Not to say Faith hadn't had reason to shoot the bastard; he'd hurt her badly enough with his bare hands before, and it was well-documented. But this would be cleaner if he'd carried a gun or...

Ah. The knife had fallen out of his hand and lay in the shadow just under the bed. It was an ugly one with a thick black rubber grip, designed for the military or hunters, if Ben was any judge. The blade was at least eight inches long. He was willing to bet it would turn out to be the same knife Hardesty had used on Charlotte.

Oh, yeah. This one was open-and-shut, but he knew that wouldn't make it any easier for Faith to live with what she'd done tonight.

He retreated as carefully as he'd entered the room. Now, how the hell had the son of a bitch gotten in? The easiest way would have been to knock out a pane of glass on the back door and reach in to unlock the new dead bolt, but he hadn't done that. He clearly hadn't made enough noise to wake either Don or Faith until he was upstairs and so close that in another few seconds Faith could have died.

Ben swore under his breath, pausing at the top of the stairs to get a grip on himself. He couldn't let anyone see him falling apart at the idea of that knife descending toward Faith Russell's breast. Or her throat.

Or—God—would Hardesty have wanted to carve up her face to punish her?

He actually shuddered and wanted to go back and kill the bastard all over again. He wished he'd done it in the first place. He could handle killing in a way he was terribly afraid Faith wouldn't be able to. Especially not when the man she'd shot was someone she'd once loved.

Finally confident he could hide everything he felt, Ben went downstairs where both his officers waited with thinly disguised anxiety.

"Have you looked for the point of entry?" he asked.

Both heads bobbed. Burgess and Meagher exchanged a glance. Jason Burgess, who'd been a cop for two whole years, was the one to answer. "Yes, sir. The laundry room, sir."

The door was behind the stairs. The window above the washer and dryer was missing its glass. The frame wasn't large; it would have been a squeeze, but doable. This might have been the only room in the house with a closed door, which would have helped make the entry quiet. Also, Ben determined by prowling, the staircase and a storage space beneath it that was packed with boxes lay between the laundry room and the living room where Don had been sleeping. The pile of boxes would have offered dandy sound insulation.

He went outside, fetched a flashlight from his car and circled the house, where he found a painter's stepladder under the window. The glass had been removed almost whole and leaned carefully against the house. Cut, presumably, although he didn't see a tool.

He wondered if Hardesty had intended to reclaim the

ladder once he was done inside and drive away to start his life anew, freed of his vicious compulsion once Faith was dead. Or would he have sat down on the side of the bed and called 911 himself, then waited for the arrival of the police as domestic abusers who killed sometimes did? Unless he proved to be carrying a handgun, too, which Ben wouldn't know until the medical examiner was done with the body and photographs had been taken, Ben doubted Hardesty had intended to commit suicide, another popular option. Stabbing yourself would be a lot harder to do than pulling a trigger.

Satisfied with this first survey, Ben walked back around the house to find all his guests had arrived. He showed the medical examiner upstairs, and encouraged the crime-scene techs to start outside with the ladder and cut window, then returned to the living room. He hoped Faith was up to talking to him now.

Don was back in his hospital bed, the sheet and a thin blanket over him. On the sofa, Charlotte sat beside Faith, holding her hand. Gray stood with his back to the window, watching the two women. They all looked at Ben when he walked in.

"He got in through the laundry room," he told them. "Took out the window glass neat enough, I'm betting he used a cutter. He either found a stepladder in one of the outbuildings or brought his own. It's still standing under the window."

"We have one," Don said. "It's damn near as old as the girls. Getting pretty rickety. Wood, with lots of paint splatters."

Ben shook his head. "This one's wood, but newish. Maybe he picked it up at his mom's house."

"Oh, no," Faith breathed. "Has anyone told his mother yet?"

Trust her to worry about someone else.

"No," he said. "I'll do that eventually. The medical examiner is here right now, and the photographer is taking pictures. It's going to be a few hours before we can move the body out of here."

Faith seemed to shrink. Ben felt cruel, but had no choice but to keep on being cruel.

"I need to ask you some questions," he said.

She swallowed and raised her gaze to his. "Your, um, officer tried earlier, but I…" She closed her eyes briefly. "I couldn't."

"I understand." He tried to make his deep, rough voice as gentle as possible. "Why don't you just tell me what happened in your own way?"

"Yes. Okay." She did, with some stumbling and halting and trembles. Something had woken her up, she didn't know what. "I haven't been sleeping well," she admitted. "I wake up every time Daddy goes to the bathroom, or a truck rumbles by on the highway, or the house settles."

Ben nodded.

At first she'd thought that's all it was, one of those sighs an old house makes. Then she heard a creak, and what she thought was something brushing the wall outside her bedroom. So she'd reached for her phone.

"And then I saw him in the doorway. It was dark, but he was darker, and I knew it was too late to call anyone." Her breath came in agitated pants. It was all Ben could do to stay five feet away and let Faith's sister comfort her. "I told you I keep my gun under the extra pillow at night."

All he could do was nod again. His entire body seemed to be locked tight, absolutely rigid. All he saw was Faith, her blue eyes dark with remembered fear. He had his back to Don, and Gray and Charlotte were no more than blurs on the periphery of his awareness.

"I pulled it out and lunged to turn on the lamp. He was rushing forward, a knife in his hand. He was almost at the bed…"

Charlotte made a soft sound of distress. Gray jerked, breaking Ben's concentration.

Faith was hunched as small as she could make herself, her gaze still pinned to Ben's as if she couldn't look away. "I pulled the trigger," she finished, barely audible. "Twice. Or…or three times. I don't remember." The blankness was coming back into her eyes, shock tugging her back under. "I saw…blood. He…he staggered and dropped down."

"What did you do then?" Ben asked quietly. His hands, he realized, were balled into fists at his side. He could only imagine what her father was thinking and feeling.

"I screamed and scrambled off the far side of the bed. I fell down. I looked under the bed and I could see him on the other side."

"Your gun?"

"It was still in my hand."

"All right," he said. "Then what?"

"I pushed myself to my feet and made myself circle the bed. I was holding the gun. You know. But my hands were shaking so much, I could see it wavering up and down."

God.

"Did you touch him?"

She shook her head. "I could see his face…." What little color she'd had disappeared, just like that, and suddenly she sprang up. "I've got to… Got to…" She clapped a hand to her mouth and fled.

Char raced after her.

"Couldn't this have waited?" Gray asked.

Ben looked at him. "You know it can't."

He knew he hadn't succeeded in hiding everything he felt. Nobody was that good. Gray studied him for a moment, then dipped his head in acknowledgment.

None of the three men said another word. Five minutes passed before the two women returned, Faith leaning on her sister. "I'm sorry," she whispered, and let herself be settled on the couch again, the comforter wrapped around her.

Without prompting, Faith resumed her tale. "I edged out of the room, even though I wanted the phone on the bedside table. I was afraid to get that close to him. I knew he was dead, but…I guess part of me still thought he'd wake up and grab me. Dumb."

"Not dumb. Smart. He *could* have been faking it. Getting away, calling the police, that was smart."

After a minute she nodded, although Ben doubted she was convinced.

Her voice was grave now, and small, like a child telling a story about something so bewildering and horrific she didn't really understand it herself. "I ran downstairs. I fell the last few steps." Faith paused. "I suppose I'll have bruises. I can't feel anything right now."

"Did you call from the kitchen?"

She shook her head. "Dad was yelling my name and I went to the living room. I told him what I'd done and he said he'd call, but I thought I should do it. And then

I waited here until there were knocks on the back door and someone yelling, 'Police.'"

"The shots are what woke me," her father said, and Ben turned so he could see him. "And Faith screaming." He shuddered, not surprisingly. There was a lot of that going on tonight. "I reached for the phone and managed to knock it to the floor. By the time I got out of bed and found it, Faith had rushed in here." He looked at his daughter. "I took the gun from her. I guess you'll find my fingerprints on it, too. But the way her hand was shaking…"

Ben had already spotted the Colt, lying on the bedside table. "Did you take it by the barrel or by the grip?"

"Ah…" Don mimicked reaching out, and they established that he had never held it by the grip or touched the trigger.

Ben turned back to Faith. "Did you see that it was your ex-husband before you shot him?"

"Yes."

"How was he holding the knife when he came at you?"

She stared at him.

He took the TV remote from the bedside table and demonstrated the two choices, blade pointing up, as Hardesty had undoubtedly held it when he'd sliced Charlotte, or down, with the clear intention of stabbing from above.

Gray moved to lay a big hand on his fiancée's shoulder. He didn't like the memory of what that knife had done to her.

"Down," Faith said, lifting her hand. "He was going to stab me."

"You did what you had to do," Ben told her, as calmly as he could. "You'd be dead if you hadn't shot him."

Unbelievably, she began to shake her head and kept shaking it as if she couldn't stop. "I don't know. Once I turned the light on he must have seen that I had a gun, and that's when he rushed forward so fast. Before that, he might've meant only to scare me."

"You don't believe that," Ben said incredulously over the voices of everyone else's protestations. Her face was still so white, he stepped forward and laid the back of his hand on her cheek. "You're cold again."

Her head was still shaking like a pendulum slowing but far from run down, and she'd started to rock. "I don't know," she whispered. "How can I know?" Her gaze lifted to his. "He's dead? I really killed him?"

"He's dead, Faith. But you have nothing to be sorry for." He crouched in front of her and laid a hand on her knee. "Nothing. Remember how close he came to killing you before you divorced him."

"But he was angry…."

"Remember what he did to Charlotte."

The rocking was becoming more pronounced. "He might have been…"

"Damn it, no!" His sharpness had them all staring. Faith quit rocking. "He was angry this time, too. He came to kill you, Faith. You saved your life, and maybe your father's, too."

He could tell she hadn't considered what Hardesty would have done if Don Russell had confronted him when he came down the stairs.

As if the words were wrenched from her, she said, "I never really believed…"

"You'd have to use the gun?"

She nodded.

Again, there might as well have been no one else in the room. They only looked at each other.

"Didn't you?"

"I did," she whispered brokenly. "But I didn't."

Ben would have given anything to hold her right now, but instead he stayed where he was, squatting in front of her. "You did the right thing," he repeated.

But God almighty, he wished she hadn't had to.

After a minute he took his hand back from her knee and scrubbed it over his face. He rose to his feet and looked at Gray.

"Can you take Faith and Don home with you?"

"I planned to," the other man said, in a way that told Ben exactly nothing about what he was thinking.

From the doorway behind them, someone said, "Chief Wheeler?"

He turned his head. The medical examiner, whom he had met only a couple of times since he'd taken over as police chief in West Fork. "Just a minute," he said, then told Gray, "Watch her for symptoms of shock. She needs to be kept warm."

Gray surprised him then by reaching out and gripping his forearm. One hard squeeze that felt like…sympathy. He'd seen too much, Ben realized.

"We'll take care of her. I assume you'll be by in the morning?" Gray asked.

"Count on it."

"Don't worry about Faith," Gray said. "Do what you have to do."

Ben nodded, allowed himself one more look at Faith's face, white and shell-shocked, and made himself turn and walk out of the room.

CHAPTER FOUR

"I'LL STAY WITH YOU," Char offered, hovering beside the blown-up air mattress in Gray's library. She offered a wavering smile. "Sleepover."

Charlotte had demanded her own bedroom when the twins were ten years old. In the years after that, however, sometimes one sister or the other desperately needed to talk or just to have this one person in all the world close. "Sleepover?" she'd suggest, and they would share a double bed the way they had when they were young. In the trauma of the past couple of months, they'd done that a couple of times. Just the soft sound of Char breathing beside her was a comfort to Faith.

Tonight, Faith wanted no one.

An image of Ben flashed into her mind, and she remembered the way he'd held her cradled on his lap, his hand on her nape, pressing her face against his shoulder. His throat had been so temptingly close, she'd inched her face over to warm her cold nose against his skin and breathe in his scent, soap and sweat and man.

No. She didn't want him, either. But a stricken feeling inside told Faith that she might not have been able to resist him if he'd actually been here.

Faith shook her head. "No, please. I'm not sure I can sleep, and…I need to be alone."

"Are you sure?" Char kept hovering.

"Yes. Please," Faith repeated.

Wearing a pair of flannel pajamas borrowed from Gray, cuffs and sleeves rolled, she sat on the edge of the bed. Despite the hot, sweet tea Char had plied her with, Faith was still cold. She felt chilled to her marrow.

At last her sister nodded reluctantly and hugged her. "Wake me up if you want me, Faith. I mean it. Okay?"

Faith nodded because it was expected of her. "Good night."

Gray, she saw, waited in the hall. He looked as worried as Char did. Faith wondered vaguely what they saw that scared them so. Dad, thank goodness, must have already gone to bed in the guest room. Still recovering from his injuries, he'd needed the better bed.

It was a huge relief when Gray and Char withdrew, turning off the overhead light. She heard them go down the hall to their own bedroom, but there was no click of a door closing—they wanted to be able to hear her. She should have felt reassured, but she didn't. She didn't feel much at all, or at least nothing...normal. There was a hollow place inside her that was new. It was like an ice cave, terribly cold, a place where her breath might freeze.

When Faith lay back on the mattress and pulled the covers over herself, she left the bedside lamp burning. She'd never minded the dark before, but she had a feeling it would be a long time before it would seem comforting to her again.

If ever.

Despite the comforter and the blanket Char had added, Faith shivered.

I'm so cold.

She couldn't seem to tear her eyes from the open door to the hall. When she closed her eyes, she saw the dark rectangle of the doorway to her own bedroom, and then the deeper shadow of a man within it. Her eyes snapped open again.

At last she got up and shut the door. After a minute, she dragged a chair away from the desk and braced it at an angle under the knob. At least nobody could get in without making a lot of noise. She hoped Char wouldn't try and become alarmed.

Back in bed, she pulled the heavy weight of covers up to her chin and lay still, listening to the silence. Gray's house, which he'd designed himself, was new and lacked the old farmhouse's sounds of settling. The silence seemed even denser because the multilayered house was built literally into the bluff, so that this lower floor not only had earth beneath it but behind it. The highway was too far away for her to hear the scant evening traffic. Houses on the river bluff were set far apart, all on at least five acres, with woods in between to muffle any sound of barking dogs, voices or cars coming and going. Faith couldn't decide if the quiet would be soothing or unsettling long-term.

Not that she'd be here for very long. She had to go home soon. Preferably tomorrow. If she put it off, she might lose her nerve. Faith wasn't sure she could ever sleep in her bedroom again, though. She thought she might move into Char's. Char had only been spending the occasional night anyway, and then only because she was anxious about Faith.

For better or worse, Char could quit worrying about Rory.

A shudder gripped Faith, one that rattled her bones.

Oh, God. I killed him. I pulled the trigger.

Even though her eyes were open, she saw his face in that moment, rage transformed into astonishment at the sight of the gun leveled at his chest. And then…and then, fear and pain. Blood blossoming. Him stumbling. Because his momentum continued to drive him forward, she'd shot again. And again, she thought. At least three times. Her ears rang with the *crack, crack, crack.*

Her fingernails bit into her palms as she felt the gun jump in her hands again. So powerful. So lethal. So much more terrible even than she had imagined. Death dealing. Like a movie, images kept running through her mind, inescapable. Blood spurting. The light going out of his eyes even as he stopped abruptly, then dropped, shaking the bed as he toppled against it. *Thump.* The heaviest, darkest sound she'd ever heard.

Faith gasped, shook, clutched the bedcovers with desperate hands. She stared blindly and thought, *What if he came only to threaten me? To try to frighten me into going back to him?*

What if he had never intended to kill her?

She couldn't imagine how she would ever know the answer to that question. How she could live *without* knowing it.

Faith wasn't absolutely sure whether Char and Dad and Gray and Ben really did think she'd defended herself the only way she could, or whether they were just saying that because there was no going back from what she'd done and they were determined to reassure her.

What would she have done if she *hadn't* had the gun beneath the pillow?

Screamed and thrown herself off the bed. Grabbed for a weapon, any weapon. The chair, perhaps, or she would have likely kept the baseball bat close at hand.

Would she have made it off the bed, if the force of the bullets slamming into his chest hadn't slowed Rory's momentum? Shivering, shivering, she didn't know.

She kept replaying it, from the moment she heard the *shush* of something brushing the wall outside her room. What could she have done differently? But it was too late to change anything. Tonight, she had killed. She'd chosen to shoot dead the man she had once believed she loved. The man she'd married.

What about your wedding vows? Do you ever think about what you promised?

She curled into as small a ball as she could manage, hugging herself. *Yes!* she wanted to scream. How could she forget them?

But Rory had made promises, too. He was supposed to cherish her, and he hadn't. He'd hurt her, over and over. Terrified her, stalked her, assaulted Char. Faith wanted, oh, she wanted so much, to believe she'd been right to defend herself in such a final way.

But what if it was all bluster? The time he had almost killed her, his fists rising and falling, slamming into her until she was like Raggedy Ann, bouncing and flopping, her consciousness seeping away, that time he had been in a towering rage. He'd lost all control. He'd wept the next day, she had been told, and said over and over, "I never meant to hurt her. I never meant it." Slipping into her house tonight had been *planned*, which was different. Yes, he'd punched Char the other time, and even lashed out with the knife and cut her, but Charlotte was Charlotte, taunting him. Tonight, he'd had a plan. He had been moving in silence, in the cloak of darkness. What if he had intended only to sit on the edge of the bed, leaning close until an awareness of the mattress dipping awakened her. He might have touched the tip of the knife to her throat while he whispered of his anger. He might have left her eventually, with perhaps a last, near soundless reminder that he could come back any time, that no mere locks would keep him out. That she was *his*.

Faith shook harder. Her teeth chattered now.

Oh God oh God. She couldn't have kept living like that, waiting for him to come back. Even if she'd fled to Phoenix or Tampa Bay, the way she'd sometimes imagined, he could have followed her.

He had no *right*, she told herself fiercely. She would almost rather have died than go on that way, fear hunched beneath her breastbone and rising to clog in her throat. She simply couldn't have borne it.

It was his fault. All his fault that she'd had to kill him.

But she was the one who had to live with it.

Sleep was not going to come to Faith, not now, when only the lamplight held off the darkness, and not later, when the pale light of dawn crept around the edges of the blinds.

How can I ever sleep again? she asked herself, and didn't know the answer.

TELLING A MOTHER that her son had been shot dead was a hell of a way to start a morning. Especially when Ben hadn't made it back to bed last night.

He wasn't surprised when Michelle Hardesty collapsed, wailing. He had to catch her and half carry her to the chintz sofa in the front room of the ranch-style house where she'd raised Rory, her only child.

Thinking that she'd done a helluva bad job didn't keep him from feeling pity. He'd seen enough grief to guess that losing a child might be the worst thing that could happen to a person. Ben had known a cop whose sixteen-year-old daughter had been killed by a drunk driver. Thirty years later, Noah's face still changed when he saw a girl that age. The grief had still been there, and would remain, undulled, for the rest of his life.

Ben was eventually able to determine that she had a sister in Mt. Vernon, whom he called. She was able, thank God, to come immediately, although he had to wait the half hour it took her to drive there. She took over kindly and efficiently. When he left, she was rocking her sister in her arms and murmuring, "Oh, Chelle. I'm sorry. So sorry. That's it, cry. It'll do you good. Cry."

Profoundly relieved to have escaped, Ben got in his car but didn't start the engine right away. He'd need to come back and talk to her, see if she might be more forthcoming about her son's whereabouts this past six weeks once she got over the shock. He knew damn well she'd been hearing from Rory. Defiance had made her chin jut when she lied to him every time he had talked to her.

Yeah, he'd be back, but he would have to give her a day or two. Maybe longer. The only urgency now was inside Ben.

He'd try talking to the sister, too, he decided. Maybe they confided in each other. Maybe she knew where her nephew had been lurking since he drove away from his job and apartment in West Fork. With a little luck, she wouldn't be as eager to excuse his behavior.

But he wouldn't be able to tackle Fay Bishop for a day or two, either, since her sister would need her.

His eyes were gritty and a headache rose up his spinal column to wrap his skull. There wasn't anything else for him to do right now. With a homicide case, he might have attended the autopsy, but cause of death was no mystery here.

The biggest mystery had been how Rory had gotten to the farm; his truck was nowhere to be found. A couple of hours ago, however, they'd discovered a car that turned out to be stolen. It had been left in a turnoff designed for farm tractors a few hundred yards down the highway. Easy walk for Rory.

Ben's stomach was roiling. He'd get something to eat to settle it, he decided, and then he would go see Faith.

Had she slept at all?

Knowing the answer, he grunted. He remembered too well the hellish doubts and second-guesses that had kept him awake the two times in his career he'd had to shoot to kill. He'd been vindicated in both cases, but that hadn't kept him from trying to figure out what he could have done differently. Violent death was always ugly. Even cops and soldiers were haunted by what they saw and what they'd done. A pretty kindergarten teacher who'd never wanted anything but to stay in her hometown and raise a family with her husband was ill-equipped to live with the sight of violence. He dreaded finding out what the act of killing would do to her.

With a sigh he started the car. A few minutes later, when he walked into Clara's Café, conversations stopped and everyone, waitresses and customers alike, turned to look at him. *Oh, hell,* he thought. Word of last night's happenings at the Russell farm had obviously spread like wildfire. Plus, here he was unshaven, wearing jeans and yesterday's T-shirt, his sockless feet in athletic shoes, when people were used to see him wearing his crisp blue uniform.

Should have gone with the drive-through at McDonald's instead. Or just gone home. His cupboards were pretty bare right now—he ate out a lot—but he could have found something.

He gave a vague nod of general acknowledgment and showed himself to the first empty booth he saw, the middle-aged waitress following with the coffeepot and a menu. He scanned it while she poured, and ordered immediately in hopes of hurrying things along. If only he could render himself invisible.

"Chief Wheeler." The hearty voice belonged to Harvey Dexter, chiropractor, current president of the West Fork Chamber of Commerce and, to Ben's private dismay, member of the city council. Dexter had stopped at Ben's booth, his gaze deeply concerned. The look was one he'd perfected, probably a stock in trade when he contemplated his patients' neck and back problems. Sixtyish, graying but fit, he also exuded good health, likely another necessity in his trade. "Heard we had a real tragedy last night," he said.

We? Ben thought with a savagery that took him aback.

He unclenched his teeth. "Gossip is making the rounds, I gather."

"Is it not true, then?"

Ben met his eyes. "I don't know what's being said."

"That Faith Russell killed her husband."

His mood deteriorated further. "Ex-husband. The divorce was final over a year ago. After he nearly beat her to death."

To his credit, Dexter seemed chagrined. "Sorry. I knew that. I've also heard that he, uh, didn't want to accept their marriage was over."

"Stalking a woman is one way to express the sentiment, I guess. Putting her sister in the hospital is another one." Goddamn. He wasn't helping matters here. Ben rubbed his forehead for a moment and said, "Hardesty broke into the Russells' place last night. She heard a creak in the hall or she wouldn't have woken up in time. He had a knife lifted to stab her when she shot him."

"No question it was self-defense, then?"

"None," Ben said flatly. "She'd be dead if she hadn't had the guts to buy a gun and learn to shoot it."

Dexter frowned. "I hope Don didn't get hurt."

Ben made himself relax. He didn't much like Harvey Dexter, but it seemed the man actually was concerned about the Russells. Chances were, he'd gone to high school with Faith's father.

"No, he's fine. Pretty shaken up, of course. He and Faith went home with Van Dusen last night."

"Good, good. It's been one thing after another for Don." Dexter looked as though he meant to say something else, but instead he nodded. "Faith's a nice young woman. I'm real sorry it came to this."

"Me, too."

The waitress arrived with Ben's breakfast, and Harvey went on his way. Ben hunkered down and ate as quickly as he could without giving the appearance of gobbling. He hoped that his hunched shoulders and grim mien held off any other curiosity seekers.

In the end, despite hushed voices, no one else worked up the courage to approach him. He didn't wait for the check, instead tossing down more than enough money to cover the bill and tip, and strode out with a sense of relief.

Definitely should have chosen the drive-through.

Part of him wanted to go straight to Faith, but he made himself detour by his home to shower, shave and change. He wouldn't be able to do anything about the tiredness that gave him a hollow-eyed look, but he couldn't imagine she'd find him reassuring the way he was.

In the shower, he bowed his head and let the hot water pound down on the back of his neck. Not until the water was starting to run cool did he turn off the shower, step out and towel himself dry.

He hesitated, almost reaching for his uniform, but he thought it would put some distance between them, remind her that he was there in his professional capacity, not as a friend.

Friend. He gave a sardonic grunt. Who was he kidding?

Okay, forget friend. Still, he didn't want her to see him only as a cop. He'd tried that, having spent the past six weeks doing his best to convince both of them that their relationship wasn't and couldn't be personal. He'd convinced her, to the point where she just might hate him. He'd utterly failed to convince himself, however, despite his best intentions.

Damn it, she was too good for him. Too gentle, too pure, too unsophisticated. Nothing in his life, neither his childhood nor his career, had made him the right kind of man for her. He'd made too many mistakes, unleashed his temper too often, despite his duty as a representative of the law to remain dispassionate. No surprise that he seldom slept without a nightmare. From the moment he'd met Faith, he'd been afraid he would taint her if he let himself succumb to temptation and get too close.

But she needed him now. He understood the darkness she would have to learn to live with in a way neither her friends nor family would. He had to offer her that understanding, whether she liked him or not.

He opted for some chinos and a clean black T-shirt then headed over to Van Dusen's place.

He'd only been to Gray's a couple of times, but remembered the way. Within weeks of taking over the job in West Fork, he'd had the community mapped out in his mind. Given an address, he could drive straight there without hesitation. As long as it was his town, he was determined to know it well.

He rang the doorbell, wondering if Gray had taken the day off, but it was Charlotte who opened the door.

"Ben." She looked glad to see him, which came as something of a surprise to him. She hadn't been much friendlier than her sister in recent weeks. Either she'd gotten mad because he'd failed to eliminate Hardesty as a threat to Faith, or she sensed that he'd hurt her twin. He wasn't sure which. But something definitely eased on her face now because he was here. "Come in. Faith and I are just finishing breakfast. Have you eaten?"

He stepped in. "Yeah. Thanks. I'd appreciate some coffee, though."

She appraised him more carefully. "I don't suppose you got back to bed last night, did you?"

"No."

She bit her lip and said in a low voice, "I don't think Faith slept at all."

"No, I don't suppose she did."

Charlotte hesitated, then led the way toward the kitchen.

This floor of Gray's house was open. Ben knew there was a home office with walls and a door, but otherwise the living room, dining area and kitchen all flowed into each other, separated by furniture and function rather than any kind of partition. A river rock fireplace dominated one side of the room, while floor-to-ceiling windows looked out at the deck and the valley below on the south-facing wall. Gleaming bamboo floors united the spaces. The place was spectacular.

Today, Ben saw nothing but Faith, sitting at the table. He felt a familiar lurch in his chest made more painful by the fact that she looked even worse than he'd expected.

"Hey," he said, keeping his deep voice soft. He pulled out a chair across the table from her. Behind him, Charlotte went into the kitchen and he heard the sound of a cupboard door opening.

Faith had been looking at a piece of toast she was shredding. Crumbles dribbled from her fingers onto the plate. Charlotte might have finished breakfast, but all Faith seemed to have done was push the scrambled eggs around and demolish the toast.

At the sound of his voice, her head lifted with aching slowness. Her eyes found him, but took longer to focus. Her forehead creased. "Chief Wheeler." Pause. "I suppose you have more questions."

"No more questions."

She kept gazing at him with seeming perplexity. "Then why are you here?"

The honesty of her surprise was like a quick knife sliding between his ribs. The hell of it was, he deserved it.

"To see how you're doing. To talk to you."

"I'm fine. Just…anxious to go home."

She actually sounded like she meant it. He turned to look at Charlotte, who set a mug of coffee in front of him. She gave a small, helpless shrug.

"Somebody is going to have to clean up the mess first. Replace the window glass, too."

"And who do you think that will be?" Faith asked.

God damn. She really thought every burden in the world was hers to carry, that she'd be the one to scrub her ex-husband's blood from the floorboards.

Charlotte sat down, too. "Me," she said. Her voice was hard. "I can clean up Rory's blood without a qualm. You are most certainly not doing it, Faith. And Gray's already called the glass company."

Ben nodded. "Where's Don?"

"He had a bite to eat and went back downstairs to lie down." Charlotte pushed her own plate away and crossed her arms on the table. "He's looking pretty ragged this morning."

"At least he can handle stairs now," Ben observed. Although he bet the process of getting up and down had been slow and painful.

Charlotte nodded. Faith was now frowning at her sister. "I can't let you do that by yourself."

"You can and you will. For God's sake, Faith!"

"Why don't you stay here for a few days?" Ben suggested.

Faith shook her head. "No. Dad and I will be more comfortable once we're home. I won't let Rory keep me out of our house."

Incredulous, he stared at her, trying to decide if she was being strong and determined, or delusional. He wished she'd at least try to eat that breakfast. He'd have sworn another five pounds had dropped off her in the few days since he'd stopped by the barn. Her face was gaunt, her cheekbones too protuberant, her chin sharp. Her astonishing eyes looked sunken, shadowed. Even her hair had somehow lost vitality and shine, like drying corn husks. His gut twisted, and he wanted nothing in the world so much as to take her home with him and do nothing but pamper and soothe her.

Some of the sharpness engendered by his fear for her gave his voice an edge. "You didn't eat a bite, did you?"

She glanced down at her plate. "Of course I did."

"Uh-huh. Faith, I know what you feel like this morning, but you've got to take care of yourself."

She lifted her face and met his eyes, her own eerily empty. "Isn't that what I did last night?"

Ben stood abruptly and circled the table, pulling out the chair beside hers and sitting in it so that his knees bumped her thighs and he was close enough to see the lines of strain beside her eyes and every separate, dark gold lash. "Last night you did what you had to do," he said quietly. "Now you need to keep doing it. When's the last time you really ate? I remember thinking when I first met Charlotte that she was living on nerves. Now I see the same thing in you."

She shook her head.

"Yes." He lifted a hand to stroke her face, as if by

molding the shape of bones and flesh he could help her see herself more truly. "There's not much left of you."

As though by rote, Faith repeated, "I'm fine. I just want to go home."

How much less fine would she have to be before admitting anything was wrong?

Across the table, Charlotte made an incoherent sound and sprang to her feet. "If I make you a raspberry smoothie, do you think you could get that down?"

Again, it seemed to take Faith ages to transfer her attention to her sister, but finally she nodded. "I'll try. If that will make you feel better."

Charlotte gave a fierce nod. "It would."

"Okay."

Moving like a whirlwind in the kitchen, Charlotte began pulling ingredients from the refrigerator and in moments was feeding them into a blender. Ben kept watching Faith, who seemed to have put him completely from her mind. She was struggling, he suspected, to hold on to one thought at a time, to deal with the demands of one person. Her exhaustion was absolute, her innate dignity all that was holding her together.

What she needed was a sedative. Which he knew damn well she'd refuse to take. Ben's eyes narrowed. Would it be ethical to slip something in the smoothie? Her dad might have something with him that would knock her out... But Charlotte already had the blender whirring, and Ben didn't think he could move fast enough.

Frowning, he decided she'd have to collapse sooner or later. She might be better able to sleep in the daylight.

Charlotte turned off the blender and carefully poured the raspberry-red sludge into a glass and carried it to the table. "Here, honey," she said, in an uncharacteristically tender voice. "Now drink. You promised."

After a minute Faith picked up the glass and sipped, then took a longer swallow. "Thank you," she murmured.

Charlotte looked at Ben. "Can you stay for a while? If it's okay, I can go to the house right now."

Not liking the idea of either of them scrubbing up blood, he argued, "I can do that."

She shook her head. "I know where cleaning supplies are, and I can toss the bedding in the wash. Dad's, too. Maybe get some other housecleaning done, if you can hang around for a couple of hours. Talk her into napping."

As if their conversation was simply white noise she could easily ignore, Faith was taking small drinks of the smoothie and staring blankly into space.

"I can stay," Ben promised. "Don't worry."

Charlotte gave an almost laugh. "Yeah. Right. Don't worry. Okay. Faith, honey." She waited until her twin focused on her. "I'm going over to the house to do some things. You finish every drop. Then talk to Ben. Or take a nap. I'll be back in a couple of hours."

That roused Faith from her lethargy. She pushed back from the table as if to stand up. "I can…"

"No, you can't. I won't let you. Just…let me do this, okay?" Her sister hurried around the table, gave her a quick, hard hug, and then grabbed her purse and bustled out of the house.

Faith sat very still. She didn't look at Ben when she said, "You don't have to stay. I'm not going to throw myself off the bluff or something."

"I'm not going anywhere." Ben didn't move either.

"Finish the smoothie, like you promised Charlotte, and then we'll talk, or you'll nap. Two choices. Either are okay by me."

She looked at him from those sunken eyes and said, "You can't make me." Then she went back to sipping her drink and pretending he wasn't there.

His jaw clenched. She might think she could get rid of him that easily, but she was mistaken. He wasn't going anywhere. Not now, not in the days to come. Not as long as she needed him.

And she did need him, even if she hadn't figured that out yet.

CHAPTER FIVE

FAITH AWAKENED SLOWLY, reluctantly, surprised when she had to slit her eyes against sunlight flooding the bed. Could she possibly have slept so late?

She stiffened, memories tumbling back. She was at Gray's house. In an effort to escape from Ben, she'd come downstairs to the library and the air mattress that had been her bed last night. She couldn't bear to have him keep watching her, his eyes dark and somehow tender. Certain she couldn't sleep, she had picked out a book from Gray's collection and lain down. Had she even made it through the first page? She must have conked right out.

Fully awake now, Faith became aware of two things. She'd fallen asleep on top of the bedding, but she was now covered. And she heard someone else breathing, slow and deep, so close she could feel it on the nape of her neck.

She wasn't alone on the air mattress, which explained why it felt so firm; Ben's weight was compressing the other side.

Apparently, when Ben said he wasn't going anywhere, he really meant it. She'd acquired a shadow.

She tried very hard to work up some anger. It took some nerve for him to climb right into bed beside her. But anger didn't want to stir; she couldn't even seem to summon annoyance. She felt too numb, except when she stole sidelong peeks at those memories of last night. And then she felt…

No. Don't remember.

Faith squinted to see the clock on the DVD player, and was surprised to discover that it was now mid-afternoon. Char must have gotten back hours ago.

Wincing at the idea of her sister having taken on the gruesome task of cleaning up Rory's blood, Faith tensed to slip out of bed. Preferably without waking Ben, who must still be asleep to be breathing like that.

Moving carefully, she inched off the mattress, then stood and gazed down at the man who lay sprawled on his back atop the covers, definitely still sleeping.

He looked oddly defenseless with his eyes closed and his lean face relaxed, one arm above his head, the other splayed to one side. He'd been up all night, too, she remembered. Although he must have stopped at home at some point, because she was pretty sure he was wearing different clothes than he had been in the middle of the night. Plus, given how dark his hair was, he'd have a heavier growth of beard if he hadn't shaved. She hadn't noticed earlier. She'd avoided looking at him at all this morning.

Something inside her softened as she studied him. Last night, he'd seemed to know exactly what she needed. She hadn't wanted anybody to touch her, but she remembered the way she'd soaked in his body heat when he insisted on holding her anyway, how comforting the steady beat of his heart had been. If she were completely honest with herself, she had felt bereft when he'd lifted her off the safety and comfort of his lap.

She should leave him to sleep, but she kept standing

there, disconcerted by how different he looked without irritation drawing his heavy, dark eyebrows together, or frustration compressing his mouth. Had she ever seen him smile with delight or amusement?

Charlotte probably had, Faith thought with a pang. She'd probably even heard him laugh. The only emotions Faith seemed to stir in him were exasperation, pity and guilt. She couldn't decide which she hated the most.

With no warning at all, his eyes opened, and her pulse took an uncomfortable leap. They stared at each other for a moment that stretched too long. *He* didn't seem to be confused about where he was, or slow to wake. It was as if he'd known exactly where she was standing even before he opened his eyes.

"Trying to sneak away?" he asked.

"Exactly where would I sneak away *to?* I don't have a car here, remember? Or were you really afraid I was going to fling myself off the bluff?"

He still hadn't moved a muscle, just lay there watching her. "I didn't think you should be alone."

Faith let out a huff of annoyance, surprised to find she could feel something after all. "You expected me to curl into a ball and sob?"

"No. I was afraid you'd have nightmares."

Oh.

She had to wait a moment for the lump in her throat to ease before she could speak. "I didn't."

"You will," he said softly.

Faith wrapped her arms around herself and, without another word, turned and walked out. She heard the rustle as he rose to his feet behind her, and could all but feel him breathing down her neck on the way upstairs. A part of her wanted to whirl and order him to back off.

That would have required too much effort, though. What difference did it make if he was right behind her? He'd go away soon enough. He could probably hardly wait to go away. Ben Wheeler was great to have around in a crisis, but not interested in hanging around afterward.

At least, not hanging around *her*.

Charlotte came out of the home office when Faith reached the top of the stairs. Her gaze was anxious.

"Did you have a good nap?"

"Apparently. I seem to have slept for five or six hours."

"I hope that doesn't keep you awake tonight." Char looked past her sister to Ben. "You got some sleep, too?"

"Yeah, thanks. Although I think that mattress has lost some air."

Char smiled. "I doubt it was really designed for two. Especially when one of the two is as large as you are."

"I'm not complaining," he said amiably. "I didn't expect to get more than a catnap."

Faith asked, "Where's Dad?"

"Still downstairs in the guest room. I took him some lunch earlier. He was reading, but it wouldn't surprise me if he's taking a nap, too."

Faith cleared her throat. "Did you...?"

Understanding her with no trouble, Char met her eyes. "Yes. I left your quilt spread out on the lawn, though. I didn't want to put it in the dryer." She paused. "I think I managed to get all the blood out of it."

The quilt had been pieced and hand-quilted by their great-grandmother in a flower-garden pattern, the cheerful pink and green and yellow fabrics faded to softer hues by the years. The Russells had several quilts

Great-Grandma Abigail had made. Faith's mother had always been careful about washing them, and especially about drying them. Eighty-year-old fabrics could be torn easily, even by the weight of the wet quilt hanging from a clothesline.

Faith hated knowing that she would never want to sleep under that particular quilt again.

Feeling the pressure of Ben's gaze on her even though she didn't look at him, she said, "I'm thirsty," and went to the kitchen. She was very conscious of a low-voiced exchange between her sister and the police chief; he was probably making his excuses now that there was no need for him to stay.

But no. Char said brightly, "You must both be starved. Let me heat up some soup and make sandwiches."

"I wouldn't mind," Ben said, and Faith knew he had decided she wouldn't eat if he wasn't there to insist.

With a sigh, she sat down at the dining-room table and waited docilely, still refusing to look at him. She wished he wouldn't look at her, either. She must be a sight, puffy eyes and hair frizzed by the pillow and pulling out of her braid. She was sure the contrast with Char was painful. Them being identical twins would make it especially plain. Char had obviously showered and changed after getting back from the horrible task she'd insisted on taking over. She now wore jeans and a cap-sleeved T-shirt that exposed tanned arms that had more muscle than when she'd come back to West Fork two months ago. Her cheeks were a healthy pink, her short hair cute. She'd even made the effort to put in tiny hoop earrings, which she didn't always.

Faith had seen herself in the mirror that morning, after she'd showered. She'd averted her eyes quickly.

If the image in the mirror had been a photograph, she wouldn't have recognized herself in that gaunt face with purple bruises under eyes that seemed to have receded.

She hadn't been able to bring herself to care much, though, and she didn't now, either, beyond the passing, wistful realization. What difference did it make what she looked like, so long as she could pull herself together enough not to frighten her students come Monday morning?

Monday morning, she realized in dismay, was *tomorrow*. Oh, God. Could she laugh, or even smile, with the kids? Offer gentle hugs, wipe faces clean, feel genuine pleasure if Kevin finally gained the hand dexterity to shape his capital *A?*

She could take a day or two of sick leave. No one would mind.

Yes, but what would she do—sit at home and replay events? Work in the barn, and wonder if every person who stopped by came to gawk?

Would people come to gawk?

Faith didn't realize she'd asked the question aloud until Ben, who'd sat directly across from her at the table, said, "Yes."

Her eyes widened. "Yes, what?"

"I'm guessing half the people in town will make an excuse to stop by the farm. And you're going to get reporters, too, the minute you're home. The only thing holding them off today is that they don't know your sister is involved with Gray, so they haven't managed to track you down." He sounded grim.

"Oh, no," she whispered. "I didn't think of that."

He reached across the table and took her hand. His

was large and warm and enveloping. "We can go one of two ways."

Char, in the background, had been listening. Now she brought a plate of sandwiches and set it between them. "Two?"

"Well, three, I suppose." His eyes met Faith's, all but forcing her to focus on him. "You can say, 'No comment.' Over and over and over."

She nodded, imagining hordes of reporters complete with TV cameras chasing her from her car into the school, sitting outside the farmhouse waiting for her to emerge. Which was silly, of course; what had happened to her, what she'd *done,* wasn't so very unusual. It wasn't as if *People* magazine or CBS news would have even the slightest interest in her. No, all she'd have to worry about was someone from *The Herald,* and maybe *The Seattle Times.* Oh, Lord. And possibly local television news crews. She had a sudden, awful picture of a KOMO news helicopter hovering over the house.

"Or you can talk to reporters one by one. Give them what they want."

She shuddered, ignoring the bowl of soup Char placed in front of her.

"Or—" Ben's gaze penetrated her defenses "—my recommendation, which is that you hold a press conference of sorts. Get it over with, get them off your back."

She stared.

Char snapped, "Or option four, she can stay here until they lose interest."

He shrugged, his eyes never leaving Faith's. "That might work, if Faith is willing. It means not going to work, though. Not going *anywhere.*"

Already she was shaking her head. "I can't just…sit. I'd go crazy."

His fingers tightened on her hand. "We can set it up for tomorrow. At city hall if you'd rather not have them at the farm."

I can't do this. I can't.

She wanted to hug herself again and begin rocking, but she didn't want to retrieve her hand from Ben's. She would never again ask for comfort from him, but found she was too weak not to accept it when he pressed it on her. He was so large and solid and sure of himself, she felt as if she was borrowing some of that strength when they were touching.

Charlotte had poured them each a glass of milk now.

"I have school tomorrow," Faith said.

Ben shook his head. "In fairness to the district, you've got to get this out of the way before you go back."

Her spurt of rebellion fizzled quickly. She seemed not to have the fuel needed to keep it alive. After a minute, Faith nodded. "All right."

"I'll make the calls," Ben said. "And I'll be right there with you to answer as many of the questions as I can."

"All right," she said again, numbly.

"What I want you to do," he told her, "is stay here with Charlotte one more night. You and your dad both. Out of sight. Call and ask for a substitute to take your class tomorrow. We'll do the press conference, and then I'll ask that your privacy be respected thereafter. It might be best if you hang a big closed sign at the barn—"

"I can't!"

"Or hire someone else to work there. Keep staying out of sight, just for a week or two."

"I'll take over," Charlotte said, sitting down with them. "I can run anyone off who isn't whipping out a checkbook to buy something."

"I hate to ask you..."

"Damn it, let's not do this again." Her sister's jaw had set in a familiar way. "One for all and all for one. Remember?"

Faith sniffed, a pathetic sound she despised herself for making. "Yes, but it seems to have been awfully one-sided lately."

"I'm doing it for Dad, too."

Faith knew perfectly well that was a sop to her conscience. Char was rescuing *her,* not Dad. Dad, she increasingly feared, would have been willing—might actually like—to sell out. Her determination was all that was keeping the Russell Family Farm in Russell hands.

Part of her wanted to give up, too, but Faith had the dim sense that she'd have nothing left if she surrendered. Work and more work, the steely determination that kept her going, was all that kept her from having to acknowledge the emptiness of her life. It was as if she hung from a cliff, her hands slipping on the rope, burning her flesh, but if she let go she'd be in dizzying free fall. If she managed to keep her grip, she kept thinking maybe eventually she'd be able to start climbing. Or even discover that someone was pulling her up.

"Thank you," she said.

Char's eyes narrowed. "Now eat."

Ben let go of Faith's hand. Reluctantly, she thought in surprise and puzzlement. She saw his fingers flex and almost curl into a fist for a moment, before he reached for his spoon.

Obediently Faith dipped her own spoon into the cream of tomato soup and began sipping at it.

PEOPLE WERE SUCH GHOULS.

Charlotte wasn't shocked, unlike Faith, who would have been. Charlotte *was* getting pissed, though. Even people who'd known the Russell twins their entire lives were stopping by with the thinnest of excuses to ask questions, their eyes avid. Charlotte knew damn well they were grabbing their cell phones the minute they got into their cars so they could tell everyone they knew, "I was just talking to Charlotte Russell..."

As if she'd told a single one of them anything of interest.

The only plus was that they felt obligated to buy something. What other legitimate excuse was there for walking into the barn? Most spent peanuts; they picked up a jar of jam, or a head of lettuce, or a couple of potted asters to replace flagging summer annuals. Still, it added up. Monday's receipts would be, she was willing to bet, among the highest of the summer, for what was normally the slowest day of the week.

At two o'clock Marsha arrived to take over so that Charlotte could be at the press conference.

"Tell anyone who asks that you don't know a thing," she told their part-time employee.

"I don't." Her face creased in worry. "Um...is Faith okay?"

"She will be."

I hope.

Faith was not okay right now. Charlotte would have been relieved if her sister had broken down sobbing, or wanted to get drunk. Anything but her single-minded insistence on going back to her life exactly as it had been. When she wasn't repeating that yes, she was sure she wanted to go home, and of course she'd be ready for the classroom tomorrow morning, Faith tended to sit with her head bent, gazing at her hands. Charlotte didn't know what she was thinking, or if she was thinking at all.

Ben had stayed for a couple more hours yesterday, although Faith had mostly ignored him. He'd left when Gray got home. Gray had walked Ben out to his car, and they'd stood there talking for quite a while. Gray had been frowning when he finally came in.

"I hope he knows what the hell he's doing."

"Do you think this press conference is a bad idea?" Charlotte had asked, after stealing a glance to be sure Faith couldn't overhear.

His gaze resting on her sister, Gray said slowly, "I don't know. God knows how she'd stand up to being stalked by a bunch of reporters."

"Not well."

"No." But Gray's frown had lingered, even when he'd bent his head to kiss her.

Charlotte knew Gray didn't trust Ben the way he had before Rory started terrorizing Faith. She wasn't sure what had actually been said, but the tension between them when they were together was strong enough to give her goose bumps. Gray blamed Ben, whom he had hired, for not keeping her and Faith safe. She didn't think that was entirely fair; in between attacks, Rory could have been anywhere. But Gray wasn't rational on the subject, and she hadn't tried to intervene.

Something had changed, she thought, the other night when Gray had seen how affected Ben was by Faith's devastation. But it might have been a case of too little, too late. When they were children, Gray had lost his twin brother in a tragic accident. In the aftermath, his parents had divorced. The man Charlotte was going to marry took family seriously. Faith was her sister, and therefore he'd take care of her, too. He wasn't any happier than Charlotte was about the way Faith had been working herself to the bone.

Charlotte had never been to a press conference of any kind, so she didn't know what to expect. Ben had arranged to use the room at city hall where council meetings were held. When she slipped in unnoticed at the back of the room, she found about a dozen people waiting with reasonable patience. Two local TV channels had sent reporters and camera operators, and a couple more photographers, presumably from newspapers, held cameras with huge lenses at the ready.

Charlotte jumped when someone placed a hand on her lower back, but turned her head to see Gray. He looked sexy in a dark suit that emphasized his broad shoulders and lean, athletic build. He nuzzled her ear briefly, not saying anything.

Ben and Faith entered from a door behind the tables where the city council members sat during public hearings, his hand on her elbow. He was in uniform, and Faith wore a skirt and blouse borrowed from Charlotte. Her hair was rolled smoothly into a chignon on the back of her head. She'd applied makeup, but it didn't help much; her bones were still painfully prominent, her pallor and the deep purple circles beneath her eyes impossible to hide even with foundation. She looked utterly composed, which made Charlotte's heart ache.

Ben steered her to a seat, then took the one beside her.

He introduced himself, then in spare, unemotional language described the events that had led to Faith having to shoot her ex-husband.

"Ms. Russell will make a brief statement," he said, "after which we'll take questions."

Faith looked at the reporters calmly, as if there weren't flashbulbs going off and TV cameras pointing at her.

"I was in an abusive marriage," she said starkly, her voice husky but also steady. "Like too many other women, I thought I could change so that I didn't make him angry. Or *he* could change. Fifteen months ago, my then-husband beat me so severely that I couldn't lie about how I'd gotten hurt. I wasn't willing to lie anymore. I had to stay in the hospital for over a week with a fractured skull, broken arm, broken collarbone and broken ribs, one of which had punctured my lung. If a neighbor had not called 911, I would not have survived. I left Rory and filed for divorce. He chose not to accept my right to leave him. Two months ago, his attempts to convince me to come back to him escalated into violence. He attempted to burn down the barn on our family farm. He broke in and assaulted my twin sister in the belief that she was me. At that point, I purchased a handgun and began practicing at a range. I knew the police could not offer me twenty-four-hour-a-day protection, nor did I expect them to do so. I believed..." Here her voice hitched for the first time. "I still believe, that Rory intended to kill me. For the past two months, I have existed in fear of my life. Two nights ago, I woke up just as he entered my bedroom with a knife. I shot him. It was…" her throat moved in a swallow, and Ben laid a hand on her shoulder "…it was something I prayed I would never have to do. He gave me no choice. I now have to live with that horror."

Questions flew, many of which Ben was able to answer. What was the reaction of Rory's family? Had Faith gotten a restraining order? Was there any question about whether the shooting had been in self-defense? Was she angry at how ineffectual the police had been in protecting her?

Charlotte felt Gray tense at that question. If Ben did the same, it wasn't visible.

"No," said Faith calmly. "When an abusive man is obsessed enough, something like a restraining order means nothing to him. It's a piece of paper. Yes, it gives police a tool under the right circumstances. As for police being ineffectual… Do you have any idea how many women in our own county currently have restraining orders in an attempt to stop a man who wants to hurt them?" She paused. "Do your research and find out. There is simply no way the police can protect all those women. Or know which ones are truly threatened. It became apparent to me that only I could save myself, if Rory came after me again. That's what I did."

Ben rose to his feet, his hand still resting on her shoulder. "No more questions. I'm going to ask you to respect Ms. Russell's privacy as she recovers. If you have follow-up questions, please call me, not her." He nodded, waited until she stood, too, and then ushered her out of the room with a hand between her shoulder blades.

Gray murmured in Charlotte's ear, "Time for us to make a getaway, too, before anyone notices you."

She nodded vigorously and turned to leave. "Though there's not as much resemblance between us as there used to be, is there?"

"No, she looks like hell." Gray glanced down at her. "You heading home? Back to the farm?"

"Farm."

"I'll walk you out." He was silent and appeared pre-occupied until they reached Don Russell's rusty old pickup truck that Charlotte was currently driving. Her own car was still garaged in San Francisco where her condominium was up for sale. She supposed she ought to fetch it, but she hadn't wanted to leave Faith long enough to fly down and drive back. Gray had been so busy with his two jobs, she couldn't ask him to take several days off to keep her company. And Dad wasn't ready to get back behind the wheel of his pickup yet, anyway, although he would be soon.

Maybe, Charlotte thought, she could talk Faith into going with her. It would be good for her to get away. And the drive back would give them time to talk. To really talk.

Something told her that right now, Faith would say no. She didn't want to confide in anyone, not even her twin sister. She had sounded self-possessed and even force-ful when she'd given her statement today, but Charlotte knew perfectly well that her sister had only done what she had to do to get rid of the press. How much of what she'd said she actually believed was another question.

Charlotte felt quite certain, for example, that Faith was still unsure about Rory's intentions. She was not convinced that shooting him had been her only choice. Those doubts infuriated and frustrated Charlotte, who knew that Faith would be dead if she hadn't had that gun under her pillow and been willing to use it.

Faith, she believed, had crept inside herself where no one would gainsay her right to feel guilty. She wanted to go home partly so she could be alone. Dad was a quiet man; he'd watch her worriedly, but he wouldn't say much. Mom had always been the talker, Dad the silent support.

But silence wasn't what Faith needed right now, in Charlotte's opinion.

"You can lead a horse to water," she muttered.

Gray raised his eyebrows. "Should I even ask the context of that?"

Charlotte sighed. "Faith."

"She and Don are really going home this afternoon?"

"So she says. I think Ben has been persuaded to drive them."

"I don't like it."

Charlotte let herself lean against him, just for a moment, and felt his arms close securely around her. "Who does?" she mumbled against his red-and-black striped silk tie.

"She won't listen, will she?"

"No. Not yet, anyway."

He swore, kissed her and stayed where he was on the sidewalk until she'd started the truck and pulled out.

How did I ever get so lucky? Charlotte asked herself, looking in the rearview mirror at the man she loved. *And why can't Faith, who deserves happiness more than I do, be as lucky?*

CHAPTER SIX

FAITH DIDN'T WANT HIM. Didn't want to believe she needed him.

Not that Ben could blame her. Hadn't he done his damnedest to shut her out these past two months? To make clear that he was available only in his capacity as a law-enforcement officer? She'd gotten the message, loud and clear. Why would she look at him now with anything but surprise when he tried to be a friend—or more?

But she did need him. Even Gray conceded as much, when he stopped by Ben's office on his way to work on Friday.

"Did you know she went back to teaching Tuesday?" he demanded, standing in the open doorway. "For God's sake, she could barely put one foot in front of the other!"

"Yeah, I know," Ben said wearily. He wasn't sleeping well. He'd had one hell of a nightmare last night, one that had him racing through the night toward the Russell Farm, knowing Hardesty was in the house, unable to warn Faith. In the dream, he had heard the gunshots just as he broke through the back door. He wasn't prepared, sleeping or waking, for the anguish. *Too late...* He'd awakened gasping for breath, swearing.

"Don says she's refusing to talk about it. She wants to

pretend nothing happened. She makes dinner, chatters about her day. Moves her food around on her plate. He doesn't think she's eating enough to keep a field mouse alive."

"If she'll listen to anyone, it's Charlotte." But he knew better, even as he said it.

Gray shook his head. "She's dodging Charlotte."

Ben gritted his teeth and met the mayor's stare. "What is it you think I can do?"

"Talk to her. She responded to you that night. We all saw."

Shooting to his feet, Ben snarled, "You think I haven't been trying? That I just walked away?"

Gray's eyes might as well have been steel. "Isn't that what you've done before?"

An obscenity escaped his lips, but he couldn't turn his rage on the other man, not when he deserved every brutal punch of it himself. Voice hoarse, he said, "I have continued to make myself available above and beyond what my job demanded. If you're saying I didn't start a personal relationship with Faith… Yeah, you're right. I had my reasons. I don't owe it to you to share them."

Gray broke first, bending his head abruptly and pinching the bridge of his nose between his thumb and forefinger. He cursed under his breath, then said, "You're right. Hell. This is killing Charlotte. I shouldn't take that out on you."

After a minute, Ben sank back into his chair, which squeaked under the weight of his body. "I've been by to see her at least once a day. So far, she hasn't been very receptive."

Gray stared at him. "I didn't know that. She didn't tell Charlotte."

"She doesn't want me there. Faith seems to have a talent for denial."

They both knew he wasn't just talking about this past week, or even the past two months when Hardesty was stalking her and she didn't want to believe he'd really hurt her. To all reports, during her entire marriage she had convinced herself over and over again that the son of a bitch was truly sorry he'd hit her and that he wouldn't do it again. Black eyes, broken bones, God knows how many bruises she'd hidden from public view… Through it all, she had forgiven him and pretended for the benefit of her family that everything was fine.

Ben didn't understand why. Could she possibly have loved the man that much? Had a capacity for forgiveness so vast?

It was one of many answers he intended to get, once Faith realized he wasn't going anywhere.

"What if she collapses?" Gray asked.

"That might not be a bad thing." Ben had been thinking about it. "She's a stubborn woman. That may be what it'll take to get her to realize she can't go on the way she is."

Gray swore again and finally went away. Ben guessed he was worried about Charlotte as much as Faith. She was likely running herself ragged, putting more hours into the farm business than she could afford and probably staying too many evenings, too, in hopes her sister would talk to her, lean on her, cry.

Ben had lost all ability to concentrate on the personnel schedule for November he had been attempting to draft. He finally shoved it in a drawer. If there was one thing he could do to help Faith Russell find peace, it was to figure out where Hardesty had been hiding and what his intentions had been. He'd felt he had to give Hardesty's mother a few days to grieve before he pressed her again for what she knew, but he'd done that now. And maybe it was ruthless of him, but she might give up more now, while she was stunned and vulnerable, than she would if he waited too long and she managed to shore up her belief in her son's innocence.

When he knocked on the front door of Michelle Hardesty's modest rambler, he saw the curtains twitch and then waited for a good two minutes before he heard the dead bolt being turned. The door opened a crack, revealing half of a face almost unrecognizable from his other visits.

"Mrs. Hardesty," he said gently. "May I come in? I need to talk to you."

She stared at him for a painfully long time before opening the door and unlocking the screen. When she disappeared from sight, he took it as an invitation and stepped inside, the screen door creaking as it snapped shut.

He had always suspected that Michelle Hardesty was a nice woman who really did believe her son was being falsely accused. She'd wanted to hate Faith, but Ben had seen cracks in the facade a few times. In her midfifties, she'd kept herself up well, with soft brown hair cut chin length and likely colored at the salon, a round pleasant face and a tidy home. Today, her face was ravaged, her hair looked as if it hadn't been washed in days and she wore a nightgown, down-at-the-heel slippers and a thin wrapper with a coffee stain down the front. By the time he followed her into the living room, she'd sat down on the sofa and seemed to have forgotten he was there. That thousand-yard stare, he thought, wasn't much different than Faith's.

Feeling manipulative as hell, he got her to talking about her son, reminiscing. She took out a photo album and showed him baby pictures and newspaper clippings of Rory in his high-school football uniform. He stopped her before she could reach wedding pictures; Ben didn't want to know what he'd feel at the sight of Faith wearing white and gazing up with shining faith—yeah, damn it, he had to use that word—at the man who would be beating the crap out of her only a few months down the line.

Instead, he flipped back a few pages to a team photo and asked who the other boys were. "I suppose I know some of them," he murmured.

"Yes, that's Lenny Phillips." She touched the face of a boy kneeling in the front row. "He has a Farmer's Insurance office here in town."

Yeah, that rang a bell, although Phillips had definitely put on some weight since high school.

She pointed out several others he'd met, including Ken Carlisle who'd fenced Ben's backyard for him after he'd bought his house.

When he asked about Rory's friends, she seemed to have forgotten who she was talking to or why he was interested. A couple of these boys had grown into men who still played slow pitch with Rory, maybe had beers after games, but Ben had already talked to most of them. One name was new to him—J. P. Hammond—but he didn't take his notebook out; the last thing he wanted was to remind Michelle Hardesty that he was the cop who'd been trying to jail her son.

She turned another couple of pages and showed him a photo of Rory in a headlock, the boys both laughing.

"Rory still goes elk hunting with Noah Berger," Mrs. Hardesty said, not seeming to notice that she was going to have to be changing verb tense. "Them and Jimmy Reese. I don't know if I have a picture of Jimmy. They weren't real good friends until after high school. Jimmy is a couple of years younger, I think."

"Elk hunting, huh? That's not something we have where I come from."

"Oh, they go down to Oregon, camp for a week every year. Jimmy got one three, four years ago. They all shared the meat." Her mind seemed to drift, and Ben could tell she wasn't seeing the album open on her lap anymore. "Noah's wife always went—nice gal—but I don't think Faith went but for the first year. Rory didn't like that." Mrs. Hardesty swallowed hard, perhaps remembering what Rory did to his wife when he wasn't happy with her. Or maybe all she was thinking about was that her son wouldn't be getting together with his high-school buddies to elk hunt ever again.

"This Noah Berger and Jimmy Reese," Ben said casually. "Do they still live here in West Fork?"

She shook her head. "Jimmy is over in Bremerton. He has a good job at the shipyards. Noah...well, I'm not sure. He was in Boise, but I think Rory mentioned him moving. I just don't remember."

Idaho. Ben felt a surge of exhilaration.

"Have you let Rory's friends know what happened?"

She gazed at him without interest and shook her head.

"Have you gone through your son's things?"

"I can't," she whispered. "I just can't."

He hardened himself enough to say, "Mrs. Hardesty, I have to ask again if you know where Rory has been staying since he left his job and his apartment."

"I don't know!" she screamed. "What difference does it make now? You need to leave! I'm done talking to you." She covered her face with her hands. The album slipped from her lap and hit the carpeted floor with a thud. "I'm done."

After a moment he stood, said, "I'm going now, Mrs. Hardesty. I'm very sorry for your loss," and let himself quietly out the front door.

He felt like scum, as he often did when he was just doing his job, but he was also aware of the heightened sensations of a hunter who had just scented new spoor. He ran the names through his mind, including the first one. Hammond. J. P. Hammond. He could get the full name from school records. Three new names gave him something to work with, especially the last two. If Rory had stayed friends with Reese and Berger, why hadn't Faith mentioned them?

With a glance at his watch, he saw that he'd have to get a move on if he was going to waylay her at lunchtime. He'd done so on Tuesday; Wednesday she must have scooted out the classroom door on the heels of her kids before the bell had quit ringing and hid for the next half hour. He sure as hell hadn't been able to find her. Thursday he'd stayed away in hopes she'd lower her guard. He'd have stayed away today, too, if he had thought she would actually eat lunch.

After a stop at a new café on Park Street, he drove to the school, parked in a visitor's slot in front, checked in at the office and then strode down the still-empty corridor to Faith's classroom. He made it just as the bell clanged.

The door was flung open and kids poured out. Ben let them go by, then blocked the doorway. Faith came to a stop only a few feet away.

She wore chinos and a three-quarter-sleeve knit shirt that made him painfully aware of how prominent her collarbone had become. And her cheekbones—damn, they could cut glass. In contrast, her eyes were dull.

There might have been a hint of exasperation in her voice, though. "Chief Wheeler."

He lifted the bags in his hands. "Lunch."

A small frown knit her forehead. "Why do you keep trying to feed me? I bring a lunch from home."

"Uh-huh."

"I do."

He advanced into the classroom and closed the door behind him, resisting the temptation to lock it. "Then where is it?"

"We have a teacher's lounge."

They did, but he'd learned the two days he'd gone hunting for her that she definitely didn't spend her lunchtime in it.

"My lunch is better anyway," he said. "Sit."

A flare of rebellion on her face encouraged him, but it died too quickly and she turned and went back to her desk, sinking docilely into the chair behind it. He set the bags down on the desk and dragged the one other adult-size chair over.

"Smoothie." He presented it to her. The café, called The Pea Patch, was into organic, vegetarian food. This smoothie, blended as he watched, was full of healthful ingredients. "Corn chowder." He put the container in front of her and peeled off the lid.

It was damn good chowder, he discovered when he started on his own. After a moment, Faith picked up the plastic spoon and began to eat.

"You been in The Pea Patch?" he asked.

She looked up with vague surprise. "No, but they've been buying corn from us. And pumpkins. I guess Carol Lynn is making pumpkin pies from scratch."

"So this is probably made with Russell Family Farm corn."

She blinked bemusedly and gazed at her bowl. "I suppose it is."

"Me, I tend to be a meat eater." He kept a careful eye on her as he rambled on, his voice relaxed and unthreatening. "But corn chowder is one of my favorite foods. Guess I should learn to make it myself."

After a long pause, she said, "It's not hard."

He smiled at her. "Why don't you make it the next time I come over? Say, tomorrow night? The corn is almost past for the year, right?"

"Most of it is already." She seemed not to have noticed that he'd lured her into accepting him as a dinner guest. "I suppose I could find a few ears in the maze. We don't harvest that field."

"I'll count on it," he said with satisfaction, even though he hated the fact that she couldn't get worked up enough to tell him to go to hell. "You ever made pumpkin pie from scratch?" he asked.

"Well, of course." Looking surprised, Faith paused with the spoon partway to her mouth. "It's not the same out of a can."

"I didn't know people still did that."

"That's because you're from a big city where no one grows pumpkins. When you live on a farm, you grow as much of your food as you can."

He liked the idea of her making that pie for him, but supposed it was too early to hint at an invitation to Thanksgiving dinner.

She finished the chowder and started in on her smoothie, seeming to have forgotten his presence. He talked a little more, about the rainstorm forecast for the weekend, his worries about keeping the streets safe for trick-or-treaters come Halloween and Gray's battle with the city council to get another couple of stoplights installed downtown. If Faith was listening at all, he couldn't tell; her head was bent, her braid fell over her shoulder and that fragile collarbone, and her expression was far away.

He couldn't decide if that distance was healthy, a sort of cotton batting she'd wrapped herself in, or whether she was trying to pull herself so deep inside, no one would be able to touch her. He remembered the way she'd grabbed the stool that day in the barn as if she intended to brandish it at him, and would have preferred her rage and anguish even if it was turned on him.

Suddenly frustrated even though he knew she needed patience most of all, he rose to his feet and bundled his lunch leavings in the bag.

"Thank you for lunch," she said politely. "Was there something you wanted to ask me?"

"No. But I'm here, Faith, when you want to talk."

"I'm fine," she said automatically.

God damn it. If he heard her say she was "fine" one more time...

"I'll look forward to that corn chowder tomorrow night," he told her, and walked out.

SHE KNEW EVERYONE WORRIED about her, but she wished they wouldn't. Couldn't they see that what she needed most was to be left alone? Like a wounded animal crawling into a hole, it was instinct, her way of protecting herself.

Her father seemed to understand the most, but even so she felt his unhappiness like a weight. His eyes were so sad when he looked at her, as if he blamed himself.

Charlotte was...well, it was miracle enough that she was here. Faith never let herself forget that, even when she was ungrateful enough to wish that Char would go home to Gray. After ten years of near-estrangement, her sister was here and wanted nothing so much as to take care of her. But they were twins. Shouldn't Char, of all people, understand that Faith didn't want to talk about what happened?

And Ben. He was the most annoying, even though she saw him the least of the three. He came the closest to making her feel things she didn't want to. Faith tried to convince herself that it was just because she wouldn't have even known him if it weren't for Rory stalking her. Everything he'd ever had to do with her was linked to Rory. She was only a loose end to be tied up. Or else he felt guilty; she wasn't sure. Either way, the minute he was satisfied that she'd put it all behind her, he would be gone. And maybe *that* was why emotions stirred uncomfortably close below the surface when she saw Ben. She had wanted to be more to him. Now, it made her angry that she couldn't get rid of him, when he'd had a way of always disappearing back when she wanted him to come around.

Saturday was awful. Faith worked out in the barn, and it had to be the busiest day of the year. But people came to gawk, not to shop, and she could hardly bear it. She slid away from questions, smiled emptily at sympathy and felt as if her skin was being peeled away from her body, one excruciating inch at a time.

Char would have taken care of today, Faith knew, but she'd worked all week and it wasn't fair to her.

Dad hobbled over midafternoon, took one look at her face and said, "I can take over for a while. You need to go lie down, honey."

"I'll be all right," she said, glancing at her watch. "It's only two more hours until we close, and I can nap then if you don't mind a late dinner. Or making do yourself."

"Ben mentioned that you'd promised him corn chowder tonight."

The dim memory swam upward. "Oh, God. I think he invited himself."

"Go rest."

"Really, I'm fine..."

"I can work the damn cash register!" Real anger crackled in Daddy's voice. "Get out of here."

She went. Remembering she hadn't eaten lunch, she paused in the kitchen, but then continued upstairs. She never reached the second-story hallway without her gaze being drawn to the closed door of her bedroom, but she had moved into Char's room. Some of her clothes were still in her old closet, but she had enough to get by for now. It was ridiculous not to be able to walk in there—Char had cleaned and aired the room, so there wasn't even a bloodstain on the wood floor. But Faith just couldn't. Even thinking about her room—even that brief, involuntary glance at the closed door—made her remember. Just a flash, before she buried it—the moment she'd stiffened when she heard the whisper of sound out in the hall, or the blacker darkness that filled the open doorway, or...

With a shudder, Faith mentally yanked the covers over her head, like a little girl sure she'd be safe if she curled in the dark, warm cavern of her bed.

Now I know I'm not safe.

She hurried into Char's bedroom—no, *her* bedroom now—and stretched out on the bed.

Which was awfully uncomfortable. Char definitely had gotten the worst of the bargain when they were ten years old and Mom decreed that Faith would get the new mattress and Char the old, since she was the one who insisted on having her own room and not sharing anymore. That was nineteen years ago, and the mattress had been gently aging even then, having been Grandma Peters'.

I should buy a new bed, Faith thought, but knew she wouldn't when money was so tight. But no matter what, she'd never sleep in her bed again, not after seeing Rory's lifeblood pour out onto it. Feeling it shudder as his body fell against it on the way to the floor.

She lay there, eyes wide open, and pretended she was resting. She was desperately tired; she knew she was, and that it showed. But she had seemingly lost the ability to sleep. She didn't think she'd slept soundly since those few hours on the air mattress at Gray's house, when Ben had sprawled beside her. Somehow, even though she had been unconscious of his presence, he had made her feel safe.

Daddy had moved back upstairs to his room this week, and had called to have the rented hospital bed picked up. Getting up and down the stairs was hard for him, but there was no denying the comfort of being able to hear his snores right across the hall. Even so, she couldn't sleep. It seemed every time she dropped off, electricity jolted her heart and brought her, gasping, awake. It was as if she'd set an internal alarm to save her from the nightmares waiting on the other side of the curtain of sleep, and she couldn't figure out now how to turn it off.

Or whether she dared turn it off.

She lay stiff, trying to decide what time Ben would arrive and how long it would take her to pick some corn and peel the potatoes. Maybe she'd get up now and make a pumpkin pie, too. Not just for him; Daddy would like it, too. It might ease the sadness that aged him more and more every time she looked at him. He'd loved Mama's pumpkin pie.

Faith's half hour of rest hadn't energized her at all. She felt so weary, she thought of herself encased in rusting metal like the Tin Man. She might be losing weight, but her body was so heavy, she had to think about every step. Holding her head up required an effort.

Nonetheless, she let herself out the back door, keeping the house between herself and the barn so Dad wouldn't spot her. Picking out a pumpkin took only a minute; she left it on the doorstep and went to the field for a few ears of corn that didn't look overripe.

Scooping out pumpkin guts was mindless but satisfying, the smell sharp. After cutting the pumpkin into pieces and baking it, she reduced the pulp to a creamy texture with the help of the Cuisinart, then went to work adding all the sugar and spices.

The pie was baking when Dad came in the back door and she saw by the clock that it was already five-thirty. His face was gray with fatigue, but it lightened when he took a sniff.

"Pie?"

"Ben's never tasted one from scratch," she said. "He got me to thinking about how long it's been since I made one." She kissed her father's cheek. "Now why don't *you* go lie down for a few minutes?"

"I think I might." He set the money bag on the counter. "I didn't count."

"That's okay. I'll do it later. Or tomorrow."

He nodded and trudged on to the staircase. She all but held her breath as he climbed, laboriously moving the crutches, then hitching himself upward.

What if he fell? He should still be sleeping downstairs, she thought with a clutch of guilt. She sank down wearily at the kitchen table. How many lives had been damaged because Rory wouldn't let her go?

Did he really love me that much?

Something in her revolted at the idea. Whatever he'd felt, it wasn't love. Obsession maybe. Faith cringed, as she had a thousand times, at the idea that she'd inspired an emotion so sick. Was something wrong with her, to have made her own twin flee from her and then her husband want to control and hurt her? It almost had to be her, didn't it?

She was so deep in her brooding she jumped when the timer went off. Dad had gone upstairs over half an hour ago! It was almost as if she'd blanked out. Shivering, Faith rose and lowered the oven temperature, then started mixing up biscuit dough. She had drop biscuits on a cookie sheet to go in the oven as soon as she took the pies out.

She'd begun husking the corn when, through the kitchen window, she saw Ben's SUV pull in and park beside her car. He wasn't in his official vehicle. Nor, when he got out and slammed the door, was he wearing his uniform. He'd apparently gone home and changed into jeans and a dark green T-shirt that hugged his broad shoulders. He didn't move immediately, instead gazing toward the house with an unreadable but somber expression on his face. After a moment he squeezed the back of his neck with one hand as if to relieve tension. Only then did he come toward the back door, his stride long and athletic.

Despite everything, she responded to the mere sight of him. She made herself back away from the window, her heart pounding. He didn't feel the same about her. He was here because he felt responsible for her. What she had to do was convince him that she was doing fine, and he'd go away.

She needed him to go away. Faith didn't want to feel anything right now, and especially not this longing that could mean nothing but more pain in the end.

He rapped lightly on the glass pane of the back door and came in when he saw her, not waiting for more of an invitation. "Hope this is good timing."

"It's fine. I'm letting Dad lie down for a bit before dinner."

He opened his mouth and then closed it. "Is that pumpkin pie I smell?"

She went back to peeling the husks from the corn.

"I thought I'd give a city boy a treat. And Dad, too. He seemed pleased."

Ben bent low to inhale the aroma of the pies cooling on the counter, then leaned one hip against the counter edge beside her. "I'm pleased, too," he said, his voice low and somehow soft despite its craggy texture.

She wished he wouldn't stand so close. "Excuse me," she said politely, and when he moved back she reached into an upper cupboard for a large bowl. Unfortunately, he resumed his spot the minute she closed the cupboard door and picked up a paring knife.

"Can I do anything?" he asked.

"Well…I suppose you could peel the potatoes, if you want." Keeping him busy seemed like a good idea.

She'd already set a small heap of Yukon Gold potatoes on the counter. Now she handed him a potato peeler and got out a cutting board. He washed his hands and went to work right beside her, which was almost more disconcerting than having him watch her. As she sliced corn from the cobs into the big bowl, she kept stealing sidelong glances at his strong brown forearms and the dark hair on them, at his wrists that had to be twice the thickness of hers, at hands so large and yet deft as he peeled and cut the potatoes into cubes.

He had held her with those arms; she'd rested her cheek against his chest, and his big hands had moved over her so tenderly it made her heart ache to remember.

Then don't, she told herself harshly. *You can't afford to.*

By the time she measured water into a soup kettle and turned on the burner of the old gas range, then scraped the potatoes into it along with the celery, onion and green pepper she'd diced, Faith had squelched the unwelcome moment of weakness. It was worse to be held and then abandoned than it was not to have anyone to lean on in the first place.

Ignoring him wasn't easy, though, with those dark eyes watching her so damn thoughtfully, as if he was trying to read every flicker of her emotions. The sound of the timer gave her an excuse; first she took the biscuits out of the oven and then, as she added the corn and milk to the chowder, she sent Ben upstairs to wake Dad.

"It takes him a while to make it downstairs."

"Stairs are a bitch with crutches," Ben agreed.

"You've been on them?" She was immediately mad at herself for asking.

"I was wounded in the leg a few years back." He didn't move for a moment, his gaze resting on her face, but when she didn't react he turned away and she heard him start upstairs.

A shudder passed through her. *Wounded.* That sounded as if he'd been knifed or shot, not injured in a car accident or something normal. She shouldn't be surprised. He must be nearly forty, which meant he'd been a cop for many years. He'd implied, if not said, that he knew what it was like to kill someone.

Dad had been drafted and sent to Vietnam, but his skill at keeping tractors and farm combines running meant he'd spent his enlistment working as a mechanic, not patrolling or fighting. Faith knew a couple of guys her age who'd been in Iraq, but had no idea whether they'd been in combat, never mind actually killed anyone. It was an awkward question to ask someone. Would it even help to find out what other people felt?

And it had to be different when the person you shot to death was someone you knew. Someone you'd once believed you loved. And when you were face-to-face and saw the moment of death in his eyes.

She closed her eyes tight and held herself very still. *Don't think about it,* she told herself desperately. It had become her mantra. *Don't think about it.*

Ben was making himself available. He *wanted* her to talk to him. Faith thought, at least, that he'd be honest with her.

But her anxiety at the idea was so great, she heard herself gasping for breath as she clung to the handle on the refrigerator door. She couldn't talk about it again! She just couldn't.

I can think about it later. Maybe a week from now, or a month from now, or six months from now, she'd want to talk to somebody. But she wasn't ready yet, and nobody could make her do anything she didn't want to.

The anxiety eased enough for her to remember that she was supposed to be getting the whipping cream out of the refrigerator to add to the chowder. Oh—and butter, for the table.

It was Ben who was making her so tense. Once she fed him, he'd go home and leave her in peace, at least for another day or two. Maybe longer than that, if she could convince him she really was fine.

Her chest squeezed with pain, and Faith had to wonder if she would ever really be fine again.

CHAPTER SEVEN

IT RAINED on Halloween. In fact, the skies had opened the Saturday before and never closed again. Faith had counted on sales for the week being the highest of the year. But Mr. Barth declined to bring his wagon or Clydesdales over to get drenched and slosh through the mud for the few brave families who decided to visit a pumpkin field in the rain. Nobody wanted to go through the maze. If people were buying pumpkins that week, it was from the covered areas in front of Safeway and Thriftway. On one memorable day that week, not a single car had pulled into the farm. Marsha just shook her head when Faith asked how the day had gone. On All Hallow's Eve, Faith didn't even light the dozen jack-o'-lanterns clustered outside the barn doors.

The evening was quiet, the windows pelted with heavy rain as she—and Dad, too, probably—pretended to watch TV. She felt the weight of his gaze, and kept her face wooden. She knew what he was thinking. *Knew* it. The receipts this month didn't even justify paying Marsha's part-time wages, much less Char taking so much time away from her highly paid software designing job.

Panic beating in her chest like great black crow's wings, Faith stared blindly at the television screen.

We could be open just weekends.

But that new produce stand had opened in town, on the corner near the farm co-op. It was more conveniently placed for locals. And there were now two antiques stores in town. They probably wouldn't make it; small businesses usually didn't. But in the meantime, they would suck more customers away from the Russell Family Farm. Halloween was one thing the farm did really, really well, and this year was a bomb. Even last week, before the rain began, she'd noticed a big drop-off in families wanting to go through the maze or browse the pumpkin patch. The barn had been busy enough with nosy people, but the genuine customers had quit coming. Real bloodshed and tragedy detracted from the atmosphere of family fun she had promoted. Even at school or the grocery store, some people stared at her, but Faith hadn't been able to help noticing that others—sometimes people she'd known for years—didn't want to meet her eyes.

The business wasn't enough to keep the farm alive. And Dad hated it anyway. She knew he did. She was the only reason he hadn't given up and sold the farm two years ago.

He was watching her again, the bags under his eyes and his expression making her think of a basset hound. Her fingernails bit into her palms. She should say something. They ought to talk about it. But Faith felt as if someone was ripping her heart out of her chest. It was stupid to let a piece of land mean so much to her; a ramshackle farmhouse, a cluster of aging outbuildings, even if it had all belonged to her grandparents before her parents, even if this was where she'd grown up, where she...belonged.

Just as it was stupid to have this terrible fear that she

would tumble off the edge of the world if she didn't have the farm to cling to, her fingernails digging into the river delta soil.

She was having trouble breathing, but she couldn't let her father see. Jumping to her feet, Faith said, "I'm going to clean up the kitchen and read for a while, Dad. I'd better do a load of laundry, too." She kissed his grizzled cheek and hurried out of the living room before she crumpled.

Of course, she couldn't do that in the kitchen, either. He'd hear her, or walk in on her. And if she went up to her room and cried in bed he'd wonder why she hadn't loaded the dishwasher and wiped down the counters. So she'd have to do that before she could break down.

But by the time the kitchen was spotless and she'd gone upstairs to collect dirty clothes to start a load, she was almost numb again. No breakdown tonight, she thought dully. It was better this way.

Dad's hesitant footsteps stopped behind her just as she started the washer.

"Faith?"

Anguish rushed back, flooding her chest until her ribs all but creaked. *Not now. Please, please, Daddy. Not now.*

"You're going up to bed?" she heard herself say brightly, not turning. She measured laundry soap out and dumped it in. "I grabbed the clothes from your hamper, too."

After a moment he said, "All right, Faith." Resignation weighted his voice. "I guess I will go up. Don't stay up too late."

"Of course not," she assured him, her cheer as real as the bright red tomatoes at the grocery store, the ones that might as well be made out of plastic for all the taste they had.

Once again, she listened as he made his slow, awkward way upstairs. He clumped to the bathroom, then back to his bedroom. He didn't shut the door. He never did anymore. Neither of them did, as if they had to hear each other breathing at night to feel safe.

Then why don't I? she wondered. *Why do I only feel safe when Ben is near?* Hadn't her daddy always been there for her? But it seemed to her that he could only keep the little girl safe, not the woman she was now. He hadn't been able to save his wife, or the farm; he hadn't been able to do anything to at all to protect Faith from her monster of a husband.

And that was her fault, too, of course, because she'd never *told* her father that Rory hurt her.

Silence settled upstairs and she stood gripping the sides of the washing machine and staring at the rainy night through the window Rory had come through. Faith didn't even know when the glass had been replaced. Probably Ben or Gray had arranged it the day after.

The blur wasn't all rain on the windowpane; tears had begun to fall, and Faith couldn't seem to stop them.

It was all over. Everything was over. There was no point in even opening tomorrow. No—there was. They'd want to sell as much of their inventory as possible. They could start with a twenty-five percent discount, then go to fifty percent, then higher. An auction would take care of the farm equipment.

The unsold pumpkins could rot; the fields would never be plowed again. They would be bulldozed. The house and the hundred-year-old barn, too. She could see it now, the earth stripped raw, an asphalt road with curbs and sidewalks winding through land that had once been a farm. Small stakes topped with bright plastic flags would mark the boundaries of lots where houses would be built cheek by jowl. Or maybe even apartment complexes, like that development on Woods Creek over behind Safeway.

Her decision was abrupt. She'd cover up the maze sign out on the highway. Tonight, just in case the rain let up before morning and someone wanted to try it out. And the sign that said Fresh Organic Produce, too, because there wouldn't be any more.

She couldn't remember where they'd stowed the piece of plywood that had covered the maze sign until the corn had grown high enough. Maybe she could cover both temporarily with black plastic garbage bags. They always kept a box of them here in the utility room.

But she couldn't find it, her search increasingly frantic, her frustration rising until she choked on it. She wouldn't wait until morning. She wouldn't!

Finally, she discovered the box fallen behind the dryer, empty. Her throat closed.

Well then, she'd take *down* the sign. They'd always kept an ax and a saw in the covered woodbox behind the house, next to the back steps.

Faith didn't bother with a raincoat or boots. Who cared if she got wet? She had the presence of mind, but just barely, to carry a flashlight so she could find the saw. The lid to the woodbox slipped from her wet hands and thumped back down, but she couldn't imagine Daddy would hear it, not with his bedroom on the other side of the house.

The narrow yellow beam of the flashlight led her across the wet grass to the highway. There wasn't any traffic. Probably no one had gone out tonight. Ben would be relieved; he'd been so worried about trick-or-treaters and about teenagers out pulling pranks. All of them would have stayed home safe and warm and dry instead, Ben included. She was pathetic, out here in the dark and cold rain, sobbing as she fell to her knees beside the sign, planted on two sturdy 4x4s buried deep in the earth.

Faith sawed until her arms ached. The serrated blade kept binding in the wood until she screamed with rage. Finally, once she'd gotten far enough through both uprights, she threw herself at the sign and felt the wood crack as the whole thing fell, her with it.

She lay, half stunned, atop the sign, until she could make herself push to her knees, then her feet. She dragged the sign and uprights behind her and dropped it beside the back steps, then went back and attacked the fresh-organic-produce sign in turn. Her arms and back ached, but she couldn't let herself stop until this sign, too, toppled. It was all she could do to get it to the back steps. She almost wept anew to realize she'd forgotten the saw, but she made herself go back for it and restore it to its place in the woodbox. As if it mattered whether it rusted in the rain. Most of the tools would go in the estate sale they'd hold before moving.

Faith was shaking by now, so cold she couldn't feel her feet. She let herself in the back door and stood dripping inside, shivering and rocking in place. Blood soaked one arm of her shirt, she noticed, as if it had nothing to do with her. She'd probably torn her skin on a nail. Which didn't matter—she'd had a tetanus shot not that long ago, when she'd stepped on a nail when she was hunting for something in the back shed.

I don't know if I can get up the stairs, Faith thought.

If she had to call for Dad, he'd think she'd gone crazy. And he would be right. She had. But she didn't want anyone to know that, any more than she wanted them to know how much she hurt inside, how desperate she had been for one single thing in her life to be right.

I have Char back. That's right.

But tonight it didn't feel like enough. Faith wasn't even sure she believed in the reconciliation with her sister.

She didn't believe in anything. Not God, not justice and, most of all, not herself.

But if she wasn't truly crazy, then she had to take care of herself. She couldn't let her father find her here, collapsed, come morning.

If she were the Tin Man, her joints had now locked and the tears had corroded her face. Somewhere inside, she found enough strength to stagger, finally, to the utility room and with shaking hands strip off her wet clothes. Scrabbling in the hamper, she came up with her own dirty jeans and a mercifully thick sweatshirt of her father's and struggled into them. Thank goodness she'd put in a white load and not dark, or there might have been nothing at all to wear in here.

The washer had reached the spin cycle. She put her back against it and slid down to sit on the floor. The rumble and rhythmic vibration were somehow a comfort, as if she were a newly weaned puppy missing her mother who had found an artificial heartbeat.

Her mouth opened in a silent wail, and then she buried her face in her hands and let go.

BEN COUNTED the unexpected peace of Halloween as a blessing. Despite the rain, he'd double-shifted his officers and been out patrolling himself. A few determined trick-or-treaters in rain slickers ventured to neighbors', their accompanying parents huddled on the sidewalks beneath umbrellas, the yellow beam of flashlights faint beacons through the downpour. By seven-thirty, even that modest burst of activity had ended. He'd sent the extra officers home and had a good night's sleep himself.

He'd seen less of Faith this week than he wanted, and hadn't had time to do more than make some inquiries of other police departments about the names he'd extracted from Michelle Hardesty. The rain had brought flooding—not from the river, still too low to top its banks although now turgid and brown, but from overwhelmed storm drains. Patrol cars with flashing lights were stationed to block streets that were a foot underneath water and to protect the utility workers trying to clear drains and ditches. A school bus had ended up stuck axle-deep in a dip in the road and the kids had had to be carried through the water to another bus. There were two calls about rats, of all damn things, apparently driven to scuttling up to the limbs of trees and onto windowsills, where they scared the crap out of residents. To top it all off, the roof on Ben's house had sprung a leak, and he'd spent a nightmarish couple of hours in the dark on the slippery, steep-pitched roof trying to anchor a heavy plastic tarp to keep out the rain until he could get a roofer out to work on it.

The endless dark gray, wet skies felt symbolic. He wondered whether the incessant downpour was depressing only to him because he was used to the endlessly blue skies of Southern California, or whether the gloom would be weighing on Faith, too. The one day that week he'd trapped her in her classroom for lunch, and the one evening he'd stopped by at the farm, she'd said only, "We're used to rain."

But there was rain, and then there was *rain*. He hadn't minded last winter's drizzle as much as he'd expected. But, for God's sake, would this deluge never end?

Sunday morning, he was up early. He had today off, unless unexpected disaster struck, but after a quick breakfast he drove around town anyway, needing to see that it was still peaceful. After a quick survey, he turned onto the highway, drawn by a pull so great he couldn't stay away from Faith even if he was unwelcome.

He'd put on his turn signal and slowed for the first, muddy pothole when he noticed the gaps in the plywood signs along the road verge. Ben stopped and set the emergency brake, then despite the rain got out and walked over to see what had happened. Had a car plowed off the highway and taken them out? He saw immediately that they'd been sawed off, and crudely. Occasional ruts torn in the lawn showed they had been dragged to the house.

What the hell…?

He got back in his SUV, shook the water from his hair and drove up to the house. The closed sign remained on the barn door. He frowned. Would Faith not be opening on Sundays, now that Halloween was past? God, he hoped she'd take a day or two a week off. Maybe her sister had persuaded her to use some common sense.

Yeah, right, he thought wryly. How likely was that?

Gray's black Prius was parked beside Faith's battered Blazer. Ben pulled in behind the Blazer. He should probably go away, now that he knew Charlotte was here, with or without Gray, but he wasn't going to. He was being tugged forward by some force beyond him.

Ben didn't like knowing exactly what that force was. He had been fighting it too long, and something told him he'd just lost the final battle.

No one was in the kitchen. He knocked on the back door and waited until Gray appeared from the direction of the living room. He raised his brows at the sight of Ben and opened the door.

"Has something come up?"

"No. Just...stopping by." He kept his voice low. "What's with the signs out by the highway?"

"Faith took them down last night."

Ben swore. "Last night? In the pouring rain?"

Gray didn't look any happier than he felt. "Yeah. We're...having a family meeting right now."

"I should leave, then." But his feet didn't want to move.

"I think the rest of us would be glad enough to have you here."

The rest of us. In other words, except for Faith.

"I'm not family."

"Technically I'm not yet, either."

"Don't be ridiculous."

"They're talking about selling the farm."

God, no. To Faith, it would be like another death. *No.*

His reaction was instinctive, and surprised him. He wanted the burden lifted from her, would have said it would be a good thing, but he knew that Faith couldn't handle it. Not now. Not yet.

"No." He shook his head. "She's not ready."

"She called the meeting. She says she is."

Without another word, Ben walked past the other man and into the living room. The hospital bed was gone, he saw, the sofa restored to its place. Don was in a wing chair in the bay window. The two sisters sat on the sofa, near enough to touch, but not doing so, their separation palpable. Faith sat with her spine utterly straight, her hands quiet on her lap. Ben was willing to bet her fingers were rigid, the outward serenity of the neatly folded hands as deceptive as her frequent insistence that she was "fine."

All three heads turned when Ben strode into the room, and he thought he saw relief on Don's face and even perhaps Charlotte's. Faith stared at him as if she didn't know who he was.

"Can we help you?" she asked politely.

His gaze boring into hers, Ben said, "You wouldn't surrender two months ago, or two weeks ago. Why now, Faith?"

She didn't pretend to misunderstand. "The rain. And..." her voice cracked "...what happened. We needed October to be successful. It wasn't."

Damn. The weather, not in anyone's control, had conspired to join that weasel Hardesty to render Faith completely powerless. It wasn't right. It wasn't fair.

"I'm sorry," he said, as gently as he could. He couldn't help thinking how many times he'd said that to her, and how little good it had done.

She gave a dip of her head in acknowledgement. She couldn't react any more than that, he guessed, without falling apart completely.

"Everyone but me seems to have known this was inevitable. I just…" Her voice drifted, and she swallowed hard. "This is home."

"I know." God help him, all he wanted was to take her into his arms and absorb all of her grief, all of her disappointment, all of her pain. He crossed the living room, and Charlotte scooted sideways to leave the middle cushion of the sofa open for him. Ben was mildly surprised that she'd made way for him, but right this minute he didn't care why she thought he could do something for her sister that she couldn't.

He sat down beside Faith and laid his hand over hers. They were as tense as he'd expected, and chilly to the touch. She jerked, as if in surprise, and looked at him with seeming helplessness.

"There's more to it," Don said. "I was developing some arthritis anyway, but I'm not coming back from having that tractor roll on me the way I should have. Faith can't run the place herself, we can't afford to hire much help and I may not be able to do the hard work anymore."

He'd said all that flatly, but cords stood out in his neck and on the backs of his hands. Watching his daughters, women, do what he couldn't would have been hard for a man of his generation. Of any generation, Ben thought ruefully; men weren't programmed to watch their women work themselves to the bone while they laid back in comfort. Ben glanced around and saw Charlotte biting her lip and Gray watching Don with compassion. Faith, Ben thought, was least affected by her father's words, because she had known what he was enduring. And now, on top of everything else, she felt guilty for making him endure it.

After a decent pause, Ben cleared his throat. "When?"

Standing in the doorway watching, Gray said, "Don plans to call a couple of real-estate agents tomorrow. Find out whether it's better to wait for spring, or go ahead and list the farm."

Ben nodded and looked at Don. "Where will you go?"

Don cleared his throat. "I thought I'd buy a house in town. Where else? Faith has a job, and now that Charlotte's back for good…"

The jolt of fear Ben had felt was idiotic; of course Don and Faith wouldn't be pulling up roots and moving across the country, or whatever the hell he had imagined for a second. He resisted the urge to rub the heel of his hand across the ache in his chest.

"The business?" he said, looking back at Faith.

Her eyes were so dark, he could have fallen into them. They seemed to struggle to absorb any light.

"We'll stay open for a few weeks, try to sell as much inventory as we can." Her mouth twisted. "Going-out-of-business signs should be a draw."

He nodded, suddenly aware that Gray had been completely silent and Charlotte mostly quiet. He should apologize to all of them, say, *I should butt out.*

Looking around, Ben did say, "I'm sorry. I interrupted. I'll shut up and let you go on with your meeting." But he didn't move. If anything, his hand tightened, especially when he felt one of Faith's swivel to grab hold of him as if she was suddenly afraid he was going to stand up and walk out.

Not happening, he thought, and felt the burning in his chest that he wished was heartburn but knew wasn't.

He hadn't just lost the battle; he was waving a white flag that probably had his heart painted on it.

He just wished he thought Faith would accept the flag and everything that came with it.

After that he sat beside her, holding her hand and letting them talk. It was all so damn prosaic, as if they weren't discussing the misery of cutting up the carcass of an animal they had all loved. Gray recommended a couple of real-estate agents; Don knew who to call to set up an auction for the tractor and tools and other farm equipment. Faith planned to phone a couple of the restaurants in town and offer what was left of the produce and the pumpkins. Charlotte and she decided to paint some signs that said Twenty-Five Percent Off and Fifty Percent Off and Going Out of Business to post out on the highway.

"We can do it this afternoon," Charlotte said. "If you're sure, Faith?" Her look held a question.

"It's time." Only the tremor of her hands betrayed any emotion at all.

When the discussion had wound down, Ben said, "It's almost noon. I'd like to take you all out to Sunday brunch. My treat."

Charlotte gave him a grateful smile, pretty enough on her gamine face to make him wonder again in passing, as he had dozens of times, why she'd never attracted him when her sister did. They were identical twins, after all. But he knew better. Whatever it was about Faith that pulled him so powerfully had nothing to do with her looks, or very little, anyway. Right now, the bruises of exhaustion shadowed her eyes and her hair was pulled back so tight it must hurt, and he still ached with the knowledge of how much he loved her.

Simple as that. Foolish as that. This was a woman who was being destroyed by the one violent act she'd been driven to commit. He would never be able to let her glimpse the dark places inside him. But after seeing her suffer these past weeks, he knew he could live with that. He could live with anything, so long as he had her.

And the only thing that gave him hope he'd have a chance was the way she clung to his hand.

"That's kind of you," her father said to Ben's invitation. "It would be good for all of us."

Gray and Charlotte hastened to agree. Faith opened her mouth to excuse herself—Ben knew damn well that's what she had in mind—but he shook his head at her.

"You know I'm too stubborn for you," he murmured close to her ear, and her eyes flashed irritation and acquiescence both. They were blue again, he saw with relief.

She snorted, shook his hand off and stood. "Fine."

Her favorite word. His least favorite.

They all put on raincoats. Faith tried to maneuver herself to go in Gray's Prius, but Ben gripped her arm and waylaid her. "Ride with me," he said.

Seeing her dad already getting in with her sister and Gray, she turned to Ben's SUV without argument. He wished she'd snapped at him. As it was, she stared out the side window during the drive and gave monosyllabic responses to his couple of conversational forays.

Don had suggested the River Fork Steakhouse, which he claimed did an excellent brunch. Ben would have been just as happy to go elsewhere, as the last time he'd been here was the one-and-only time he had taken Charlotte out on a date. Her glance as he held open the door for everyone told him she was thinking the same, and Gray's sardonic expression wasn't much better. Gray had walked in that night and seen the woman he was falling in love with dining out with his police chief. He hadn't been a happy man. Never slow on the uptake, Ben had realized that Charlotte had gone out with him to make a point, perhaps to herself as much as to Gray. Sure as hell not because she was drawn to Ben. Just as well, since he'd only asked her because he was scared to death of what he felt for her shyer, sweeter sister from first sight. The night had been a debacle all around.

Today, they were seated right away. Apparently the rain was keeping even the regulars home. The brunch was a nice spread, and everyone seemed to relax some now that they were away from the farmhouse that held too many memories for the Russells.

In an effort to make conversation, Charlotte turned to Ben. "You must live here in town, Ben. Are you renting, or did you buy when you took the job?"

"I bought." He spread cream cheese on a toasted bagel. "One of the old houses up on the hill. Seemed like a plan at the time."

His tone had apparently been morose enough to capture even Faith's interest. "You're sorry?"

"The furnace crapped out first. That was last winter. Then I got tired of having to go flip a breaker again every time I plugged my electric razor in." He rubbed a reminiscent hand over his jaw. "I went back to a good, old-fashioned razor for a while, but that ticked me off, so I finally called an electrician out. Had to have a new electrical box and half the wiring replaced. Now I've got a leak in the roof, which is at least thirty years old. Yeah, I'm starting to have some doubts."

Gray was laughing. "You should have had me design you a house."

His fiancée elbowed him. "Those old houses have charm."

"It would have more charm," Ben grumbled, "if my budget had been spent on refinishing floors and moldings instead of a furnace and wiring."

Faith, at least, was listening. Why did he suspect she'd prefer a turn-of-the-century fixer-upper to anything modern, however much character the architect managed to give it?

Gray flashed him a grin. "So, how's the plumbing?"

"It groans."

"Ours does, too," Don admitted, a reminder none of them needed that their old house was likely to meet the blunt end of a bulldozer. The state of the plumbing wouldn't matter.

Faith laid down her fork, but she *had* eaten. Not as much as Ben would have liked to see, but some. He swore she was still losing weight. How had she had the strength to saw through those uprights last night and then haul the heavy signs all the way to the house?

When he'd paid the bill and they were leaving, she said, "There's no point in you coming back out to the house, Ben. I'll just ride with Gray and Charlotte."

"All right," he said, but drew her to a stop. When she lifted a wary gaze to his, he asked, "Are you sleeping at all, Faith?"

She stiffened. "What makes you think I'm not?"

With one fingertip he touched the betraying, deep blue smudge under one of her eyes.

After a moment she said, "I refuse to take sleeping pills."

Frustration suddenly gripped him. "Do you know what I'd like to do right now?"

Her teeth closed on her lower lip, betraying nerves. She shook her head.

"I want to take you home with me and tuck you into my bed for a nap. I want to lie there next to you, just like I did that day at Gray's house." He wouldn't even have to be touching her. He'd be satisfied just watching her sleep, like he had that day before he'd finally dropped off himself.

Color touched her cheeks and he thought he saw yearning in her eyes before they shied from his. "That's just weird."

He smiled at her. "Maybe. Of course, that's not all I want, but it would be a start. Just…knowing you were sleeping soundly, right there next to me."

"I don't understand you," Faith whispered.

His own voice low and husky, Ben said, "I'm willing to give you a chance to, any time you're ready."

A shiver traveled through her, and then she lifted her head and tugged her arm free from his hand. She met his eyes, her own stripped of emotion. "Your guilt isn't comfortable for either of us. Get over it." With that, she turned and walked away.

Frustration boiling in his chest, Ben had no choice but to watch her go.

No, she wasn't interested in taking that white flag of surrender from his hands. She didn't trust him.

For good reason.

He couldn't figure any other way to convince her but with persistence and one hell of a lot of patience, both of which he'd already been employing without notable success.

Ben just wished he could see an alternative to wearing her down, when, in his opinion, she was about as worn down as she could be without giving up altogether.

It was a minute before he unlocked his 4Runner, got in and backed out of the parking spot.

CHAPTER EIGHT

"OH, CHAR." In a rush, Faith's blue eyes filled with tears. "You look gorgeous."

The two women stood before a tall mirror in the generously sized dressing room of a bridal shop. The wedding was only two weeks away, and Faith had been the one to insist they go on an all-out shopping expedition. Given recent events, when Charlotte had thought at all about needing a wedding dress, she'd just figured she would find something at the nearest department store.

But now, gazing at herself in the mirror, she was astonished to feel her chest fill with emotion. Okay, damn it—she *did* want to look beautiful for Gray when she walked down the aisle to him. Not traditional-bride beautiful, which meant lace-encrusted pearls and miles of stiff white satin skirt and veil that just didn't suit her. But this dress...

It was reminiscent of the 1920s flapper era, with a dropped waist and silk the color of gentle ivory, as if aged in a cedar chest in the attic. The thin straps were sewn with rhinestones, as was the very edge of the bodice. Otherwise, the dress relied entirely on drape. Fabric cut on the bias lovingly outlined her breasts, lingered at her hips and shaped to her thighs when she moved experimentally. It fit her perfectly, as if made for her.

And Faith—Faith was glowing, which she hadn't done in weeks, maybe even months.

Charlotte's chest burned at having to contain so much.

She didn't know if she could express any of it, and didn't even try. Instead, she twirled to peer at her back. "Dare I ask how much it is?"

Faith laughed and then sniffed. "Within your budget, or you wouldn't be trying it on. Hmm…" She studied Charlotte in the mirror. "I wonder if we couldn't do something flapper style for a headpiece, too. A band of some kind, with glittery fringe, or…"

The saleswoman, who had been standing back smiling, now narrowed her eyes and studied Charlotte, too. "With your short hair… Hats aren't common in weddings these days, but… You need a cloche. They were very popular in that era." Her hands shaped the hat she envisioned as if it sat on her head. "A soft fabric, ivory like the dress, with perhaps a vintage brooch on it. It could anchor a veil if you want one…."

"I don't," Charlotte said decisively.

The woman nodded. "You might have to hunt online for the kind of thing I'm imagining, but there are a couple of vintage clothing stores in Seattle. You could get lucky."

They did get lucky. Charlotte hadn't been sure how she felt about the idea of wearing a hat—it wasn't as if she often did, and she had doubts that one would go with her wedding dress anyway—but at the third vintage clothing shop they went into she found a soft, ivory wool cloche. They showed the shop owner the dress, and she produced a brooch that was a spray of brilliant rhinestones to match the ones on the dress. "And perhaps a feather," she murmured, and found one—or stole it from some other hat—that curved rakishly when clipped on with the brooch. They all sighed with pleasure at the sight of Charlotte wearing it and gazing into the mirror.

"Now shoes," Faith said firmly.

Today was the first time Charlotte had seen Faith come out of herself since Rory's death. From the moment she'd decided that they *would* go shopping, she had been just a little bossy and startlingly decisive.

They ate a late lunch in the café at Nordstrom, having chosen a dress for Faith there. Charlotte smiled at her sister over the table. "Do you remember when we went shopping for prom dresses our junior year?"

"Oh, Lord," Faith groaned. "I kept picking pink with ruffles, and everything you liked cost the world."

Charlotte grinned. "I always did have expensive taste, didn't I?"

Of course, she hadn't been able to *buy* any of those elegant, stylish dresses she'd coveted so. The Russell family budget hadn't been up to that challenge. Heavens, thinking back, the cost of outfitting two girls for a prom had probably just about killed their parents, even though they'd both ended up sewing their own dresses.

"I'll bet Mom and Dad couldn't afford to have another kid after us," she mused. "With twins, they couldn't take advantage of hand-me-downs like they would've if we'd been stair-stepped in age. And every time one of us grew and needed new shoes or a winter coat or whatever, so did the other."

"We did get hand-me-downs from the Smiths and… oh, from Lisa! I *hated* having to wear her clothes!"

Funny, Charlotte hadn't known that. Probably there hadn't been anything wrong with the clothes at all, but neither of the twins had liked the daughter of their mom's best friend. And the idea of showing up at school in something any of Lisa's friends would recognize hadn't been very welcome to Charlotte, either.

But apparently less so to Faith.

"Because you cared what you wore," she realized. "And I really didn't most of the time."

Faith snorted. "In fifth or sixth grade, you'd have worn your soccer shorts and jersey to school, if you could have gotten away with it."

"Yeah, and it was okay if they were muddy, too."

They both laughed, remembering their very first soccer practice when Faith had fallen in a mud hole and realized her pristine white shin guards were now filthy and would never be pretty and white again. Trying to make her sister feel better, Char had taken a slide into the same mud hole, as if she were stealing second base. Of course, unlike Faith she'd laughed at how dirty she got. Their mother, rolling her eyes, had made them sit on newspapers for the drive home.

The thought made her smile waver. "I wish Mom could be here."

Faith clasped her hand. "Me, too." After a moment she said softly, "Maybe none of this would have happened."

None of what, exactly? Charlotte wondered.

"Would you have told Mom about Rory?" she asked.

Faith removed her hand under the pretext of picking

up her spoon. "I don't know," she said after a minute. "Maybe." Her mouth twisted into a small, painful smile. "Or not."

"I've never understood...."

"I know. I guess...I don't either. Not altogether."

Charlotte nodded, not wanting to press the issue. It mattered now only because she knew that her sister had to learn to open up to somebody if she was going to survive this last tragedy whole. And despite all the ground the two of them had regained, Faith wasn't talking to her twin. Not really.

"Ben's around a lot," Charlotte remarked, seemingly at random.

Faith didn't quite meet her eyes as she picked up her half sandwich. "He feels guilty."

"Are you sure that's all there is to it?"

"What else would it be?" Faith asked flatly. "He seems to think he can put me back together again, like Humpty, and satisfy his sense of responsibility. I can live without his brand of superglue."

Charlotte watched her. "Can you? I think you ought to at least talk to him, Faith. Unless you're willing to find a counselor who has experience in working with victims of violence."

"I wasn't the victim this time."

Her own appetite deserted her on a wave of anger. "Sure you were. You *are*. And you need to come to terms with it, Faith." This might be cruel, but she had to say it. "You're crumbling day by day. That makes you a victim as long as you let yourself be flayed by remorse you shouldn't be feeling."

Her sister was silent so long that Charlotte's resolve faltered and she longed to say, *I didn't mean it.*

Faith's gaze met hers. "Easier said than done. You didn't pull that trigger. Or see the blood, and the way his eyes…" She swallowed and set down her sandwich. "Today is supposed to be about you. Can we not talk about this anymore?"

Charlotte all but tumbled from her chair on her way to hug her sister, hating the new fragility of a body that had always been slender but strong. "You're right. I'm sorry. Darn it." Now *her* eyes threatened to overflow, and she had to blink hard to quell the impulse. "Shoes," she said. "We still don't have shoes. And stockings. Something pretty."

Faith's smile might have been strained, but it was real. "Definitely something pretty," she agreed. "And you can't show any of it to Gray. You need to let me take it all home, so he doesn't sneak a peek."

"He wouldn't…"

"He would."

"And anyway, that's a silly tradition."

Faith grinned at her, far more naturally now. "Traditions survive for a reason. Come on, you want to blow him away, don't you?"

She found herself smiling back. "Yep. But you know he's already broken with tradition, don't you? Moira is going to be his best man, so to speak."

"Good for him."

Charlotte thought the same. She and Moira Cullen, Gray's partner in their architectural firm, had become good friends. She *was* Gray's best friend, and should be standing beside him when he made a lifetime commitment to the woman he loved.

Charlotte, of course, wouldn't have had anybody but Faith. She'd always assumed it would be Faith beside her, just as she had stood up beside Faith at her wedding, despite her puzzlement at her sister's choice of husband. No matter what had gone wrong between them, they were still essential to each other.

Once, she would have felt smothering panic at the idea of the bond that had united them from the womb, a bond she doubted *could* be severed as long as they both lived. Now, she felt a sudden, unexpected surge of joy, because she had Faith to help her choose her wedding dress, because she would be there, smiling, when Charlotte gave her life into Gray's keeping, as he gave his into hers.

The thought was absurdly romantic and not at all like her. But Charlotte reached out and laced her fingers through Faith's and tugged her toward the first display of shoes.

"I love you," she said.

Faith gave her a quick, hard hug and a scratchy, wobbly, "I love you, too."

FAITH GRIPPED the steering wheel of her Blazer with fingers that absolutely didn't want to let go.

This was the worst idea she'd ever had. She could not walk up to Ben Wheeler's front door and ring the bell. She had literally broken out in a cold sweat now that she was parked in front of his house.

Panting, she thought, *Oh, God. Oh, God. What was I thinking?*

What she'd been thinking was that Charlotte was right: she was now *letting* herself be a victim, and she hated that. Talking to someone might be the first step toward healing. Ben had offered. In a way, if she took him up on that offer, she'd be using him, but in return he'd get some satisfaction from having helped rescue her. It would assuage his guilt, soothe his hero complex. Right?

Yes, but I should have called.

She hardly ever did anything on impulse, but after brooding all morning as she manned the cash register at the barn, she'd asked her dad if he could take over for a couple of hours.

He'd looked mildly surprised but didn't ask any questions, only nodded. "Take all the time you need," he said in his gruff, kind way.

Of course, the odds were that Ben wasn't home. She'd told herself that as she drove over here after calling Gray to find out where Ben lived. Now she couldn't tell for sure, because there was a detached garage and the door was closed. His 4Runner might be inside.

With fatalistic certainty, she knew she was going to chicken out and wait until the next time he came to her. She'd feel, somehow, less vulnerable that way.

But Faith had no sooner made up her mind that she was going to drive away than the front door opened and Ben walked out, coming straight to her Blazer. On the sidewalk, he stopped, shoved his hands in the pockets of his well-worn jeans and waited as patiently as if he had all the time in the world.

Heart drumming, she unwrapped her fingers from the steering wheel, took her key from the ignition and got out. He neither touched her when she got to the sidewalk nor said anything.

She let out a puff of breath. "You saw me sitting here."

"Kind of got the feeling you weren't going to make it to the front door."

"I was…having second thoughts," she said with dignity. As much dignity as she could salvage, considering he'd caught her being a coward. "I realized I shouldn't have just dropped by. You might have company, or…"

His dark eyes saw right through her. "I've made it pretty clear I'm available to you any time. Anywhere." He held out a hand to her. "Will you come in, Faith?"

She stared at his hand, big, tanned, powerful. She knew its warmth, how gentle he could be with that hand. Taking a deep breath, Faith put hers in it, felt his clasp. "Yes," she whispered. "Okay."

As if she were a child, he led her up the front walk. She was aware on some level of his house, its gingerbread trim, a wide, deep porch and beveled glass sidelights framing a door with an oval glass inset. The house was just a little shabby, with paint that needed renewing and a yellowing, patchy front lawn, but she could imagine loving it. It puzzled her, because it didn't seem to fit the man who'd chosen to buy it.

Inside, the hardwood floors did need refinishing, the molding was too dark and the wallpaper in the entry peeled. But the potential was wonderful, and she could see how Ben had been seduced. This was a grand old lady, built when West Fork had been settled by lumber barons. The farmhouse where Faith had grown up was different, built in the 1920s to be utilitarian. It was a good, solid, practical house, perfect for its purpose of sheltering a stolid farming family.

Except…Faith no longer felt sheltered there. There were ghosts even outside her bedroom. In the hall, where Rory had attacked Charlotte when she came out of the bathroom. In the utility room, where he'd broken a window to gain entrance. In the dining room, where the cherry bomb had exploded her sense of safety.

Mom's ghost was everywhere, too, not just for Faith, but for Dad. Perhaps, she realized for the first time, that's why he was ready to sell and leave. Her parents, she believed, had loved each other deeply. Perhaps without Mom, Dad didn't have the heart to stay in the home that held too many memories and only the wounded remnants of his family.

Ben waved his fingers in front of her face. "I've lost you. What are you thinking?"

Blinking, Faith said, "Just…having a minor epiphany. About Mom, Dad, home." She shook herself, took a deep breath. "I came… I hoped I could talk to you. Char says I have to talk to somebody." Embarrassed, she realized how sulky that had sounded.

Ben's mouth curved in amusement. "So you chose me."

"I don't want to see a therapist," she mumbled.

His smile widened. "So I'm the lesser of two evils. Or maybe three or four."

Now that he wasn't holding her hand, she wrapped her arms tightly around herself. "If you didn't mean it…"

"Oh, I meant it." His voice lowered to a soft growl. "Would you like a cup of tea or coffee?"

"You have tea?" she said in surprise.

"I do." He led the way through a dining room to the kitchen, seeming to assume she'd follow.

An "Oh" escaped her when she saw the kitchen, even though it desperately needed a complete do-over. Some idiot had replaced whatever original cabinets had been in here, probably in the 1940s or '50s, at a guess. The existing cabinets were ugly, painted a yellow that was nicked and scratched to reveal the olive green beneath. Ancient vinyl covered original hardwood, too. But the proportions were perfect, with high ceilings and a generously sized bay window at the back that formed an eating nook and flooded the room with southwest-facing light.

Ben gave her a wry look as he turned on the faucet to fill a tea kettle and the pipes grumbled and groaned. "I did tell you the place needs major work."

"Oh, but it's worth it! You have a huge yard, and those big old trees, and oak floors." She stopped. "Well, you must have fallen in love with the place."

"I don't know that I'd put it that strongly." He turned on the burner and looked around the kitchen as if seeing it through her eyes. "But…yeah. There's something about this house. I could be living in a brand new-rambler that didn't need any work at all, and instead…" He shrugged. "I suppose it was part of whatever insanity that made me throw over a career with the LAPD for this gig in a small town that isn't even on the way to anywhere."

He moved restlessly now, thumping down mugs on the counter and frowning as he turned away from her to take out tea bags.

She frowned a little herself. "You're not happy here?"

"Happy?" He gave her an odd look. Opened his mouth as if he was going to say something, closed it, then after a pause said, "The jury's still out."

"Oh," Faith said again, bothered by how little she actually knew about Ben Wheeler and how incurious she'd been. She'd wanted him from the first time she saw him. Needed him. Let him shake her confidence and bruise her heart because he'd given her such tenderness and then withdrawn it so abruptly. But she had also been awfully self-absorbed. With reason, maybe, but still... Why should he respect her?

The desire to flee took wing in her again, and she actually backed up a step or two before she stopped, hearing Char's voice.

You're crumbling day by day. That makes you a victim as long as you let yourself be.

She met Ben's eyes, saw that he'd known very well that she was losing her nerve. Not letting herself change her mind, she marched to the round oak table nestled in the bay window and sat down. "I like a teaspoon of sugar in my tea."

Ben smiled, as if to himself, and lifted the whistling kettle to pour. "Good to know."

DAMN, he couldn't believe his eyes when he'd seen her sitting out there in front of his house in that beat-up black Blazer of hers.

Ben had been trying to talk himself into spending the afternoon stripping the wallpaper in the living room. It was a crappy job; he'd already done it upstairs in two of the bedrooms. The living room was going to be a bitch, which was why he kept putting it off. He could have paid someone to do the work, but there were enough things, like plumbing and wiring, that he couldn't do, so he felt obligated to take on the ones he could. He hadn't gotten very far on the house. He'd had a condo in L.A., and hadn't realized how much time he was going to have to spend on basic maintenance, like mowing and fertilizing the lawn, cleaning gutters and getting the garage into shape so he could actually park in it. And then there was the job; in his first months, he'd found the department so shoddily run he hadn't taken any entire days off.

Today, he'd been letting frustration with Faith get him down. He had needed to take on something that would make him sweat, give him aching muscles. Only…he'd glanced out the window, and there she was.

He'd frozen, standing back so she wouldn't see him. Waiting, until he realized in sudden alarm that she must have been in the middle of talking herself out of whatever urge had brought her here in the first place.

Now she was planted at his kitchen table, wrapping her fingers around the mug of tea he'd set in front of her. Fiddling with the string of the tea bag, swirling it in the hot water, gave her something to do. If she'd noticed her tea was raspberry herbal and had no caffeine, she hadn't commented. Ben put the sugar bowl and a plate for the used tea bags on the table, then sat down himself.

"You aren't sleeping, are you?" he said after a minute, when she kept gazing, mute, at the mug.

Faith shook her head. The movement made her braid slip over her shoulder and down over her breast.

He made himself keep looking at her face. "Nightmares?"

"Sometimes." She looked up at him with eyes that seemed a darker blue than usual, as if desperation deepened the color. "Mostly…I have trouble falling asleep at all. Or staying asleep. Just as I'm dropping off, I get zapped and jolt awake. It's like…being poked by a cattle prod. I'd swear my body doesn't think I'm *supposed* to sleep." Her words tumbled over one another, as if she couldn't stop them now. "And if I manage at all, after an hour or two, zing! I'm awake again. My heart will be thudding, and adrenaline is shooting through me." She hunched her shoulders. "I talked to Dr. Pauley—he's been our family physician forever—and he gave me a prescription for sleeping pills, but…" She let out a gust of air. "I suppose I'm afraid I'll keep needing them. And I thought eventually I'd get better on my own."

"But you're not. And it's been weeks."

She bristled. "You think I don't know that?"

"For God's sake, you can't heal without sleep!"

"I thought…" She ducked her head and swirled the tea bag again. "That is… Did you have trouble sleeping, after…?"

"Hell, yes." He hadn't had anyone to hold him at night then, either. Not someone he could trust.

The thought jarred him momentarily, and he frowned. Trust to do *what?*

Aware that she was watching him now, he said, "For me it was mostly nightmares." He moved his shoulders uneasily. "I still have 'em once in a while.'"

"Really? How long has it been?"

"I've had to shoot to kill twice in my career. Once was early on. Has to be sixteen, seventeen years ago. It was a traffic stop. Taillight out, just me walking up to the driver's side to issue a friendly warning. Turned out the guy had a warrant for murder one out on him. He opened fire, winged me with the first shot. I returned fire and hit him in the head."

Her eyes were huge and dark again, and he had the belated thought that maybe she didn't need to hear the details. He could hear her breathing, but she didn't say anything.

"Second time I was working Vice and a partner and I were involved in a big drug buy that went bad. My partner was killed, I was shot again. I took out a couple of them."

Seeing his partner die, that was what had lingered in his nightmares. Figueroa had had a young, pretty wife and an eighteen-month-old girl, the cutest little thing. Man, Figueroa had loved them. Ben was still angry, wondering why the guy had put in for Vice, why he'd taken such chances when living or dying should have mattered more to him. Maybe he'd just been young enough to believe himself immortal; from the look on his face as he went down, he hadn't expected it. The complete surprise still sent a shudder through Ben.

"And you had nightmares both times?" Faith asked carefully. She was finally squeezing the tea bag around her spoon and depositing it on the plate.

Doing the same, he nodded. "I had to see a police psychologist. And there were guys I could talk to who'd gone through it."

"Char wants me to see a therapist."

"It wouldn't hurt," he told her. "Depending on how you go into it."

"Dad leaves his door open. So I can hear him snoring." She smiled faintly. "And he really does snore. It... um, helps a little. Knowing he's there."

"Are you sleeping in your bedroom?"

She shook her head. "I just can't. Char cleaned up all the blood, of course, but...I can't."

She might get pissed at him for saying this, but he thought he needed to. "Moving may be a good thing."

"I...had the same thought. Which doesn't make me feel any better about having to give up, about losing the farm. It's home. It's always been home. Can you understand that?"

Her expression was so beseeching, he couldn't resist reaching out to touch her hand. "I'm trying. But I've never had a home. Not the way you're talking about. I grew up in different circumstances." And he sure as hell wasn't going to tell her about the crime-ridden neighborhoods where his mother had found rooms or an occasional apartment in which to raise her son, about the foster homes that followed when her heroin addiction stole her ability to be any kind of parent at all. This house in a poster-perfect small town was the closest thing to a home he'd ever had, and he still didn't know why he'd come looking for it.

"Different?"

He shook his head. "Moving a lot."

"Oh." Her gaze became unfocused. "I think I was born wanting everything to stay the same. Life to be predictable. I never imagined anything but having a life like my parents'. Mom was a teacher, too. Did you know that? She quit after Char and I were born. Well, I get why. Imagine suddenly having two babies in diapers! Looking back, I can see that I was trying to model my life after hers. Rory came along at the right time, so I married him. I assumed we'd take over the farm from my parents eventually." She fidgeted with her spoon. "I guess none of this has anything to do with why I can't sleep, or why I feel as if…"

She couldn't seem to finish, so Ben did it for her. "As if your life makes no sense at all anymore."

Faith blinked. "Yes. I guess that's it."

"Of course it has to do with why you're so adrift now. If you hadn't married Rory, it wouldn't have all ended the way it did. I'm guessing you're pretty tangled up trying to figure out why you did choose him, why you didn't see him for what he really was."

"Yes." The word was strangled. "Oh, God. I don't understand myself at all."

Just like that, she was crying. Despite everything, he'd never seen her lose control like this. As if horrified at herself, she clapped her hands over her face, but her body shook and tears spilled between her fingers.

Ben moved fast, circling the table, lifting her and settling with her on his lap. He might have expected her to struggle, but she didn't. She burrowed her face into his throat, grabbed hold of him as if she'd never let go and sobbed.

He found himself rocking her, as if she were a distraught child, the motion coming naturally. With one hand he massaged the nape of her neck, her braid bumping his knuckles. With his other arm he held her tight, making sure she'd feel completely secure and protected.

"It's okay," he murmured, over and over. "Let it out, honey. Just let it out."

She felt almost boneless by the time she went still, as if exhaustion had finally claimed her. He was glad. A man didn't get that many wishes come true, but today he had every intention of lying beside Faith and watching her sleep.

He stood, cradling her in his arms, and walked back through the house.

She stiffened and then began to struggle. "What are you doing? Ben! Let me down. Where are you going?"

"Hush," he murmured against the top of her head.

"Remember what I said that day? You need to nap, and it'll be in my bed."

Taking the stairs with her in his arms was effortless. She weighed next to nothing, alarmingly little, as if her substance had slipped away along with her defiance and strength.

"I can't go to bed with you! Are you crazy?" She had the sense to quit struggling while he climbed the stairs, but resumed when he reached the second floor. "Ben!"

"Just a nap," he said. "Would that be so bad?"

He shouldered open his bedroom door and carried her to the bed. With one hand he swept the covers back and deposited her on it. Her face was puffy and blotchy and indignant, and he felt the familiar cramp under his breastbone he got each time he looked at her. Only this time it was stronger. So much stronger it hurt.

"I…" She swallowed. "You won't…?"

"Just nap." Instinct had him keeping his voice low, the way he might have sung a lullaby.

He sat down by her feet and took her shoes off, then stood again and tucked her under the covers. When he went to the windows and lowered the blinds, she only watched him.

Finally, he unfastened his shoelaces and kicked off his sneakers. In the dim light, he could see that her eyes were still big, like a baby owl's, but she hadn't protested again. Ben got under the covers, too, still wearing jeans, T-shirt and even socks. He wanted to gather her in his arms, but he didn't. Instead, he stroked one finger down her still damp cheek, pushing a strand of hair back, behind her ear. And he smiled.

"Sleep, baby. Just sleep. I won't go anywhere."

"You're weird," she said again, her voice sounding funny.

"Yeah." He caressed her cheek again. "I know. But go to sleep anyway. You're safe. You can trust me."

"I know," Faith whispered. "I do know that."

"Good." His thumb wanted to touch her lips, but he didn't let it, just stroked her cheek again, softly.

After a minute her eyes closed. She tucked her hand under her chin and relaxed.

As the afternoon wore on, Ben lay there at her side and watched her sleep. Even though it occurred to him that maybe he should call her dad and let him know where she was, he didn't. Because he'd promised. He wasn't going anywhere.

CHAPTER NINE

FAITH AWAKENED SLOWLY, as if swimming up through the shifting, flashing waters of her dreams. Even as consciousness returned, she felt clearheaded in a way she hadn't in weeks.

She frowned. Why did she feel so *good?* Had she actually slept? At last?

And then her eyes opened and she saw the big man sprawled beside her, a pillow doubled under his head to give him some elevation over her. Her heart bounded in the moment of confusion. Ben?

A smile softened his hard mouth. "Hey," he murmured.

Memory flooded back and she blurted, "Oh, my God."

He grinned. "Yep. We did the nasty. We slept together again."

With his eyes still smiling and that devilish grin carving a dimple in one lean cheek, crinkling the pale scar that ran from the crest of his cheekbone up one temple, his dark hair tousled, he was the sexiest man she'd ever seen and she was almost speechless.

Almost. "Oh, my God," she said again, then in shock, "What time is it?"

"Ah…" He rolled over to look at a clock his body blocked from her sight. "Five-thirty."

"Five-thirty? In the evening?" She sat up fast enough to make herself dizzy. "I told Dad I'd be back hours ago!"

"Give him a call. Tell him you're staying for dinner."

"I'm not." Barely letting her vision clear, she swung her feet over the side of the bed and looked for her shoes.

"Sure you are." Ben's voice, behind her, was almost gentle. "Why wouldn't you? Isn't your dad capable of opening a can of soup?"

"Maybe I don't want to." Faith couldn't look at him. Slipping on her shoes and tying them was a good excuse to avoid his gaze.

"And why wouldn't you?" he said again. He'd settled on an armchair and was putting on his own shoes.

Swallowing, she took a quick survey of the room. His bedroom. Where she had spent the last—*oh, my God*—six hours sleeping on his bed.

The ceiling was high, befitting the age of the house, but slanted at one end, above a dresser. The walls were textured as if they'd been plastered and were painted a creamy white, and the molding and baseboards had obviously been stripped and restained a warm, maple brown. Only the wood floor itself still needed refinishing. He'd covered a good part of it with an oval braided rug in a plain navy blue. The bed was enormous; king-size, she guessed, which made sense given his height. It and the large, upholstered armchair were the only signs of luxury in here.

"You need paintings," she said. "Something."

He looked around. "Yeah. I just haven't figured out

what yet. And, hell, it's not as if there aren't other things to spend money on."

"The roof," she remembered.

Ben grimaced. "The roofer has been and gone, patched it up. He thinks it will hold up for the winter, but I'll need to get a new roof come spring or summer."

"Oh, dear." She remembered her parents agonizing when they'd had to put a new roof on the farmhouse about fifteen years ago. It had been a financial calamity, the first of many, she thought now.

Ben stood. "How do you feel?"

Her standard fallback—*fine*—almost popped out, but the truth was, she felt amazing, as if the blood pumping through her fizzed with tiny bubbles, like champagne.

"Good," she admitted. "I don't like being bullied, but, um, for some reason I let go and really slept." Faith felt heat climbing her cheeks. *Some reason*. They both knew what it was. Hurriedly she asked, "Did you nap?"

The intense satisfaction on his face should have annoyed her. Instead, it made her wonder if that's how he'd look after sex. Except…more.

"Maybe dozed," he said.

Maybe? Did that mean… "You didn't stay all afternoon, did you?"

"Sure I did. I said I wouldn't leave you."

He'd lain there and watched her sleep. For hours. Oh, God. Did she snore? Drool? Snuffle? She couldn't possibly have been a pretty sight.

So what? She'd given up wishing he thought she was pretty long ago, hadn't she? He was a cop. The one who'd rushed to her aid over and over.

The one who hadn't been able to stop Rory.

Her breath started coming faster, thoughts of Rory reawakening anguish.

Exasperation in his voice, Ben said, "Damn it, Faith, put the brakes on whatever you're thinking about."

Startled, she met his dark eyes. "How did you—?"

"You started humming like an electrical wire." He gripped her arm, hoisted her to her feet and started her for the door. "Come on. You can help me make dinner. That'll get your mind off your troubles."

"I can make dinner at home, thank you," she snapped.

"I gave up my afternoon for you. You owe me dinner."

At the top of the stairs, Faith pulled her arm free of his grip. "Oh, play the guilt card! You claimed to *want* me to come talk to you."

"And I did." He flashed another grin. "I still do. Over dinner. We didn't actually get much talking done, you know."

No, they hadn't. She'd cried, and then... And then he'd swept her off her feet and carried her up to his bed.

Purely sexual hunger cramped between her legs. Faith hurried ahead of him down the stairs, wanting to hide her face. She knew she was blushing again.

The trouble was, while she'd wanted him from the beginning, she had no idea how to handle him in this mood. She wasn't actually very experienced with men. There'd been one semiserious boyfriend when she was in college, and then Rory. And her relationship with Rory had been more...comfortable than passionate, until that inexplicable anger of his had destroyed it.

For the first time ever, it occurred to Faith to wonder

whether her lack of passion had had something to do with his anger. Had he sensed that she wasn't giving him something he needed? That she was capable of more, and holding back on him?

But she wasn't! She hadn't known then that another man could stir something so powerful, so...unsettling in her. She had loved Rory.

Or, a voice seemed to whisper in her ear, *you thought you did.*

No! She would not feel guilty for something she couldn't help. She would have been faithful and loving and content, if only he'd been the man she had believed him to be. If, later, she had felt even the faintest stirring of these alarming feelings when she met the new police chief—and that was a big *if,* because she might never have had occasion to meet Ben Wheeler at all— she would have stifled them. Firmly and completely, because she was married and that was that.

Her spurt of anger surprised her.

I was a good wife. I didn't deserve the back of Rory's hand, or his fist.

And she had never, never, ever deserved the raised blade of that wicked knife.

Assuming, the voice whispered again, *that he ever intended to use that knife for anything but to scare you.*

No! She hadn't deserved even that. Still, Faith was chilled.

"May I use your phone?" she asked politely, at the foot of the stairs.

"It's in the kitchen."

She followed him, conscious of the late afternoon sunlight pouring in the west-facing bay window. Ben leaned against the kitchen counter and crossed his arms, unapologetically listening when she dialed and said, "Dad?"

"You okay, honey?"

"Yeah. I just, um, came to Ben's house, and we got talking, and…" *I fell asleep. He* made *me.* Yep. She was going to say that. "I'm sorry I didn't call."

"It's fine. I'm glad you went. Char came by and helped me close up. She brought hamburgers, fries and milk shakes. We went ahead and ate. Don't know what shape yours will be in…"

"I suppose I'll stay here for dinner, then," Faith said grudgingly. "Ben suggested it, but I didn't want to desert you."

"I'm fine," her father said gently. "I was just going to turn on the news."

Did he sound *pleased?* Her gaze shifted to Ben, who wasn't trying to hide a certain smugness.

"I'll see you in an hour or so, then," she told her father, and ended the call. Then she raised her eyebrows at Ben. "What do you plan to feed me?"

He smiled. "Do you mind simple? I was just going to have a hamburger and baked beans."

"If I'd just gone home, I could have had a hamburger from Tastee's," Faith grumbled. "Char brought some by."

"Mine are better."

They were, too. He chopped up onion and added it with a splash of Worcestershire sauce before shaping the patties and putting them on to cook. Faith opened a can of baked beans and cut up some broccoli. Ben produced a package of buns and a nice ripe tomato to slice on top of the hamburgers once he melted cheddar cheese on them. Everything smelled fabulous; she was swallowing saliva before they even sat down.

It must have something to do with the tiny pop of champagne bubbles in her veins, Faith thought. She'd slept soundly, and now she was *hungry*.

They talked during dinner, but not about Rory or anything profound. It was more as if they were feeling each other out, exchanging tastes in movies and music and books, political convictions, things like that. As if, she was disconcerted to realize, this was a first date and they were trying to discover whether they meshed. But it was more than that, at least on her part. Now that she'd surfaced from her own misery enough to realize she really didn't know anything about Ben, she felt an urgency to find out everything. This was all superficial, but necessary.

A little stunned by her burst of understanding, she eyed him shyly and wondered if this whole conversation was completely casual for him, or whether it was possible he felt something similar. Only...if he was really attracted to her, the way she was to him, why had he stayed away so long? It had to be guilt on his part, the way she'd already decided.

The light in his brown eyes as he watched her didn't look like guilt, though. It gave her a shivery, stomach-clenching feeling that scared her.

He pushed his plate away and said, in a deeper, rougher tone, "We really didn't talk."

She began to shred what was left of her hamburger bun. "That's not true. It helps just to hear that what I've been going through isn't unusual."

"It isn't. But I can help you only so much. I didn't know the men I killed. I'd never cared about them. And

I'm a cop. I chose a job that meant carrying a gun, and I've spent the past twenty years prepared to use my weapon. I'm guessing it's the last job in the world you'd have chosen."

She couldn't look at him now. She felt ashamed. "It's true it wouldn't be my nature. I suppose I never would have gotten in such a mess if I'd been brave enough to stand up to Rory in the first place." Her shoulders jerked. "To kick him out when he hit me a second time. Char never would have tolerated…"

Ben reached across the table and took one of her hands, holding tight. "You aren't Charlotte. There's nothing wrong with that, Faith. Her nature isn't better or worse than yours. The first time I met you, I thought—" He stopped.

She looked up, saw the muscles in his jaw knot.

He let go of her hand abruptly. "It doesn't matter. My point is, the world wouldn't be a better place if everyone was a fighter."

She opened her mouth to say, *I should have had more pride than to let him think it was okay to hurt me when he felt like it.*

It was her great shame. Why hadn't she had more inner strength, more sense of her self-worth?

Faith didn't know. Yes, she'd always measured herself by Charlotte, and had always come up short. She felt as if her twin, her other half, didn't want to be with her, didn't even like her….

But that was just an excuse, and she was getting tired of making excuses. Which might be a good sign, Faith thought. People did change. She could be stronger. Maybe she already was, in a way. She couldn't imagine ever again putting up with anything close to what Rory had dished out. In fact, she hadn't. She'd done what she had to to stop him. Maybe, horrible as it had been, she should be proud of herself that she had finally fought back.

Ben's gaze had never wavered from her face, although he'd stayed quiet and let her work things through in her head. Now he said, "There you go again, off by yourself."

"What did you think, the first time you saw me?"

"*That's* what you were thinking about?"

She narrowed her eyes. "You shouldn't start something if you're not going to finish it."

After a minute, he said slowly, "Spring. One of those first days when the sun feels warm on your face if you stand in just the right spot and tilt your face up. A few of those early flowers are opening, so pretty but somehow…tender. Tiny green shoots opening bravely even though they're not sure they'll survive late frosts." He cleared his throat. "That's how I saw you."

She stared at him, stunned. She would never have expected anything so poetic from him. And…about *her.* Faith wished she could be sure it was a compliment, that he wasn't saying that he'd known on sight she was too emotionally fragile to handle any problems.

Well, she *hadn't* handled what had happened very well.

Damn it! There she went again. She'd shot and killed her ex-husband. Of course she hadn't handled it well! There'd be something wrong with her if she had.

"That's…" The words dried up. "I don't know what to say."

"Nothing." Was that color tinging his cheeks? "I

just…wanted to protect you. I can't decide how I feel about the fact that I failed."

"Guilt," Faith said flatly.

His dark brows drew together. "Some, sure. But I'm realistic." He shrugged. "I've been a cop a long time. We can only do so much."

"That's why I bought the gun and practiced. I didn't expect round-the-clock protection."

"Do you know what I felt when Charlotte told me what you were doing? When I walked in at the range and saw you shooting?"

She shook her head, her breath catching in her throat.

He looked uncomfortable but said it anyway. "I thought you might be the gutsiest woman I'd ever known. And I had a suspicion you were doing it as much to keep Charlotte and your dad safe as for your own protection."

"You must have known women cops," she whispered.

"Sure. But they were risk-takers to start with. You're a kindergarten teacher who stepped way out of your comfort zone. That takes courage." His voice had dropped to a gravelly timbre. "Don't ever doubt that, Faith."

The terrible pressure in her chest made her want to cry again, but this time, she refused. Instead, she shot to her feet. "I really do need to go. Why don't I help you clean up quick, Ben. I can't leave you with the mess after you've been so nice…."

"Sure you can." He smiled crookedly. "You don't have to wash dishes, honey. I'll walk you out."

She wished he wouldn't call her "honey." He hadn't done that before today, had he? What did it *mean?* Did it just slip out, because she was a woman and they were socializing?

He'd admitted to feeling guilt at not stopping Rory. *Don't let your imagination get carried away,* she told herself.

She all but bolted to the front door and down the walkway. Ben's hand on her upper arm stopped her when she reached the Blazer.

"Faith," he said in that soft rumble.

Taking a deep breath, she faced him.

"I'm going to kiss you," he said.

"That's not a good idea." Panic made her quiver. "I'm not ready for anything like that. And…and why would you want to?"

He laughed, a low, oddly contented sound. "I can only talk myself out of it for so long."

"What…?" she started to say, but gave up when his head bent.

His kiss was gentle but not at all tentative. He just claimed her mouth, as if by right, rubbing his lips over hers, nipping, sliding his tongue along the seam until she let him in. And then he groaned with pleasure, pulling her against him until they stood thigh to thigh, her breasts pressed to his broad chest, his erection against her belly. He didn't push against her, nothing that blatant, just held her firmly in place with one hand on the small of her back while the other roamed.

Faith lost all sense of place and time. She'd never felt anything like this. The champagne in her veins had been replaced by honey, thick and sweet and languid. If not for his grip and her arms, which had somehow wrapped themselves around his neck, she doubted she could have stood. Her knees had gone liquid.

He was the one to ease back, look at her with hot dark eyes, take her mouth another time as if he couldn't help himself before slowly, a finger at a time, releasing her. She actually fell back against the Blazer.

"I'll stop by school with lunch tomorrow," he said.

"You don't have to... You shouldn't..."

He only smiled. "Drive carefully, Faith."

She was probably staggering when she circled the Blazer and got in on the driver's side. Ben waited on the sidewalk, big and alarmingly patient in the waning light. He was still standing there when she pulled away from the curb and turned at the next corner.

"Damn," she whispered. She could deal with his guilt, but this... What *was* this? It scared her more than anything had since she'd heard that whisper of sound in the hall and known that Rory had come for her after all.

If she let herself fall in love with Ben, and he didn't mean what his eyes and kiss implied, she'd never be able to put the pieces back together.

FAITH HAD REGAINED all of her poise and then some by the time Ben showed up in her room at lunchtime on Monday. Her eyes were clear, the bruises beneath them less obvious.

"How nice of you," she said briskly, when she saw the deli sandwiches and cookies. "It really isn't necessary, Ben. You saw me pig out last night. I seem to have my appetite back."

True or false, he didn't know, but she had eaten a decent dinner last night, and now she ate the sandwich and half a cookie.

"Dad signed with a real-estate agent this weekend,"

she told him. "The for-sale sign is up. Dale—that's the agent—has even gotten a nibble or two of interest already. He knew a couple people in the market for land."

Her chatty tone suggested this was all good news. And it was, in one way—but not necessarily for her. Ben's gut feeling was still that she might do better if the whole process of selling the farm dragged out until she'd said her emotional goodbyes.

Or maybe not. He'd never been in that position, never cared so much about a place, or even really a person. So what did he know?

Faith kept the desk between them, even when he rose to leave.

"Did you sleep at all last night?" he asked.

"Yes, I took one of those sleeping pills. You were right, most of my anguish has probably been exhaustion. So quit with the guilt, okay? You don't have to feed me and tuck me in anymore."

"Have to?" He smiled at her. "I know I don't."

She'd risen to her feet, too, as if prepared to dodge him if he tried to circle the desk, so he only said, "Glad to see you looking better today, Faith," and left.

That afternoon, Ben finally succeeded in tracking down Jimmy Reese, one of Hardesty's elk-hunting buddies. It hadn't been easy. The address and phone number that Information had weren't current; a Bremerton officer had agreed to drive by the rental house and reported that it was empty and that the neighbors weren't chummy and had no idea where the guy who'd lived there had moved to. Reese was still employed at the shipyards, but on a two-week vacation. Eventually his supervisor called to say that a coworker of Jimmy's had mentioned him calling. Did Ben want his cell-phone number?

Yes, Ben did. And Jimmy answered on the second ring.

"What do you think *I'm* going to tell you?" he asked, when Ben had identified himself.

"Sounds like you were pretty good friends."

"I haven't seen him in almost two years. I mean, we've talked on the phone a couple of times, but that's all."

"Mrs. Hardesty said that you and Rory and Noah Berger went elk-hunting together every fall."

"We used to," Jimmy agreed, "but then I couldn't get away from work the year before last, and Noah's wife was pregnant anyway. They've got a couple of kids now. And Rory, yeah, he was pretty tied up about Faith. He didn't seem that interested in anything else."

The guy sounded uncomfortable but not defensive, Ben thought. He'd rather have been interviewing him in person, but a trip to Bremerton would have taken damn near all day, what with the ferry ride across Puget Sound. He couldn't justify the time without more reason to think it would be worthwhile.

"Do you have a phone number where I can reach Noah Berger?" Ben asked.

"Uh…sure. But I don't think he heard from Rory any more than I did." There was a pause. "Rory's *dead*. What's the deal?"

Ben fell back on cop-speak. "We'd like to ascertain where he was living the last couple of months before the shooting. Maybe get a clearer idea of his intentions."

"You mean, you're not sure he really was going to hurt Faith," Jimmy said thoughtfully. "Shit, it must be really hard on his mom, thinking Rory..." He stopped. "Yeah, let me get you that number."

No answer at Noah Berger's house that day. Ben didn't leave a number. He tried again in the evening and a woman answered.

"I'm sorry, he's not available," she told him. "May I take a message?"

"My name is Ben Wheeler. I'm the police chief in West Fork. I was hoping to talk to him about Rory Hardesty."

"Rory?" she said. "I heard what happened. I couldn't believe Faith *shot* him."

"You knew Faith?"

"Not that well, but we all camped together once. I liked Faith. But Rory was, like, this laid-back dude. And supposedly he hit her? I don't know."

It wouldn't matter to Faith if he leaped to her defense, but irritation made him say in a hard voice, "There was no question that he physically abused her, Mrs. Berger."

"Oh, wow. Well, that's too bad. I mean, Faith was nice."

"I'd really like to speak to your husband," Ben said.

"His mom just died, and he's having to settle things, you know? So he probably won't be home for, like, another week."

"He's back in West Fork?"

"No, his mom remarried and..." She was silent for a moment as if realizing how much information she'd given freely. Sounding considerably warier, she said, "I can take your phone number and pass the message on to him. I'm sure he'll call you, um, Officer Wheeler."

He didn't ask her if she knew where Rory had been hiding out. Ben didn't want his hand tipped. Not very happy, he gave her his cell-phone number and emphasized the urgency of his need to speak to her husband.

"But Rory's *dead*," she said, with just about exactly the same intonation as Jimmy Reese had used. "So why… Well, I mean, I'll tell Noah."

Ben had to settle for that, although he didn't like it.

Hardesty's truck had to be somewhere. He'd stolen a car from a hardware-store parking lot in Everett, only a couple of blocks from the bus station. The county had damn good bus service. Or he could have hitchhiked from anywhere.

Sooner or later, though, someone would notice that pickup. The registration still listed Rory's address in West Fork. Ben would hear when it caught someone's eye. The fact that it hadn't yet made him guess it was in a garage, or at least a driveway. He half regretted not asking Lisa Berger about it.

He talked to a couple more of Rory's slow-pitch buddies that week. Ken Carlisle, who built fences and decks for a living, told Ben he'd come to dislike Rory. "I knew Faith, too," he said. "In high school. She's sweet. But after they were married, Rory'd get a couple of beers in him and talk shit about her. He got really ugly. I felt sorry for her."

Ben knew there was a reason he had liked Carlisle when he'd hired him to build a fence around his backyard.

"Don't suppose you refinish hardwood floors?" he asked.

Ken laughed. "I could do it, if it were my own house. But I'd have to rent the sander and, honestly, you'd be better off getting someone who does it all the time. I wouldn't want to put a gouge in the middle of your living room."

He hesitantly provided the names of a few more guys Rory might have hung out with, but Ben didn't have much hope for them. Once Rory got angry, his ability to make friends diminished. Faith didn't think he had any, and it was beginning to look as if she was right.

Lenny Phillips, the Farmer's Insurance agent in town, was even less help. He'd tried to sell Rory a life insurance policy, he said. "Of course, it wouldn't have paid out, not the way he died…" He cleared his throat, his round face flushed.

Ben went back to his office, where he put his feet on his desk and leaned back with his hands clasped behind his head, thinking. He was hitting nothing but dead ends. Maybe nobody had helped Rory. He could have rented a dump somewhere, hidden his pickup in the garage, and it would sit there until the landlord went poking around. Although it didn't make sense that he'd have paid rent very far in advance. Who did that? So why wasn't that landlord already poking around?

Noah Berger still hadn't called. Ben would give him another day or two.

That left J. P. Hammond, who evidently no longer lived in the area. No one seemed to know where he'd gone, and his Washington State driver's license had expired a year ago. Ben would have to widen his inquiries for Josiah Peter Hammond.

In the meantime, he hadn't learned a damn thing. Maybe Rory had driven the truck into the Columbia River where it would rust undiscovered until a fisherman caught a line on it one day. Maybe Rory hadn't left any notes, any hint at all of whether he'd gone to the Russells' house that night intending to kill Faith.

Maybe Ben would never be able to give her even this much: an answer that could help give her peace.

She seemed puzzled and even angry because he felt guilty, but the fact was, he did. *So sue me,* he thought. It didn't mean he wasn't also head over heels in love with her, because he was.

With a sigh, he sat up and put his feet back on the floor. He probably shouldn't have kissed her. He guessed he'd hoped that once Faith emerged from the fog of her own guilt and mourning for what had once been, she would notice him. He wanted to believe she had; she'd sure as hell responded that night when he had her in his arms. But by the next day, she'd put a pretty impressive wall in place and was back to trying to convince him she was fine, just fine, and didn't need him.

He'd given it one more shot during the week, stopping by the farmhouse Wednesday evening. She had been pleasant and pretended to assume he was there to help. He'd spent a couple of hours hauling boxes down from the attic to be sorted through and loading more boxes, destined for a thrift store, in her Blazer. He'd never really caught her alone.

But when he'd asked, her father had agreed that she was sleeping. He'd lowered his voice and stolen a glance at the empty doorway. He knew Faith wouldn't like having them talk about her.

But she was getting rest, and she was eating better. That was something, Ben told himself now. One step at a time. She had every reason to doubt him. He had to be patient.

Too bad for him that he'd felt way more patient before he'd kissed her.

CHAPTER TEN

WHY HAD SHE AGREED to have dinner with Ben?

Faith scowled at herself in the mirror. Now she was having to get dressed up, when she should be spending the evening working—it was hard enough packing up a house that three generations of family had lived in, but she and Dad had to pack up an entire farm, too. Barn, garage and outbuildings, all were crammed with *stuff*. Apparently, nobody in the family had ever gotten rid of anything.

But mostly, she shouldn't be going tonight because it meant shoring up her guard against Ben, who still seemed determined to rescue her.

Of course, she knew perfectly well why she'd said yes. The simple answer was that he had finally, after a week of quiet, relentless pursuit, cornered her until she had had no choice but to agree or be rude. The more complicated answer was that, heaven help her, she wanted to be with him.

Maybe it was just chemistry, his particular brand of pheromones, but he did something to her. All kinds of contradictory somethings. She felt safe when she was around Ben; the fearful part of her relaxed. At the same time, she became excited, excruciatingly, sweetly conscious of herself as a woman and him as a man, of every glance, every shift of his expression, of even small things like the way his hand wrapped around a glass or the steering wheel. She had responded to him like this from the first, and that made her wary. He'd consistently done a disappearing act every time she'd reached out to him before, so now he was being persistent, but how was she supposed to believe she could count on him?

It seemed only sensible to send "not interested" signals until he shrugged and disappeared from her life again.

But he wasn't disappearing, and when he'd stood there and said, "Will you have dinner with me tomorrow night, Faith?" she'd tried to evade him, starting with, "This isn't a good time, Ben. You know how much I have to do. Dad still isn't mobile enough to be as much help as he'd like…"

"You have to eat," he had said patiently. "You have to take a break sometimes, honey."

Damn it, there he went again. It was the "honey" that got to her. The slow, deep, rough way he said it gave her goose bumps. His voice always dropped a notch, became huskier and more intimate, as if he was turning to her in bed.

She was nuts to read so much into some imagined tone in his voice. But Faith knew perfectly well that she was going out to dinner with him because he'd called her "honey" again. And because he'd looked so kind, if also a little bit frustrated.

She put in earrings and started downstairs. Ben and Dad were talking in the kitchen. Both turned to look at her when they heard her footsteps.

Dad's face softened into a smile she didn't see much anymore.

Ben's eyes warmed and he smiled in appreciation.

Her pulse bounced. She liked his purely male approval. If nothing else, it beat the pity she'd seen on everyone's faces recently.

"Look your fill," she told them both. "I don't wear heels often."

Ben moved to meet her. Lowering his voice, he said, "You don't need them, not with legs as long as yours. But I've got to say, the effect is nice."

She'd thought so, too, when she had appraised herself in the mirror. All that weight she'd lost had her looking more like a model than a farm girl. Her little black dress bared plenty of leg, and for once she'd put her hair up in a smooth twist on the back of her head, baring her neck, as well.

She said good-night to Daddy and let Ben escort her out the door. His hand rested between her shoulder blades the whole way to his SUV, as if he thought she needed guidance.

She should have stepped briskly away from his hand, but didn't.

Pulling out onto the highway, Ben commented, "Your dad looks good."

"He does, doesn't he? He goes to physical therapy twice a week, and lately I keep catching him doing his exercises. I'm not sure he was that diligent earlier." She swallowed the lump in her throat, allowing herself to acknowledge a difficult truth. "I think he's relieved. He seems...freer."

Ben shot her a startled glance. "He told you that?"

"No, of course not." Her father, Faith had begun to realize, hadn't been honest with her in a long time. Or, more likely, he'd given up trying to be, when she didn't want to hear him.

"It's funny," she said. "He's lived on the farm ever since he married Mom. Thirty-seven years, I think. But he's not very sentimental. He's been going through all those boxes you hauled out of the attic, but I have to keep sneaking behind him to make sure he's not trying to sell something at the estate sale that Char or I would want to keep. Or, worse yet, give it away to a thrift store." She wrinkled her nose. "Partly, he wouldn't know an antique if it bit him. He sees an ugly old glass bowl, I see Carnival glass with a lovely patina of age. And the really old stuff wasn't from his family, it was from Mom's, so I guess it makes sense that he's not attached to it. He took over running the farm when my maternal grandfather died, you know. Grandma Peters lived with them until she had a stroke when Char and I were...oh, seven or eight."

"I hadn't heard that." Ben sounded interested. "Did your father want to be a farmer, or did he just fall into it?"

"I don't know," she admitted, perturbed. She'd never asked him that. It hadn't occurred to her; he had always seemed content with his life, competent, settled in the rhythms of a farm. But maybe...maybe some of his relief now was because it *wasn't* what he'd always wanted to do. Maybe this was an escape.

Had she been trying to save a heritage for him that he didn't want?

The thought was unsettling.

Ben took her to a restaurant in Edmonds, near the ferry dock. From their window table they could see lights out on the Sound and catch glimpses of arriving and departing ferries. Their table was candlelit, and conversations around them were hushed. She wondered if he'd known how romantic the atmosphere was, whether that's why he'd brought her here, or whether he'd picked it out of the Yellow Pages.

He kept conversation easy, grumbling—but not too seriously—about a city council meeting and his frustration with the budget. He talked about his wet-behind-the-ears officers, but with the rueful pride of a father, and about butting heads with Fred Mulligan, the cantankerous old guy who lived right behind the town library and hated all the comings and goings, including cars lined up along the curb for a block each way, but especially the kids walking over from school.

Faith laughed. "Old Mr. Mulligan has been complaining as long as I can remember. I was scared of him, but Char wasn't." Story of their lives. "She'd deliberately cut across the corner of his lawn while I made sure to stay on the sidewalk. He might not have known who she was, but everyone knew those identical twins were Don Russell's. He called Dad a lot."

Ben chuckled. "And you weren't ever tempted to be defiant? Just once?"

"No. I'm the original good girl."

In the pool of silence that opened after her admission, Faith thought, How was it possible that she of all people had ended up shooting a man dead? Pulling the trigger and doing it again and again while blood exploded from his chest?

She hoped she hid her shudder. It was hard to tell, when Ben's dark eyes were so often unreadable.

After a moment he said softly, "A good girl with guts."

She wanted to believe he really saw her that way. That he thought she'd had courage and not just desperation.

She wanted to believe that what she'd done had been brave and not just horrible. Convincing herself wasn't easy, not any easier than believing that Rory really had meant to kill her.

"Are you getting reconciled to the idea of moving?" Ben asked, as if he really wanted to know.

"I don't have much choice, do I?" Faith closed her eyes momentarily, dismayed at how sharp she had sounded. "I'm sorry. I'm being bitchy. Or pathetic."

"No. Honest."

He understood. She could tell, even without looking at him. "The honest answer," she admitted, "is that I don't know. I still have this huge sense of failure. You don't have to tell me it's irrational—Char does often enough. If Dad actually wants to move…then I don't even know who I failed. Maybe nobody. Maybe myself." She picked up her fork and made herself take a bite. After swallowing, Faith said, "The thing is, nothing much has changed yet. I go to school every morning, come home and work until I put dinner on, then work some more until bedtime. I have no clue what I'll do with myself after we move and my evenings are free. How I'll feel then."

"You'd be a good mother," he said, not pointedly, but as if he were making an idle observation.

Faith froze inside. She had wanted children so much. Rory and she had planned to wait a couple of years before starting a family, but once he started hitting her she hadn't even let herself think about getting pregnant. She'd made excuses when Mom asked if the time wasn't coming. She'd quit even thinking about the baby she had once longed to hold in her arms. Now here she was, almost thirty, with no prospects at all of ever having her own child.

Had Ben wanted children? she wondered. Or... She suddenly reeled, as if she'd walked into a plate glass window.

"Do you have kids?" she asked. He had to be close to ten years older than her. He could conceivably have a son or daughter almost grown.

But he shook his head. "I was married once, briefly, but we didn't get that far. Thank God."

"What happened?"

He shrugged. "She didn't like being married to a cop. I was working Vice then, and it was hard. But when it came down to it, I didn't care enough to make any changes."

"Oh."

He smiled. "Don't look so shocked. We shouldn't have gotten married at all. It was impulse on my part, that's all. Thinking I might have what I saw other men had."

He said it so easily, as if it hadn't mattered. As if he'd been an idiot to think he could have had the home and family and love he must have wanted.

Faith ached inside for him, which was a switch from aching for herself.

Ben hadn't loved his wife enough to make drastic changes in his life then, but a year ago he'd walked away from a successful career with a major metropolitan police force to take the job in West Fork. She wondered what reason he'd given himself for doing that. He almost had to be yearning for something different. But what?

She cleared her throat. "Did you ever want children?"

He didn't answer for a minute. Eyes holding hers, he said at last, "There was a time I'd have said no. Now... maybe. If it's not too late."

Her heart began to pound. Was there any chance...? No. *Don't read too much into it.* And even if he was talking about him and her, she didn't trust him, not that way.

She didn't trust *herself.* How could she, after she'd driven Char away and then chosen to marry Rory?

When she didn't say anything, Ben's expression closed, stealing her last chance to guess what he had actually felt or thought. He nodded at her cup. "More coffee?"

"No. Thank you."

He nodded. "Then I'll get the check."

They talked some on the drive home, but sporadically. Faith was very conscious of the dark and the two of them in a kind of bubble together. Things said, things unsaid, had a presence as tangible as another person. The lights of other cars would illuminate Ben's face briefly, the hard planes of it and the pair of furrows that had dug their way between his eyebrows. Then the headlight would sweep past and she'd no longer be able to make out his features. Why those furrows? Was he brooding? Angry? Frustrated again?

Faith kept fixating on his hands, as she often did. He had big hands, broad in the palm. Dark hair dusted the back of his fingers. Along with the thickness of his wrists and the sinewy power of his forearms, his hands were unmistakably male.

Oh, who was she kidding? *He* was all male, and for some perplexing reason that drew her, even though she'd have sworn her inclination had always been to want a partner and friend in a man—someone more likely to be sensitive and kind and funny than protective and sometimes domineering and capable of violence.

She stole a glance at his profile. Ben had been kind to her, she couldn't deny that. He hadn't made her laugh much, but then she hadn't been in the mood, so she couldn't necessarily blame him. And, while "sensitive" might not be exactly the word to describe him, he did see below the surface with her in a way no one else seemed to.

I'm in love with him, she thought hopelessly. Not just attracted, not just tempted, but foolishly in love. With a man driven by guilt and an overdeveloped sense of responsibility, a man who was almost forty years old and hadn't managed any long-term, committed relationships—his short-lived marriage didn't seem to count, motivated as it had been by impulse. A man who maybe wanted something deeper in his life, but didn't appear to actually understand what that was.

Even if he wasn't so complicated, even if she knew him better... She couldn't trust her own feelings, not when she'd been so horribly wrong about the only other man she'd ever loved.

She was having trouble breathing. Her chest felt tight. She couldn't love Ben Wheeler.

But then Faith thought about the two times she'd slept with him stretched out beside her, and knew that she did. What she'd felt was *trust*. Trust, and happiness, although she hadn't called it that either time.

She wanted to sleep beside him every night for the rest of her life.

OF COURSE Ben had been invited to Gray and Charlotte's wedding.

Faith preceded Char down the aisle of the church, aware the entire way of Ben sitting near the front, turned in the pew with his arm laid across the back so he could watch her measured progress. He wore a dark suit and white shirt; she could tell as much even with her eyes focused straight ahead.

Gray waited at the front, Moira beside him. Faith kept her eyes on them. She wouldn't think about Ben. Today was about Charlotte. Charlotte and Gray.

Faith had been repeating that to herself for the past hour. She hadn't been to a single wedding since her own. She wished she had. Anything to blur the memories. It didn't help that she and Rory had gotten married in this same church, the one where she and Charlotte had gone to Sunday school as children. Rory had waited for her exactly where Gray now stood, in front of the altar.

What *had* blurred in her mind was Rory's expression as he watched her come to him. She couldn't remember that at all, and was glad.

Holding sadness at bay was mostly easy, Faith was so filled with joy at her twin's happiness. How could she not be? This was one of those times when she swore she knew everything Char felt, as if in some way they were still as inseparable as they'd been in the womb.

Char being Char, she'd left any decision about what her maid of honor would wear to Faith. Left to their own devices, Faith and Moira had agreed to coordinate their dresses. Peach, they'd decided, would look good on both of them and would accent Char's ivory dress. They wanted an old-fashioned look, too. They wouldn't try to match, just go for a similar style.

The dress Faith had found was similar in length to Char's, mid-calf, but had a snug waist and full skirt. It was a peach organza, she thought, with tiny sprigs of embroidered white flowers. It was pretty, proper and somehow innocent. She realized now that she had bought it imagining what Ben would think when he saw her in it.

Today was about Charlotte.

Who was breathtakingly beautiful when she walked down the aisle on Daddy's arm toward Gray. He didn't take his eyes off her. Faith saw that Moira was watching him, too, smiling. They grinned at each other behind his back, unnoticed by the groom.

Prickly Charlotte kissed Daddy's cheek with remarkable tenderness just before he handed her over to Gray. Faith saw Daddy's Adam's apple bob as he swallowed hard. He'd been able to make the walk without crutches, and she knew that mattered to him. Did he, too, wish with all his heart that Mom was sitting in that front pew?

Gray's mom wiped her eyes in the front pew on the other side of the aisle. Both his parents were here, and his stepmother, too. This was the first time Charlotte had met them. Faith thought they seemed like nice people.

The service was short and somehow more heartfelt for all its simplicity. When it came time for the bride and groom to exchange vows, Gray looked into Charlotte's eyes as if no one else in the world existed and said huskily, "I do." Char, who had once been so terrified by the bonds of love, made her promise as if she didn't have a doubt in the world.

The minister pronounced them man and wife and smiled at Gray. "You may kiss your bride."

He swept her into his arms as if he'd barely been able to wait this long and kissed her with such hunger, everyone in the church had to feel it. Despite herself, Faith looked past them at Ben and found him watching her, not the bride and groom. The expression on his face made her heart stutter, it was so much like the longing and love and passion in Gray's eyes when he'd said, "I do."

Oh, God. She was so afraid to believe it was possible Ben felt that way. Why now, when he had avoided her for months except when he had had to go to the farm as a police officer? She didn't understand.

She didn't understand much of anything anymore. Why Rory had felt such rage, why he couldn't let it—and her—go. Why everything had changed. Why *she* had changed so much, until she'd become completely lost.

Faith tore her gaze from Ben's and looked at Daddy instead, letting him anchor her as his calm, steady presence had for much of her life. Her breathing slowed; her heart unclenched.

Gray lifted his head at last and turned himself and his bride to face the wedding guests. His arm was still around her when they started back up the aisle.

Moira and Faith stepped forward to follow. Ben stepped out of his pew toward Faith, but Daddy reached her first, offering his arm. She smiled at her father and took it. Ben crooked his elbow for Moira instead, and they followed behind.

In front of the church, Faith was very careful not to catch the bouquet of white gardenias that Charlotte tossed over her shoulder.

WHAT THE HELL WAS THE USE? Ben asked himself in bafflement and frustration after leaving Faith's classroom a couple weeks later.

They had gone out twice more since the wedding, but getting her to go was like netting a wild animal. Every time he asked her out, Faith offered excuses. Sometimes she did open up when they were together, but more often, she raised a barrier that made him think more of barbed wire than a brick wall. Did she even notice that she was drawing blood?

During the last dinner date, he had decided to lay his feelings on the line. Maybe he was being too subtle for her.

He couldn't quite bring himself to say, "I love you." He'd never said those words in his life to anyone, and the odds were good that if he did now Faith would throw them back in his face.

So after he kissed her good-night, before she reached for the door handle, he said, "Maybe you're not ready, but I'd like it if you'd start thinking about what we have going here."

She stared at him, eyes shadowed by the darkness.

Even more clumsily, he continued, "What I feel is... something new to me. I want you. No, more than that. I..."

Faith shook her head. Hard. "Don't say that. You didn't want me when I was whole. You feel guilty, and sorry for me, and... *No!*" she cried, when he tried to interrupt. "No!" She turned away from him, struggled with the door handle and all but erupted out of his 4Runner, racing to the house so fast he didn't catch her before she banged inside.

And today... Today she'd made conversation as if she were lunching with a substitute teacher, someone she was being nice to but didn't expect to run into again.

He was left with no idea whether she'd actually heard what he was trying to say.

Damn it. Maybe she just wasn't ready. He was pushing; he knew he was.

The alternative was to admit she wasn't interested at all, which meant he'd have to give up. His chest felt hollow when he imagined doing that.

She didn't need him as much as she had; she looked better all the time, even if she wasn't—and maybe never would be—the same woman she'd been before her last confrontation with Rory. She'd said today at lunch that she had quit taking the pills and was sleeping fine anyway. She no longer had the bruised, wounded look that had wrenched his gut every time he saw her. He'd noticed, when she had walked past the window in her classroom in a shaft of sunlight, that her hair shone again. He wanted desperately to see it loose around her shoulders. Spread on his pillow. She had beautiful hair, smooth and as pale as the early spring sunshine she evoked for him.

She did respond to his kisses as if she couldn't help herself, but then she fled from every one of them. She never touched him voluntarily. He suspected his invitations to dinner alarmed her as much as they did because a date inevitably led to a kiss, while she could dodge him when he dropped by her classroom or even the farmhouse in the evening because her father was present.

That gave him hope and maddened him at the same time. She wanted him, but she was refusing to let herself have him.

That might be because she didn't believe she'd ever feel anything serious for him. For her, lust wouldn't be enough.

On the other hand, he had to ask himself whether she was afraid of him on some level. She had loved and entrusted herself to a man who proved to be a monster. Was she left fearing what went on behind closed doors in other marriages? When he got frustrated, did she wonder whether he was capable of lifting his hand to her? It made his stomach turn to even think about it, but he had to.

Maybe Charlotte would know.

At city hall, a couple of people in the lobby and on the stairs cleared out of his way after startled glances. Ben knew he could look forbidding and had to make a conscious effort sometimes to strive for unalarming. He was in no mood right now to try.

Unfortunately, when he got to his office, Gray was waiting there, standing at the window. Ben couldn't even be rude, since this was the first time he'd seen him since he'd gotten back from his honeymoon.

When Ben walked in, Gray turned from the window. "I had a question—" He stopped, raised his eyebrows. "What's wrong?"

"Nothing." Ben dropped into his chair, then scrubbed a hand over his face. "Faith."

"You had lunch with her?"

"Only because I got to her classroom before the bell rang, so she had no chance to escape. If I'm late, she always makes a getaway."

"Did she expect you?"

Ben snorted. "Doesn't matter. I suspect she hides out during lunchtime every day, because I try to stop by a couple times a week."

"Charlotte said you two are seeing each other."

"We are. Because I keep pushing and pushing." He

paused and faced the bleak facts. "I don't know if I should keep on, Gray. Hell." He pinched the bridge of his nose. "I've been thinking about talking to Charlotte."

"Come to dinner tonight. Unless you have plans?"

He looked up in some surprise, meeting the mayor's gray eyes and finding compassion he hadn't expected in them. "You mean that?" he asked, hearing the thickness in his voice.

"It's not just Faith, is it? It's the job, too."

He let out a huff of air. "Sometimes I wonder what the hell I'm doing here. Yeah. Right now, I feel as if I'm beating my head against the wall on all fronts."

"Come to dinner," Gray repeated.

Unexpectedly warmed by what he knew was a gesture of friendship, Ben nodded after a moment. "Thanks. I'd like that. Uh…how was the honeymoon?" They'd gone to Kauai for ten days.

Gray gave a brief, wicked grin. "Good. Too short." He tugged at his tie as though it was choking him. "I have a late meeting. Seven tonight?"

"Seven," Ben agreed. "You had a question?"

Gray just shook his head. "It can wait." He rapped his knuckles on Ben's desk and walked out.

CHAPTER ELEVEN

MAN, HE WAS A MESS. Ben stood on Gray Van Dusen's front step with his finger hovering above the doorbell. He'd never in his life begged for reassurance from anyone, and Ben knew damn well that's what he was here to do.

He'd never pleaded for an intervention in his personal life, either, and he needed that, too.

Crap.

Ben pushed the button, then shoved his hands in his pockets and waited.

It was Charlotte who opened the door. Did she look surprised?

"I hope Gray told you I was coming," Ben said.

Startling him, she stood on her tiptoes and kissed his cheek. "Of course he did. We've been waiting for you."

He stepped cautiously inside, the cop in him doing a quick sweep even though he'd been here often enough. It stung a little that—this place was everything his aging house wasn't. The wooden floors gleamed. A bronze statue of an eagle that must have cost an arm and a leg perched on a pedestal carved from a single chunk of wood; on the wall behind it hung a rug that looked Navajo. A fire burned behind glass doors in the river-rock fireplace. Gray rose from the leather sofa and said, "Would you like a glass of wine? Bourbon?"

"Wine. Thanks."

Gray went to the kitchen and came back with a glass of red wine that had a ruby glow against the fire-light—or, hell, looked like blood from Ben's perspective. Maybe he should have gone for a bourbon and water.

Charlotte nudged him to a deep, upholstered chair, then sat close enough to her husband to lean against him once she'd tucked her feet under her.

"There's an offer on the farm," she said.

Ben closed his eyes. "Oh, damn."

"It was inevitable," Gray pointed out.

"Yeah, but…" Ben lifted one shoulder. "Winter can be slow for real estate. I thought slow might be a good thing for Faith."

"I don't know." Charlotte frowned. "Once they're all packed, the house is going to seem really empty. And having the barn closed up and even emptier…" She gave herself a shake, as if warding off shivers. "For Faith, I'm guessing living there might feel like…like the old days when someone who died was laid out in the dining room for weeks and you had to live around the body."

"Nice imagery," Gray said. "Jeez."

Ben's grunt was almost a laugh. "But effective." He took a swallow of the wine. Too sweet for his tastes, but he appreciated the heat of it in his throat and belly. "Faith has gone at the getting ready to move thing like an athlete training for a triathlon. I'd been hoping she'd see that it isn't really that urgent."

Gray set his wineglass down on the table. "And now she'll be even more convinced it is."

"What happens when she's done?" Ben asked. His

frustration tasted more like anger right now. "When there's nothing left to do? How long has she been filling every spare minute to keep from facing whatever the hell her demons are?"

"Years," her sister whispered.

He looked at her, startled. "What?"

"She started this…crusade to save the farm after her marriage broke up. After she came home from the hospital. She needed something, and Dad gave it to her." Head bent, she gazed down at the wineglass she still held, looking more fragile than usual. More like Faith. "I should have known what was happening, but I didn't." Her voice, too small and not like her, broke. "I didn't want to know."

Gray didn't say anything, but his hand had settled around her nape and he seemed to be gently massaging it. Her head turned and she rubbed her cheek against his knuckles.

Ben waited. He'd known something was wrong between the sisters, although he could see their love, too. The tension was occasional, more on Charlotte's side than Faith's, it seemed. He hadn't been able to figure out why she hung back sometimes, like the night Faith had shot Rory and the two sisters had sat on the sofa holding hands but with too much distance between them. Even if Faith had pushed her away, why had Charlotte let her?

Shame on her face but determination, too, Charlotte said, "We'd been mostly estranged for ten years. My fault."

Gray made a sound in his throat. "Char, you don't have to do this."

She gave him a twisted smile. "Yes, I do." She met

Ben's eyes. "I…didn't like being an identical twin. It really ate at me. I loved her, but I pushed her away, too. I think that makes a lot of this my fault." She shook her head at her husband's rumbles. "No, let me finish. I can't help wondering if I'm responsible for her putting up with Rory's abuse. There was some reason she didn't believe she deserved better than that. I think I left her feeling lousy about herself."

"She'd tell you that was crap," Gray snapped.

"And would you believe her?" She gave him a single, devastated look. "I thought coming home was a good thing, that we were healing each other. I still think it is. That we *are*. But…it hurts to know that she didn't call me when she needed me. And that there's a lot we can't fix." Her grimace might have been intended as a smile. "I just thought you should know, Ben. There's history here that isn't just her marriage."

He nodded. "I appreciate it. I doubt it's as simple as you've made it out to be, though. I didn't know your mother, but she sounds like a nice lady. You had good folks who gave you real bedrock." Something he wasn't always sure he believed in, but…he'd met a lot of decent people in West Fork. In L.A., those weren't the types he often encountered.

"That's true."

"So why's the responsibility all on your shoulders? There are plenty of sisters and brothers who don't get along."

Behind her head, Gray gave a thumbs-up.

She couldn't possibly have seen it, but she narrowed her eyes at Ben. "You sound like Gray. Have you been talking to him?"

He found himself smiling despite the tension that still

gripped him. "He hasn't prepped me, if that's what you mean."

Laughing, Gray kissed her cheek. "Common sense, sweetheart. What'd I tell you?"

Ben looked at the wine and again thought about blood. He clenched his jaw. "If I'd been able to arrest that bastard so she didn't have to shoot him…"

"He'd have gotten out of jail eventually. Probably sooner than later," Gray said bluntly. "Let's not kid ourselves. He'd have come after her again. The truth is, she stood up to him. She saved herself. After feeling like a victim, after having him stalk her, that has to be the best outcome."

"I've been telling her how gutsy she was, but I don't think she believes me."

Charlotte scrutinized him in a way that made Ben shift in his chair. Most of the time he was able to block out how much she looked like Faith. Well, hell; they were identical. But to him they weren't, and it was more than the fact that Faith's hair hung to her waist when it was loose from the braid while Charlotte's was cut boy short and hugged her head. It was a matter of expression, of attitude, of the wants and needs and self-doubts that lay beneath the identical bones and flesh. It was like seeing the same dress on two different women: same fabric and style and cut, sure, but it didn't fit the same.

Right this minute, though, Charlotte looked disconcertingly like her sister. Maybe it was the worry in her eyes, the softness of her mouth.

"You're not going to give up on her, are you?" she asked.

Ben rolled his shoulders. "I'm adding to her troubles

right now. That's not what I want to be doing." What he'd wanted was to take care of her, to protect her, to soothe her and love her. Instead, he upset her right when she was trying to find her footing again.

"What are, um, your intentions?" Charlotte made a face. "Not that it's any of my business, except… You weren't exactly pursuing Faith until after this happened. You asked *me* out, not her."

Well, shit. Ben hesitated. He wasn't in the habit of talking about how he felt. He knew Gray had guessed, but Charlotte, he wasn't sure of. Probably not, or she wouldn't be asking.

But why else was he here, if not to throw himself at their mercy?

"I love her," he said hoarsely. "I want to marry her."

Her forehead crinkled. "Then why…?"

Damn, he hated this. But for Faith, he'd do it.

"I may have done her an injustice, but I saw a gentle, sweet woman when I met Faith. One who kept trying to believe that bastard Hardesty was redeemable, was really a good guy underneath." Now his voice was harsh. He couldn't help it. "I couldn't see her wanting a man who grew up in foster care, who doesn't know what it's like to have a real family. A man who chose a job steeped in violence. I've killed three men. Did you know that? I've slammed more of them to the ground when I cuffed them than I can count. I have nightmares, but probably not as many as I should have. I am not a gentle man." He looked hard at Faith's sister. "Am I what you would have chosen for her?"

Damned if she didn't have compassion in her eyes. "Not when we were twenty, no. But now, I think you're exactly what she needs. Think about everything she's survived. Everything she did to survive. You *are* doing her an injustice, Ben. I've known for a long time that Faith is stronger than I am."

He nodded after a long moment. Faith was stronger than he'd ever given her credit for being, as well.

"I'm too old for her."

She blinked, then smiled. "How old are you?"

"Thirty-eight. Almost thirty-nine."

"Nine years isn't too much."

"She's trying to get rid of me, Charlotte. There's only so long a man should ignore the fact that a woman is saying no."

"Faith may be strong, but she's scared, too. Rory was, well, the only man who ever meant anything to her. That would make anyone doubt herself. And there's the way people look at her these days, as if—" She stopped.

Ben hadn't thought of that, but he could imagine. This was a quiet, conservative community. She'd shot a man down; people might think she'd done it coolly, deliberately. Especially those who had known Rory Hardesty as a likable kid and popular jock in high school. Some of the townsfolk never had been able to see Rory Hardesty as any real threat.

Of course, they knew Faith, too, but might still have trouble understanding and believing the darkness that could lurk behind any of their neighbors' front doors.

His stomach knotted at the idea of her having to flinch from curious or judgmental stares at the grocery store or library or—worse yet—when she met with the parents of her students, or even fellow teachers.

"Damn," he muttered.

"And then there's you. Faith really liked you when

you first came out to the farm. And later, after Rory threw that cherry bomb through the window and you held her on your lap as though—" She stopped again. Cleared her throat.

He was able to finish her sentence with no trouble. He'd held Faith as though she was the most precious thing in his world. And then he'd been all cop the next time he saw her.

"I was an idiot," he admitted. "Is it hopeless?"

"No, I don't think so. You have a miraculous effect on her, Ben. That day she disappeared all afternoon and then stayed for dinner at your house? She came home... different. I don't know what you did..."

He knew what she was thinking and was unaccountably embarrassed. Damned if his cheeks didn't feel hot. "Not that."

"Then what?"

"We talked." More reluctantly, he added, "I convinced her to take a nap."

Both Gray and Charlotte stared at him.

"She'd been refusing to take sleeping pills. You know that."

They nodded.

"She felt safe with me. I thought she might."

There was a long, speculative silence. Finally Charlotte said, "But she's been sleeping ever since, too, according to Daddy. Well, all I have to do is look at her to tell."

"She discovered how restorative sleep is and decided to quit being stubborn. She started taking the pills."

Charlotte frowned. "Is she still?"

"No. She said that she'd stopped."

A timer went off in the kitchen, causing Charlotte to

stir and put her feet to the floor, where she groped for her shoes. "Let me turn on the asparagus and then we'll be ready to eat."

Gray patted her butt when she rose as if he couldn't resist.

When his wife had left them, he looked again at Ben. "I could feel you seething at the council meeting."

"Is there a single city-council member under sixty?"

"Ah..." Gray gave it a moment's thought. "No. I'm hoping that'll change in the next election. I'd especially like to see the last of Luther Conrad. But I happen to know that Esther Rose is seventy-one years old, and she's smart and willing to admit there might be such a thing as new ideas."

Ben moved restlessly, crossing and uncrossing his outstretched legs at the ankles. "Yeah, Esther is okay. I guess I just didn't realize when I took the job that I'd have a bunch of old farts looking over my shoulder. I'd gotten tired enough of the politics I had to deal with in L.A., I figured as police chief I'd be calling the shots."

Gray laughed like that was the funniest thing he'd ever heard. "Just like I do as mayor? The truth is, our jobs are more like leaning our shoulders into the bumper of a broken-down old boat of a Cadillac and trying to get it rolling down the road."

Ben grunted in acknowledgement. "But is it rolling?"

"Your Caddy? What do you think?"

"You sound like a therapist," he said suspiciously.

Gray grinned. "Didn't mean to. It just seems to me

that sometimes you have to run a self-check. Did I make a difference today? This past week? The past month?"

Ben nodded.

"So what do you think? You have a bunch of young officers. Are they shaping up?"

"Sometimes I feel like I'm running a preschool." He gave a snort of laughter. "I guess Faith and I have something in common after all. But...yeah. And did you hear about the shooting while you were gone?"

Gray sat up. "Shooting?"

"Routine traffic stop, Carl Stevens got out of his unit and walked forward. He was paying attention, the way he should have been, and when the driver suddenly leaned out his window Carl took a dive behind the car. Shot missed him. The car peeled out, Carl called it in and not two minutes later a county deputy joined Carl and another one of our officers in pulling the bastard over. They did a damn fine job." He allowed himself a faint smile. "I didn't tell them how surprised I was."

Gray laughed. "Leadership in action."

"So to answer your question, I think things are coming together. I'm pushing hard with training, trying to build more camaraderie."

"From what I hear, it's working," Gray said straight out. "There's a sense of pride that didn't used to exist." He paused. "Did you know that Ronnie Peschek put in an application to Seattle P.D. right about the time you started?"

"No." Peschek was one of the few experienced, competent officers Ben had had to work with.

Gray lifted his wineglass in a kind of salute. "They offered him a job. He turned it down."

"Well, damn." Ben took a swallow of his own wine.

"I'm hearing good things about the officers you've put in the schools."

"They're young enough," Ben said sardonically. "They ought to fit in."

Sounding meditative, Gray said, "Our last police chief assigned Martin Galbreath to the high school."

Martin had retired just six months ago. He'd worn his gray hair in a buzz cut and his belt low to support a hanging belly. He was one of those guys who liked the charge of wearing a uniform and a gun, and figured a nose or eyebrow ring was justifiable cause for pulling someone in for questioning. Ben had encouraged the retirement.

"Bet he was popular."

"Oh, yeah."

"I know you're frustrated that the council doesn't want to foot the bill to upgrade from revolvers to semi-automatics."

Ben scowled. "*Faith* was better armed than my officers."

Charlotte appeared and both men turned their heads. "Dinner's ready."

They stood. In a low voice, Gray said, "You're wearing the council members down, Ben."

He stopped, looking at his boss, a man whom he'd thought was becoming a friend, back before Charlotte had come back to town to protect her sister. "Uh-huh. What about you? It wasn't so long ago you told me you were disappointed in my performance." Ben waited tensely for the answer.

Gray winced. "You know that was fear talking."

"I should have been able to find Hardesty. I *still* haven't found out where he was those last weeks."

"You're trying?" Gray said in surprise.

"Faith needs answers. I can't figure out any other way to get them for her."

All he was hitting were dead ends. Noah Berger had finally called back, but hadn't been able to tell him anything more than Jimmy Reese already had. Rory's aunt professed to know nothing, which might even be the truth, as she seemed to look on her nephew's behavior with a considerably more jaundiced eye than his mother did.

"He didn't have his cell phone with him, did he?" Gray asked.

"No. I'd like to find that phone. He might have even left a note somewhere, if he'd intended to die that night, too."

Gray gave him a sharp look. "Do you think he did?"

Ben sighed. "No. If he'd carried a gun, I'd be more inclined to think so, but I don't see him being willing to slit his own throat. If he'd planned to die, he wouldn't have had any reason not to drive his own truck. No, I think he was planning to walk right back out of there feeling like he was justified in teaching her a final lesson."

"That's my guess, too," Gray agreed.

By unspoken agreement they dropped the subject once they reached the table. It wasn't as if any of this was news to Charlotte, but there was no need to stir up her anger and guilt any more, either.

She'd made lasagna and served it with garlic bread and the asparagus. It seemed that growing up both the Russell girls had learned to cook, and to cook well. Conversation stayed on local news during dinner: plans to break ground for a Haggen store, the going-out-of-business sign that had appeared on the front window of the fabric shop, rumors that a longtime, beloved dentist was getting senile. Charlotte had the historic perspective on everyone they discussed and offered some amusing anecdotes.

Ben had the thought again that in L.A. he wouldn't have known every business owner the way he did now; he wouldn't have been tapped into every organization in town from the Soroptomists to the high-school booster club. He wouldn't have been able to worry about small but potentially lethal problems like traffic outside the high school, or cared about the upcoming school bond issue. Sometimes he felt like an alien observing a peculiar society from a sociological perspective, but talking with Charlotte and Gray tonight left him with an unfamiliar, warm feeling under his breastbone. He realized that he'd somehow become a strand of the web that made up this community in a way he'd never expected to be.

Maybe he'd become important here.

Food for thought.

At the door, Charlotte kissed his cheek again and said softly, "Don't lose patience with her."

Ben said with perfect seriousness, "I don't want to turn into another stalker in her mind."

Startled, she drew back and thought about it. "If I ever get the feeling that's how she looks at you, I promise to tell you. Okay?"

"Thanks." He hugged her, shook Gray's hand and drove home. What he'd have liked to do when he got home was call Faith, just to hear her voice. Which meant the smart thing to do was strip some woodwork.

CHARLOTTE AND GRAY HAD Thanksgiving at their house and invited Ben and Moira as well as Faith and Dad. Faith managed to avoid being alone with Ben, although she felt his gaze resting on her whenever he wasn't directly talking to someone else. As soon as she could politely do so, she made her excuses and left, unable to bear being the object of such close attention.

Faith had been telling herself she was glad the farm had sold so quickly. How miserable it would be if the whole thing had dragged out forever! A fellow teacher and her husband had had their house on the market for fifteen months before it sold. Waiting like that, it occurred to Faith, would have left her and her dad in limbo. Yes, this was definitely best. They'd made the decision. Now the break would be quick and clean.

She'd regretted taking even the one day off. This was one year when she didn't *feel* like giving thanks. She knew that was wrong; she'd survived Rory, she had Char and Dad and Gray, and that quick sale really was a blessing.

Except for Thanksgiving Day itself, she'd been working harder than ever, tirelessly sorting and pricing for the estate sale, finding ways to make a little profit on the last of the antiques in the barn and the nursery plants that had filled a quarter of an acre. As shelves emptied in the barn, she filled them again with the items she'd priced for the estate sale. The aging Tupperware wouldn't bring in much, but the vintage clothes and eighty-year-old costume jewelry might. She and Daddy had agreed to sell certain pieces of furniture, too; once November rolled into December he began looking for a small house, and she already had furniture in storage. Char and Gray hauled the antique spool bed from Faith's bedroom out to the barn and the mattress and springs to the dump. Faith never wanted to see the bed again.

She loved the dresser, though, and decided she could forgive it for being in the room. The tall beveled mirror, too, that stood on a mahogany stand. The dresser in Char's old bedroom, the one Faith was currently using, would be sold.

The seemingly never-ending decisions all felt important to her. She knew on one level that her involvement in every mundane detail was like a life jacket for her, keeping her afloat. She suspected no one but her actually cared what pieces of furniture the family kept or sold, just as it seemed no one but her had cared whether they lost the farm or not.

Of course, they weren't actually losing it, Faith had to keep reminding herself. They were selling it for an impressive amount of money. It turned out the land was even more valuable for being inside the city limits; the residents of whatever development sprang up here would be able to take advantage of city water, and fire and police services.

If the farm had been a few hundred yards west, it would have been sheriff's deputies that had come when Rory threw the cherry bomb through the window, when he broke in and attacked Char, when Faith killed him. Gray might never have met Char. Ben wouldn't have held Faith on his lap and warmed her with his big, solid body. Even though she still didn't know what to make of him, she shuddered at the idea of some impersonal deputy questioning her and perhaps at best offering rough sympathy.

Char wouldn't have stayed in West Fork if not for

Gray. *I wouldn't have survived,* Faith admitted to herself, *if not for Ben.*

So why couldn't she bring herself to trust him, to believe what he had said, his voice gruff as if he were moved?

I want you. No, more than that.

There were plenty of reasons she shied from believing in a future with him, most real, some probably imagined. How could any woman who'd been abused—had *allowed* herself to be abused—ever fully trust again? A man *or* herself? That was only number one on her list. Number two was the wounds to her self-esteem her relationship with Char had dealt. Number three, her uncertainty about why Ben wanted her now when he hadn't before.

In one way, she was putting her life back together, gaining a pound or two a week on a body that had become gaunt, sleeping at least a few hours a night if not well, holding up her head when she felt people staring or heard whispers. Some of the worry had faded from Dad's and Char's eyes when they looked at her.

Inside…inside, she knew she wasn't doing nearly that well. Denial was her watchword. *Don't think about it,* her mantra. She kept busy, tried not to think, not to remember. Her classroom was the only place she felt whole. The kids gave her that, and always had. Otherwise, she knew she was still in danger of completely falling apart. If she ever convinced herself that Rory hadn't meant to kill her, she knew she would.

But each day that passed was a victory, and if enough of them added up Faith had to believe that she *would* heal. Time was supposed to heal all wounds, wasn't it?

But she could not take one more blow. The knowledge was bone-deep. Ben could destroy her, and she didn't dare give him that chance.

The depths of her longing for him told her how dangerous he was to her. So, she was not only a coward, but weak, because she couldn't make herself send him away altogether. When he kissed her, she forgot about being afraid; when he smiled, or his dark eyes lit with humor, she ached with joy.

Eventually he'd give up, she reasoned. Or his sense of guilt and responsibility would fade, if that was what he really felt. And that would hurt, but not as much as if she gave herself to him, heart and soul.

And so she didn't.

CHAPTER TWELVE

DAD STOPPED the pickup truck beside the curb and turned off the engine. After a moment, he said, "What do you think?"

Back to driving for some weeks, he'd stopped in front of a small house in the old part of town, an odd little place, but charming. The pitch of the roof was unusually shallow, not quite flat but close, and the walls were stucco, unusual in the Northwest. Dwarfed by the larger homes on each side, the house was painted white and the trim bright blue. The previous owner had liked to garden; the narrow front yard was all flowerbeds and no lawn. Small as it was, the yard boasted a gnarled old lilac, bare of leaves, and a couple of rosebushes holding on to red-and-orange hips. Low boxwood hedges marched along each side of the concrete walkway to the front door.

A for-sale sign stood out front.

"I've always liked this house," Faith said truthfully, although it made her nervous to realize they were less then two blocks away from Ben's house. "I've never been inside, though. I don't remember who lived here."

"Lillian Ewing. She just passed away. I'm told she was eighty-eight." He was eyeing the house thoughtfully, his forearms draped over the steering wheel. "She and your grandmother were of an age. Your Grandma Peters and Miss Ewing were in a quilting group together. Never married, and she became something of a recluse these past ten years or so."

Faith managed a smile. "Shall we go in?" Ignoring her father's searching gaze, she got out and waited for him to join her.

The real-estate agent had lent her father the key, since the house was empty. Faith was glad she could wander through it without having to make conversation with a stranger.

Dad had been househunting, but he hadn't suggested she join him until today. It was nothing she'd expected him to choose, a gingerbread house without the gingerbread, a whimsical cottage that seemed to suit an eccentric old lady, not her practical, stoical father. But she could feel his eagerness; he wanted her to like this place.

On the front porch she stood aside while he unlocked the door.

"Dad," she said gently, "you know you don't need my approval."

He looked at her.

"I won't be living with you forever. In fact, maybe this would be a good time for me to get an apartment."

He didn't like that, she could tell. "I'd hoped..." He didn't finish.

"What had you hoped?" she asked with sudden sharpness.

He held her gaze. "That you and Ben were talking marriage."

"No," she said flatly. "Can we go in?"

Daddy hesitated, but after a moment pushed the front door open and stood aside for her to go ahead.

The rooms had been stripped of furniture, so their footsteps were too loud. The air wasn't musty, but felt peculiarly still, making Faith wonder how long it had been since Lillian Ewing had died.

The living room was small, with hardwood floors, a fireplace of white-painted brick and an arched doorway. On the other side of the front entry was a dining room with a built-in, glass-fronted buffet and another arched door leading to the kitchen. It was old-fashioned, but nice, the cabinets painted the same bright blue as the trim outside, while blue-and-white gingham curtains framed the double-sash window over the sink. At the back of the house were two bedrooms and a single bathroom. Out of one of the windows Faith saw that there was a detached garage off the alley, big enough for a single car and perhaps some gardening tools. And that was it.

She could live here with him for a little while. Perhaps they both needed that, but it was really a house for one person. Or for a couple. Dad hadn't dated since Mom's death, to Faith's knowledge, but she wondered for the first time if he'd begun to imagine remarrying.

Faith gave her head a bewildered shake. She felt like Alice in Wonderland, where nothing fit the rules she understood.

"I like it," she finally said, turning to face her father, who leaned against the door frame. "Wait. Is there a laundry room?"

"Back porch is glassed in. The washer and dryer hookups are out there."

"Will you want to garden?"

He tugged meditatively at one earlobe. "I think I

might. I could put some vegetables in back, maybe a row of raspberries, but I like flowers, too."

She went to him, laid her head against his shoulder and wrapped her arms around his waist. "I love you."

He hugged her. "Love you, too, punkin."

How long since he'd called her that? Faith blinked hard, eyes burning. How long since she'd told him how much she loved him, how grateful she was for his unfailing, silent support?

Too long.

After a moment she sniffed and let him go. "I say go for it, Daddy."

Looking pleased, he nodded. "Then I will. I want this to be your home, too, Faith."

"For now," she conceded, because it mattered to him. And she wasn't quite ready yet to live alone, to give up the sound of her father's snores in favor of silence.

As he locked the front door behind them, she asked, "Have you showed it to Char?"

"No. Just you."

"It's good that it's empty. You—we—won't be held up moving."

"I thought about asking if we could rent it until closing. Then we could start moving in any time."

Her anxiety swelled, but Faith nodded as if considering. "Might be a good idea."

"Why don't we get some dinner?" her father suggested. "Just you and me. Bob and Silvia asked me to play bingo with them later at the grange."

So she would be alone for a few hours. It would be the first time at night, but she thought she'd be all right. That's really what Dad was asking, without coming out and saying so. She smiled at him. "Sounds good."

They ate at Clara's Café where he and Mom had often taken the girls after church on Sunday. He had chicken-fried steak and mashed potatoes, Faith the macaroni and cheese that had been a favorite of hers as a child. Nothing had changed, not the red vinyl booths, not the collection of fanciful salt-and-pepper shakers beneath glass by the cash register. Even the waitresses were the same. Theirs called Dad by name, although her gaze skittered from Faith. Dad didn't seem to notice.

After they finished eating, he dropped her at home, waiting until she unlocked the back door and waved at him. Once inside, Faith refused to feel uneasy about the silence or the knowledge that she was alone. She couldn't afford to let herself.

Out of long habit she focused on what had to be done next. There was plenty to keep her too busy to even remember Dad wasn't home.

Why not start on the kitchen? Goodness knows how long it had been since anybody had even opened the upper cupboards, too high up for everyday use. Dad wouldn't have room for half of what was in here.

Faith was standing on a step stool, stretched to reach the back of the cupboard above the refrigerator, when she heard a vehicle pull in. Not Daddy's pickup, which ran rougher.

She wasn't panicked, not exactly, but she did climb down and felt her heart pounding a little faster as she waited for someone to appear at the back door. The porch light was on, so she'd be able to see whoever came knocking. Of course, he or she would be able to see in, too….

At the sight of the big, dark-haired man looming

outside her back door, something very like panic jolted her. Ben. She should be relieved, and was. In a way.

He rapped lightly even as they looked at each other through the glass pane.

Her pulse didn't slow, although now it hurried for a different reason. She let him in and stood back.

"I suppose Dad set me up," she said with resignation.

Ben's "Huh?" sounded genuine. Over jeans, he wore a crew-necked, rust-colored sweater that made her all too conscious of the breadth of his shoulders. He walked past her, carrying a shoe box that he set on the kitchen table. "To do what?"

If only her whole body wouldn't quake just because he was here, a few feet from her. "Nothing," she muttered.

"I don't hear the TV."

"Dad's playing bingo tonight down at the grange."

He frowned. "I figured he'd be home."

Okay, Dad *hadn't* told Ben this would be a good time to catch her alone. Faith studied him more closely, realizing for the first time that his expression was somber, as if he'd come to say something he knew would be unwelcome. He didn't step forward to kiss her, and he wasn't smiling.

She backed up until she bumped the edge of the counter. Her throat constricted, Faith said, "What?"

"I didn't know if you'd want it back." Ben nodded at the shoe box. "But we're done with it, and it is yours."

It. Her gaze darted past him to the innocuous box. Horror rose in her. She opened her mouth, but couldn't make anything come out on the first attempt. At last, in a voice that cracked, she whispered, "The gun? You're bringing back the gun?"

HIS GUT HAD TOLD BEN this was a mistake even before he'd gotten into his SUV to drive over here, but he hadn't listened. A gun owner had a right to reclaim possession of a weapon after a shooting, assuming it had been properly licensed in the first place. Faith had done everything right; the Colt was hers. It hadn't been cheap. She might want at least to resell it.

But he hadn't finished speaking, hadn't taken the lid off the box, and she was hyperventilating and staring at it as if a bomb were ticking on her kitchen table.

In a tormented whisper, she said, "The gun? You're bringing back the gun?"

He stepped forward. "I won't leave it if you don't want me to."

Her face was stricken and paper-white when she tore her gaze from the shoe box and met his. He'd never wanted to see her look like that again. "I don't want it," she gasped. "Get it out of here!"

Ben gripped her arms, feeling again her fragility. "Faith. Honey. I'll take it back out right now. Calm down."

"*Calm down?* How could you?" Wrenching free of him, she swung away and hung over the sink, her body heaving. He couldn't tell if she was sobbing or wretching.

"It made you feel safe before," he tried to explain. He didn't know if he should touch her again or not, but he couldn't help himself. He laid a hand on her back and rubbed.

Faith erupted, turning and pummeling his chest with her fists, sobs torn from her throat. Her eyes were wild, her face wet. "How could you?" she screamed. "How could you?"

His own eyes blurred as he let her hit him. He didn't try to defend himself, physically or with words. All he could do was stand there and take it while he watched anguish pour from her, the acid that had been eating her alive. She could hurt him all she wanted, if only it would make her feel better.

The outburst was violent but brief. When her knees buckled, he grabbed hold of her, pulling her against him. She buried her wet face against his shoulder and trembled from head to foot.

Ben held her as tight as he could and whispered against the top of her head, "I'm sorry. God, I'm sorry. I didn't think. I just didn't think. Blame me all you want. It's all right."

When he felt the tremors pass, he started to ease back, but her arms clamped around him and so he tightened his again. Rocking slightly, he kept murmuring soothing words, or maybe they were just sounds, into her hair.

He hurt inside, hurt so damn much he hated knowing he was also aroused, just because she was resting against him. If he didn't back up soon, she'd notice.

"It's not your fault," she mumbled, her lips tickling his throat.

"What?"

She scrubbed her face against him, dampening his sweater, then looked up. "I said, it's not your fault I fell apart."

"I should have called and asked you if you wanted the

damn thing." He sighed. "Or known you well enough to guess you wouldn't."

"How could you have guessed? I bought it, and I used it." Her eyes were puffy and dampness clung to her lashes. Her nose was red, too, and needed a good blowing.

Tenderness stirred at the sight of her face so woebegone. Ben looked past her and spotted a roll of paper towels on the counter amidst the clutter she'd apparently been removing from upper cupboards. Without letting her go, he grabbed the roll and, one-handed, pulled a sheet off.

Sniffing, she took it from him, gave a firm, undignified honk, swiped her eyes and then crumpled the paper towel in her hand. "I'm sorry. I don't know what got into me."

"It was more what needed to come out of you," he suggested.

Faith leaned back a little more to see his face better, although she kept the one arm around him as if she didn't want to let go. At his back, she had a wad of his sweater in a death grip.

"What do you mean?" she asked.

"I mean you've been tamping too much down. Not letting yourself scream and kick and rage."

Her forehead crinkled. "Why should I have to? It doesn't make sense to get mad."

"Sure it does." He gave her a little shake. "The son of a bitch just would not back off, not until he made you do something so goddamn horrible you'll never be able to forget it. Nobody managed to save you from that awful ending." He swallowed. "I sure as hell didn't. Meantime, your father's pulling the rug out from under you..."

"He has to sell!"

"Maybe so, but I'm betting deep inside you don't believe that."

She gazed up at him, her eyes huge and so blue he couldn't look away. "You're right," she whispered. "I agreed, too, and I know it's the best thing to do, but…"

"You're hurt anyway. And pissed. But you're too nice a woman to let anyone see that, especially your father."

Faith abruptly let him go and tried to step back, stopped by the counter. "How do you do it?" she asked sharply.

He should back up, too, give her some space. He didn't. "Do what?"

"See inside me?"

He shook his head. "I just know what I'd feel."

After a long moment of that disconcerting scrutiny, she abruptly bowed her head, her lashes veiling her expression. Very quietly, she said, "I'm maddest at myself."

He squeezed her shoulder. "Why?"

"I've been playing the martyr for a long time. I could have asked for help anytime. Why didn't I? Even this past year…" She gestured vaguely. "Charlotte came when I called. She would have come sooner. But me, I had to do it alone. I told myself it was for Daddy, but it wasn't, was it?"

Held mute by tenderness that had swelled until it filled him entirely, Ben shook his head.

Her stare no longer saw him or the kitchen or the here-and-now. She was looking painfully into the past. "I've been so self-absorbed."

"No." He'd heard as much as he could stand. "No. You were saving yourself, the only way you knew how. And you did a hell of a job. With a few more breaks and some more enthusiasm from your dad, you could have saved the farm, too."

"For a little longer."

Emotions swarmed in her eyes like a flock of birds blocking out the sky. "Char," she whispered. "Char happened."

"And me." Unable to read her expression, after a minute he grimaced. "Or maybe I'm giving myself too much credit."

"No." This was a mere breath of sound. She was seeing him again. "You happened, too."

Neither of them moved or said anything for a moment. Maybe thirty seconds.

Then, so quick he didn't have time to brace himself, Faith rose on tiptoe, flung her arms around his neck and pressed her lips to his. Hard. Their noses bumped, their teeth clanked together and he fell back a step so that he could wrap her in his embrace and lift her against him.

"I need you," he heard himself say in a voice he didn't recognize, and then he fit their mouths together the way they belonged.

This was no preliminary. His tongue plunged deep and hers met it. Their bodies strained together and he reached one hand down to grab her butt and knead even as his hips rocked against her.

When their mouths separated long enough for them to suck in oxygen, she panted, "Upstairs."

All he had to do was hoist her a little higher and start for the staircase. "Wrap your legs around me."

She did, and he gritted his teeth at the glory of her riding his erection. Faith kissed and licked his neck and nipped at his jaw as he climbed. A groan tore its way from his throat and he had to stop halfway up to capture that mouth in a kiss so deep he never wanted to surface.

Except he did, because, damn it, he couldn't take her here on the stairs. He had to lay her down to get her jeans off, and the bed wasn't that far away. Somehow he lifted his head and staggered upward, bouncing her against the wall once or twice. Didn't matter; the pictures had all been taken down, leaving brighter rectangles of wallpaper against the faded backdrop.

"In here?" he managed to say, bumping one of the bedroom doors open with his shoulder.

"Yes."

A few more steps, his mouth devouring hers, and they fell onto the bed. He wasn't so far gone that he didn't try to catch some of his weight on his forearms so as not to crush her, but he didn't roll to the side. It felt too good, being between her legs, his hips cradled by the clasp of her thighs.

She yanked his sweater over his head even as he fumbled with the buttons on her flannel shirt and spread it open. Ben growled to find her bra wasn't front-opening. Another deep, hungry kiss and he rolled back, pulling her atop him so he could push off the shirt and unclasp the bra.

She might still be too thin—she was still too thin—but all he saw right now was the narrow, creamy-pale length of her torso and small, firm breasts tipped with rosy-pink nipples that begged for his mouth. A raw sound escaped him as he tugged her down so he could lick and taunt and suckle those breasts, each in turn.

Faith made sounds of her own, and her hands kneaded his shoulders, fingernails making their mark. Ben looked up to see her face, her eyes a glowing, deep blue, lips swollen from his kisses, color running high over exquisitely formed cheekbones. He groaned again and flipped her so that he could strip her jeans and panties off. Then he just stared.

Her legs were glorious, long and taut with muscle. The curls at the junction of her thighs were barely a shade darker than the hair on her head. Her belly was concave above hip bones that were too prominent. He wanted her curves restored. He wanted her just a little more lush, a little less vulnerable.

She was the most beautiful thing he'd ever seen.

"Do you know how much I want you?" he whispered, his throat aching.

Her eyes flashed emotions he couldn't read. "No. I'm not so good at believing anymore."

"Believe," Ben said hoarsely. His lips a hair's breadth from hers, he said again, "Believe," and then kissed her until words were beyond him, until there was nothing but sensation.

He had the sense to sheath himself in a condom before flinging his jeans to the floor. Another time, he'd make love to her with his mouth as well as his hands, he'd explore and let her explore, but right now need drove him as if he were an addict, blind and stumbling for his fix. Faith's hands pulling him over her seemed as frantic, her whimpers and moans the flick of a match to his tinder. He parted her legs and plunged inside her, his tongue in her mouth going as deep. He'd never felt anything like this, never wanted a woman so much he couldn't have stopped if someone had held a gun to his head. The way her hips lifted to meet every thrust, even as her tongue stroked his, had his vision blurring and the end about to pound into him whether he was ready or not. Whether or not he'd given her a quarter of the pleasure she was giving him.

But just as he felt himself explode, she cried out in a climax that was the most erotic caress he'd ever felt in his life.

There was sex, he thought dimly as he collapsed on her, and then there was love.

THEY MADE LOVE one more time, after Ben unplaited her hair and spread the unconfined waves over her shoulders and breasts. He ran his hands through her hair, tangled his fingers in it, his expression rapt as though he'd never seen anything so glorious. Faith managed to block out all her doubts and just *feel*. This wasn't happiness, not exactly; happiness, to her, had always been something more placid than this storm of passion that cleansed even as it tumbled her over and over.

Ben tried to be gentle the second time. He tried to hold her back, to make her look into his eyes as he caressed her with hands that learned and exploited all her weaknesses. He didn't understand that she *needed* the thunder and lightning and whipping winds of the storm. This had to be all physical, a release as tumultuous as her wild, ineffectual attack on him earlier. She had to be swept away, so she pushed him with her hands and mouth until he broke and did the sweeping.

They started with her astride him, and ended up with him on top again, his big hands gripping her hips, holding her so he could thrust deeper. Faith heard herself scream at the end, when her body imploded. This was like dying and being reborn all at the same time.

"Faith," he groaned, as his body went rigid and then bucked. "Faith."

She was shocked to realize there were tears on the face she had buried against his chest. She didn't even know what they meant, didn't want him to see them.

When he rolled to take his weight off her, Faith slipped from his arms and scrambled from the bed, keeping her back to him as she swiped at her cheeks.

"Dad will be home anytime." She spotted her panties and jeans and pulled them on as one. Ignoring the silence behind her, she hunted for her bra and finally saw it draped over the back of the rocker.

"All right," Ben said slowly. "I can see why you wouldn't want your father to walk in on us naked."

The bed creaked when he moved.

Faith reached behind her to fasten her bra and her fingers bumped into others. Ben's bare feet had been silent enough on the floorboards that she hadn't known he was so close.

He hooked her bra for her, then closed his hands on her shoulders and turned her to face him.

"What's wrong?"

"Nothing's wrong." She wasn't much of a liar, Faith realized, and her eyes closed in near defeat. "I didn't mean for that to happen."

His fingers bit into her flesh. "I did," he said in a voice that could have scraped bone. "You wanted me, too."

She wrenched free of his grip. "I lost control in more

ways than one tonight. Do you think I feel good about that?"

Was that hurt in his dark eyes? If so, he blanked it out quickly. "You should. Letting go isn't always bad, Faith."

"I wasn't ready." She swallowed. "I'm not ready."

The muscles in his jaw spasmed. Without another word, he began to get dressed. He was sitting in the rocker putting on socks and athletic shoes when she left the bedroom and went down the hall to the bathroom.

All she could think was that she had to braid her hair again before Daddy saw her like this and guessed what had happened. She couldn't even bear to look at herself in the mirror until she'd run the brush through the tangles and begun the soothing, familiar act of braiding. It seemed essential that she restore her outer self to exactly what it had been before she'd begun to sob, before she'd beaten at Ben's chest and then pressed her mouth to his.

Fixing her hair wasn't enough. She had to splash cold water on her face, pat it dry and rub lotion where his end-of-day stubble had reddened her skin. At last she could study the Faith in the mirror and see a self she knew, a self she could live with. Only then did she unlock the bathroom door and go downstairs, barely pausing to glance in the bedroom. She'd known he wouldn't be there, that he'd have gone down ahead of her.

But he wasn't downstairs, either. He'd taken the shoe box from the table and was gone.

Faith stood in the empty kitchen, so lost in desolation she didn't know if she could make her body obey her enough to take even one step. She simply stood there, breathing in, then out, trying not to think, not to feel, not to wonder if she had finally driven Ben away once and for all. And then, at last, her muscles unlocked and she was able to walk across the kitchen to where she'd left off.

She began carefully wrapping the miscellaneous glassware and vases in newspaper so nothing would get broken when she carried the packed boxes to the barn for the sale.

CHAPTER THIRTEEN

IN ONE NIGHT, Faith had given herself to him and then rejected him with a cold finality that left Ben stunned.

He went home to his empty house, knew he wouldn't be able to sleep and decided to throw himself into a job that would give him something—anything—else to think about. He'd put off stripping the old, darkened varnish from the woodwork in the living room. That would work as well as anything else.

Ben flung open the windows and let the cold night air leaven the fumes of the chemical stripper. He worked unceasingly, stroking the stuff on one stretch of molding with a paintbrush and, while it did its work, scraping up sodden, bubbling curls of varnish with his chisel in another spot where it had already sat long enough.

He tried not to think about her and failed. Anguish, anger, bewilderment and devastation supplanted each other, circling around and around. It all came down to the same conclusion: she'd had a moment of weakness, but that was all it had been. He'd made love to a woman for the first time in his life instead of just having sex with her and all she could say afterward was that she hadn't meant for it to happen. Right before she walked out of the bedroom without even a backward glance.

Ben swore aloud, looked around and saw that he'd

stripped every inch of woodwork in the living room, including the mantel.

The place stank. *He* stank by the time he staggered upstairs as dawn was lightening the sky, dumped his clothes in the hamper and stood in the shower, letting it run over his head until the hot water was gone.

He felt older than the house when he walked into the police station a few hours later, numbly determined to do his job. He'd had sleepless nights before and had functioned fine. Ben knew from experience that he could go up to three days with no more than a snatched nap here and there. This was nothing.

And everything. He felt hollow, used up, hopeless in a way he couldn't remember ever feeling before. Probably because he'd never before been stupid enough to let himself love anyone.

DAD DIDN'T SEEM TO NOTICE a thing when he got home. His mood was genial, and after kissing her cheek and telling her not to stay up late, he'd gone upstairs to bed. The minute he was out of sight, Faith sank onto a kitchen chair and quit pretending, even to herself, that she cared which pans they kept and which they sold or gave to the Goodwill.

After a minute, she stood up and turned out the lights, leaving everything where it lay. Climbing the stairs in the dark was easy, the faint glow from the bathroom light Dad had left on enough of a guide. How often as a teenager she'd come home from dates after everyone else was in bed! She would always hope Char's light was still on beneath her door, so Faith could slip in and sit on the bed and they could talk and giggle quietly. Char would come to her room sometimes after her own dates, though less often than Faith. They hadn't shut each other out completely, not then. Faith wasn't sure how it had happened that, after they went in different directions to college, they'd quit talking at all.

She brushed her teeth and changed into flannel pajamas, then stood and stared at the bed. *He* had just been in it. Swallowing, she made herself get in anyway, even though she'd swear the sheets held the musky scent of sex, that her pillow had retained the imprint of Ben's head.

She pressed her own cheek in that imprint and closed her eyes on a soft moan. She'd been so scared; scared of everything she'd felt. How could she have held herself together for so long, and then in a matter of an hour completely disintegrated? The rage had literally blinded her, the tears scalded her, the passion... Oh, Lord. Making love with Ben had undermined her self-control like nothing else ever had.

Faith lay in her dark bedroom hugging the pillow, that everpresent fear holding her rigid. If she surrendered to all these feelings, she'd be taking the greatest risk of her life. That's what you did when you fell in love; you made yourself vulnerable. But she was already too vulnerable to risk more. She didn't know if she would ever dare.

And, while Ben had been kind and patient with her, and persistent, too, he'd never actually said, "I love you," or done more than imply that he was thinking about anything permanent.

Yes, he had wanted her. Wanted her a whole lot, she thought, her face heating as she remembered the way he'd pinned her against the wall halfway up the stairs and kissed her as if he couldn't make himself stop. As if he was desperate for her.

He'd made love to her the same way, with shattering urgency. Not at all as if it was just sex.

She'd been awful to him, afterward. Faith squeezed her eyes shut, remembering the expression on his face after she said, "I lost control in more ways than one tonight. Do you think I feel good about that?"

Tonight he'd held her, comforted her, offered her explosive passion, and she had told him it was a mistake and walked out of the bedroom.

Like a skim of frost, a new kind of fear crept over her. No matter how she'd pushed him away before, he had always come back. But this time…would he?

The next day, as she walked around the classroom supervising her kids while they glued cotton balls on construction paper cutouts of Santa's face, touching a shoulder here, guiding a hand there, smiling as she quieted an overexcited five-year-old boy, Faith realized she was only going through the motions, as she'd done all fall. She hadn't invested herself in this current crop of students the way she usually did. She should have taken a leave of absence this year.

Except, of course, she couldn't have afforded to.

New guilt and unhappiness froze her in place for a moment.

"Miss Russell! Miss Russell!"

She blinked and saw a frantically waving arm. Somehow she made herself focus on the little girl. "Yes, Carrie?"

"Kieran's gluing his beard on himself!"

At a flurry of giggles, Faith turned. In another mood, she would have had a hard time not smiling herself. Skinny, bright-eyed Kieran had indeed taken advantage of her inattention and stuck white cotton balls all over his chin and jaw.

Faith bent a stern look at Carrie, one of her least favorite students, and said, "Perhaps you should pay more attention to your own project and not so much to what your classmates are doing, Carrie." And then she handed Kieran off to a grinning aide who led him to the sink at the back of the room. Kieran, Faith decided, had lost his glue privileges until after Christmas break.

I haven't been a bad teacher. Have I? Even if, perhaps, she hadn't been able to give as much of herself as usual?

Something relaxed inside her, although her depression remained. No, she wasn't a bad teacher. In fact, she thought she was a good one, even when she'd been so sad inside that she'd sometimes imagined herself seeping blood from a thousand wounds. She hadn't lost patience, even with Jakob whose Ritalin tended to wear off before the end of the day. Delia, who it seemed no one had ever read a story to in her life, was learning her letters, and look how quiet and absorbed they all were right now. At the beginning of the school year—not so long ago—Jakob would already have knocked over the glue twice, Walter would have torn up his Santa in frustration over his own inability to achieve perfection and Eden would have vanished from her chair to be found at some point later, humming to herself under the table.

Mrs. Marshall two classrooms over would have lost patience. From the hall, Faith sometimes heard her raised voice with an edge in it that didn't belong in a kindergarten classroom.

I'm a good teacher, Faith thought defiantly. *I am. Even when I'm not at my best.* There were enough things for her to feel guilty about. This wasn't going to be one of them.

Nonetheless, it was a relief when the lunch bell rang. Although she had very little appetite, Faith took her sandwich, apple and bottled water from the bottom drawer of her desk where she had stashed it. She'd eat right here. Not that she expected Ben to come by, but if he did, she would be here. And she could at least say, *I'm sorry, I didn't mean that the way it sounded.*

Of course, he wasn't coming today. He'd have already been there, filling the doorway as soon as the bell rang. Blocking her escape, Faith knew.

He didn't come the next day, either, or the one after that. Not all week. He didn't come by the farm that weekend, either. The icy hollow inside Faith expanded with each day that passed, until she knew she couldn't bear it any longer.

BEN HAD JUST FINISHED his pitiful excuse for a dinner—boxed macaroni and cheese and a hot dog, which was bound to upset his nearly middle-aged stomach—when he heard the knock on his door. His bad-tempered gaze found the clock on the microwave. 7:46. Who the hell…?

He expected to find a neighbor on his doorstep. The way he'd been working on his house, Barton with his perfectly edged flowerbeds and the inflatable reindeer on his putting green of a lawn was probably here to complain about toxic fumes.

Ben was not in the mood for complaints of any kind.

He flung open the door without looking through the sidelight to see who was actually here. He wasn't scowling because, goddamn it, he was the police chief and as such had to be polite whether he felt like it or not. Whatever expression he had on his face vanished when he saw Faith.

A nervous Faith. She was wringing her hands, although she stilled them when she saw his gaze touch on them.

She looked good. He hadn't set eyes on her in eight days, and he was hungrier than he liked to admit, even to himself, just for a look at her. The night was cold, frost already shimmering on lawns and windshields under the streetlight. She wore jeans tucked into boots with sturdy soles and a fleece lining turned over at the top, a turtleneck and a quilted vest. Under his silent scrutiny, she curled her hands into fists and stuck them in the pockets of the vest.

"Um…I was hoping to talk to you."

He didn't know if he *could* talk. Not reasonably. But maybe he wouldn't have to. She'd come to say something, and who knew what she expected in return?

Ruthlessly suppressing the hope that had risen despite himself, Ben nodded and stepped back.

Faith edged past him into the entry. He shut the front door behind her.

She peered into the living room. "You've been working in here."

"Yes, and it reeks," he said brusquely. "We'd better go back to the kitchen."

He led the way, wondering if he looked anywhere near as ragged as he felt. Probably. When he'd shaved that morning, his face had seemed gaunt, his eyes red-rimmed.

"Coffee?" he felt obliged to offer.

"Only if you were going to have some."

He reached for the coffeepot and then changed his mind. "No."

Faith stopped in the middle of the kitchen. "I just… came to say I'm sorry."

He looked back at her as unemotionally as he could make himself. "For?"

"Saying what I did."

"That you didn't mean to make love with me?"

She nodded. "And that I didn't feel very good about it."

"Was it true?" His voice was harsh.

Her gaze slid from his. "I was…scared." Her shoulders made a helpless shrug even as she reluctantly met his eyes again. Her hands, still balled in her pockets, made lumps over her stomach. "Do you know how hard it's been to keep myself together? And then—wow—I just fell apart. I totally lost it. So no, what we did wasn't because of a conscious decision on my part. If that hurts you, I'm sorry."

"Yeah, it hurt me." It didn't feel good admitting how low she'd brought him. But what was he going to do? Pretend he didn't give a damn? "You made me realize you don't actually want anything I have to give. I've been kidding myself, haven't I, Faith?"

"I…" Her voice a mere whisper of sound, it faded entirely. She tried again. "I don't know. I don't know what you want."

"How can you not know?" When she only stared, he said hoarsely, "You. I want you, Faith."

Her face was startlingly pale, her eyes dilated. "You had me."

Ben shook his head. "I'm in love with you." That didn't seem to be enough; he said, "I love you."

She actually flinched, as though he'd announced that he intended to discard her after a few steamy nights. Ben backed up a step. Two steps. He reached to each side and gripped the edge of the kitchen counter. His knuckles were white, he was holding on so hard.

After a painfully long pause, Faith said, "I don't understand. Why now, Ben? You must have known I was attracted to you earlier and... You didn't want me. Why?"

He had to be honest. "You know nothing about my background. I'm a piss-poor risk for a woman like you. The minute I saw you, I thought you were too soft for me. Too gentle. That you shouldn't be married to a cop, any cop, much less someone like me. That you'd never sleep again if I told you a fraction of the things I've seen and done. I thought I'd only hurt you."

There was a spark of anger in her eyes. "You did hurt me, Ben. It goes both ways, you know. You held me like I mattered, and then the next time I saw you, you could have been a stranger, an officer who'd been sent out to the farm but was wishing he hadn't had to make the time to stop. *That* hurt."

"I was an idiot."

"Why did you change your mind?"

"I realized you're a hell of a lot stronger than I gave you credit for." He hesitated, driven still to honesty. "Besides...the past is done. I can live with my own ghosts without making them yours."

"What does that mean?" Faith asked.

"It means I'm not going back to L.A. I'm staying here, in West Fork. Our life here wouldn't have anything to do with the job I did before, or the way I grew up. None of that matters, Faith. I don't know why I thought it did."

She hadn't moved, but the way she was studying him was... Hell, he didn't know what it was.

"Introduce me to one of your ghosts," she said. "Tell me something that will make me understand you."

"I told you I've killed."

"On the job. When you had to."

"Which didn't make it any less bloody, or them any less dead." His voice was rough with frustration.

"How did you grow up?" she asked stubbornly.

"A drug-addict mother. Foster homes. Faith, I'll be thirty-nine years old in January. You don't need to meet my ten-year-old self."

"Aren't you curious about me at ten years old? Fifteen? Twenty?"

"Yes," he admitted, knowing he was walking into a trap but unable to help himself.

"Well, then?"

"I don't have anything pretty to tell you. My childhood has nothing in common with yours. My *life* has nothing in common with yours."

"Until I had to shoot my ex-husband."

Yeah, the fact that they'd both killed was something they shared. Something most people never experienced outside of the armed forces.

"Tell me...something." She looked soft. Wistful.

Ben felt naked. And like a son of a bitch, too, because this beautiful, injured woman was pleading with him to tell her something ugly because he'd led her to think it was important.

"No," he said around a constricted throat. "No. I'm

not going to do that to you. Faith, I love you. This doesn't matter. Trust me."

"Like you trust me?" She shook her head hard when he let go of the counter edge and stepped forward. "Whatever you're offering isn't love. I'm glad I realized it before I gave you any more of myself."

"Faith—" He felt like his guts were being torn out.

"No." She backed away, her eyes still dry but distress pinching her face. "No. I shouldn't have come." The next moment, she whirled and hurried for the front of the house.

"Damn it, Faith!" He was close behind her. "Don't make true confessions a condition on our having a relationship."

She flung open the door and paused briefly. "You want a relationship that's all about my weaknesses, my tragedies. Is that really what changed your mind, Ben? You liked playing...I don't know." Her voice hitched. "Knight errant to my wounded lamb?"

"It's not like that."

"What is it like?" Pain darkened her eyes.

"I love you. I trust you."

"Do you?" Faith wore sadness like a cloak, as she had for most of the time he'd known her. The difference was, this time it was his fault.

She pulled the door shut in his face. He opened it to see her running for her truck, jumping into it, probably locking the doors so he couldn't drag her out.

And driving away.

Once the street was empty, Ben very carefully closed the door, turned, leaned back against it and let his head fall back in a silent paroxysm of desolation.

THREE WEEKS LATER, Christmas come and gone, an
answer floated back from one of Ben's thousand inquiries regarding Rory Hardesty.

At last he had a lead on Josiah Peter Hammond, the
one of Rory's old friends who had eluded him to this
point. Of all places, J.P.—who now went by Pete, assuming this was the right guy—apparently now lived in
Nebraska. Hastings, Nebraska. A simple call to information, and Ben would likely have a phone number.

He sat in his office for the longest time staring at the
scribbled notes he'd made on the legal pad that sat in
front of him.

Faith would not want to hear from him again, not
for any reason. He couldn't blame her. He hadn't been
willing to trust her, not the way she'd meant. He still told
himself he was protecting her, not himself, but either
way it played out the same. Her life lay bare to him,
while his was closed to her. Maybe she was right. Maybe
he'd lied to himself when he'd believed they could be
happy that way, that when he woke at night shouting
he could pretend he didn't remember the content of his
nightmares.

Faith and her father had moved this past weekend,
Ben knew from Gray. The estate sale was over, the farmhouse was now empty. All the signs along the highway
were gone. Ben hated driving by more than ever knowing what was coming.

He'd given thought to looking for a new job, a new
town. However, even though West Fork was small, it was
entirely possible if he stayed that he and Faith would
never run into each other. He didn't recall ever seeing
her before the morning he'd gone out to the farm to talk
to the Russell sisters about the arson fire. Socializing

much with Gray and Char would be out, of course, but that wasn't likely to be a problem. He'd known from the get-go that their friendship was contingent on his relationship with Faith. They'd both believed Faith needed him.

It seemed they were wrong.

He looked again at the legal pad.

This is my job, he told himself, but knew better. Hardesty was dead and long buried. What difference did his last days make? His last intentions?

But they did matter to Faith. This was very likely the only thing he had to offer her. A kind of absolution: *yes, you had to kill him or die yourself.* He knew she still asked herself that question every day.

Ben muttered an obscenity and picked up the phone. Information gave him the number, but when he called it he reached only voice mail. He didn't leave a message. He'd try again tonight.

In the act of dialing, he'd shifted into cop-mode.

The fact that Hammond lived halfway across the country would suggest he and Rory hadn't maintained a close friendship. Staring unseeing at the open door of his office, Ben thought, *Uh-huh, but what about that saying about distance making the heart grow fonder?* Rory had alienated most of his buddies; maybe this Hammond remembered only the high-school friend who hadn't yet developed an increasingly violent obsession with Faith.

He'd hoped for a distraction of any kind and got lucky that afternoon. A public-utility district worker operating a backhoe turned up a human skull. The minute Ben saw it he suspected it was from an old Indian burial; the bone was brown and crumbling, the remaining teeth ground to stubs with no signs of modern dental work. Of course, an Indian burial opened up a whole other can of worms—although, thank God, not his—and work was temporarily shut down on the site while the skull went to the county coroner and calls were made to the anthropology department at Western Washington University and to leaders of local tribes.

He went home and discovered that, despite the windows he'd left open all day, it still stank from the previous evening's effort to keep himself busy. He heated a can of chili, too tired to make any more effort on dinner. The morning's resolution had crumbled; his mood was bleak enough that he hesitated over calling Hammond, but finally muttered an obscenity and picked up the phone.

"Yeah?" a male voice answered.

Ben identified himself and said, "I'm trying to reach Josiah Peter Hammond, who graduated from West Fork High School in the state of Washington."

There was a brief silence. "That's me. What's this about?"

"Rory Hardesty."

"Shit," Hammond said explosively.

Ben waited.

"What's he done?"

Interesting that he'd leaped immediately to the conclusion that his good friend Rory had "done" something, rather than fearing he'd been a victim of a crime, was missing, or was the subject of a lawsuit of some kind.

"Were you aware that Mr. Hardesty is dead?" Ben asked.

Hammond whispered another expletive. "No. God. No. I haven't heard from him in...uh, a couple months or so. I just figured he'd cooled down. Maybe went back to work."

"He called you?"

"Uh...yeah. And texted."

"What did he say, the last time you heard from him?"

"He was totally hung up on Faith. His ex. He thought he'd get her back. Then he got totally pissed when she told him she was seeing somebody else."

Ben straightened. What the hell...? Who had she been talking about? Or had her supposed love interest been fictitious? Hadn't she realized that saying anything like that to Rory was tantamount to waving a red flag in front of a bull?

And exactly *when* had she held this conversation with Rory?

"That was your last conversation with him?"

"The last time we talked, yeah. He texted me a couple of times later, though. Mostly pretty obscene. Um...just letting off steam, you know?"

"Did he threaten his ex-wife, Mr. Hammond?"

Sounding really uncomfortable, Pete Hammond said, "Well, yeah, but... It was just the kind of shit people say, you know?"

"What did he say?"

"He said he was going to kill her. I figured he was drunk. Just... God." He breathed audibly. "Did he actually do it?"

"He tried. He stabbed her sister in one assault, then came back a couple of weeks later and went for Faith. She shot him."

Hammond was clearly shaken. He kept repeating, "I didn't believe him," until Ben had to clench his teeth to keep himself from saying, *You stupid son of a bitch, didn't it occur to you to* warn *Faith?*

Instead, he kept his temper and asked if Hammond had any idea where Rory might have been staying in the month leading up to his death.

Voice subdued, Hammond said, "Yeah. He told me he'd walked out on his job and just needed someplace to…be. My aunt has this log cabin outside Gold Bar, right on the river. Really primitive. Not that big a step up from camping out, but it has four walls and a roof. Just an outhouse. My uncle really liked to fish, only he died a couple years ago and Aunt Betty hasn't done anything about selling the place yet. Rory and I used to go up there sometimes. I told him where the key was hidden so he could stay there for a while, just until he got his shit together."

Gold Bar, barely a dot on the map off Highway 2 on the way up to Stevens Pass, one of the main routes over the Cascade Mountains. All that time, he'd been so damn close, not an hour's drive from West Fork.

Suddenly enraged, Ben wanted to arrest this jackass as an accessory to Rory's crimes. He wanted to make him face Faith and explain why he'd protected and sheltered a guy who was openly threatening to kill her.

But none of that would do any good, and a part of him knew that it wasn't unreasonable for Hammond to have assumed his buddy was just shooting his mouth off. People did say things like that. "I'm going to kill my old lady" wasn't usually a real intention. Normal people didn't believe a guy who meant it. Normal people were always surprised when their son or husband or neighbor murdered someone.

Ben asked, "How do I find this cabin?" and got

directions as well as the aunt's full name and phone number so he could get permission to search the cabin without having to acquire a warrant. He thanked the other man although he didn't feel civil. He hoped like hell Rory's good *friend* suffered guilt enough to make him a better person.

Ben grunted. Too bad he couldn't remember the last time—if ever—that he'd seen anyone even try for redemption.

The next morning, he reached Betty Fuller, who gave him the needed permission while repeating, "I had no idea. To think someone was living there. Goodness. It's really not much better than a shack. I simply can't imagine. But I suppose if J.P. said so..."

Two days later, he made the drive to Gold Bar and found the cabin hidden in the woods on the banks of the river. Rory's red pickup truck, dusted with fir needles, was parked beside it. His search inside the cabin yielded nothing but fast-food wrappers torn to shreds by mice, towers of empty beer cans, a filthy sleeping bag and a duffel bag full of clothes, atop which lay a key chain, an iPod and a cell phone. No convenient note.

The battery to the phone had long since died, but Ben found a charger and not much else in the truck. He took the duffel bag for Rory's mother and plugged the cell phone into its charger in his car, hoping the hour-long drive home would be long enough.

Depression settled over him as he turned his car around and drove back down the long dirt lane shrouded by fir trees and enclosed by a tangle of undergrowth. He supposed he'd thought that, because Faith had married the guy, Rory might have been literate enough to be inclined to write out his rage. It was surprising how many nuts did.

Ben glanced at the phone, the kind that might show text messages that had already been sent. It was his only hope.

He had to make a stop at the jail in Everett, which meant he'd have to drive by the farm. From long habit, he tensed even before the curve of highway revealed the first fields to him.

But the cornfield was no more. Bulldozers had been working here the last day, or several days. He swore softly, his foot lifting from the gas pedal. The farmhouse was a heap of rubble, as were the smaller outbuildings. Most of the farmland was now raw, bare earth, nearly ready for the stakes that would mark out lots. Only the barn still stood, stark and lonely, a sagging scrarecrow leaning beside the closed double doors. Several massive pieces of earth-moving equipment were parked for the night between the barn and what had been the house.

Ben had had no idea this was coming so soon. He wondered whether Faith had known, whether she'd seen the place yet. Aching for her, he wished she never had to see it, could forever imagine her home still standing. He wished he could be the one to hold her after she did see what had been done.

Taking a deep breath, he accelerated again. He needed time to figure out the damn cell phone, access any messages and sent texts. Tomorrow would be soon enough to go by Mrs. Hardesty's to give her the pitiful few possessions her son had left behind and tell her where she could find the pickup truck. For her sake, he hoped Rory had actually owned it rather than being badly in hock for it.

Dispatch didn't expect him back today and he hadn't been called, so he drove straight home and took the cell phone in the house with him.

It came on readily. After some experimenting, there it was, the last text sent to a phone number Ben didn't recognize but guessed was Hammond's cell. The date was the day Rory had died.

2NITES D NITE. IM GunA F-ING BLEED D BITCH OUT. SHE HAD HER CHNC. SHES MYN 2 KILL.

Cold rage swept over Ben. Standing in his own kitchen, he made a raw, animalistic sound. He wanted to go back in time and save her. He wanted to be the one to *do* the killing.

But when the first wave of fury ebbed, it left behind some relief, as well. Faith's knight errant could give her the bloodied lance.

There could be no more question. Rory had not crept into her bedroom to frighten her. He'd come to stab his knife deep in her breast.

CHAPTER FOURTEEN

FAITH WAS JUST PREPARING to lock up her classroom at the end of the day when Clio Nordmann stuck her head in. Clio was a pretty redhead about Faith's age who taught second grade in a room just down the hall. They'd become friends as soon as she hired on in West Fork two years before.

"Faith! Wow. Did you see?"

Accustomed to Clio's dramatic tendencies, Faith took her coat from the hook in the closet. "See what?"

"Your farm! Surely they won't be able to build until spring. Why did they start clearing the land so soon?"

A strange numbness crawled over her. "Clearing the land?"

Clio's expression changed. "You didn't know?"

"No. The sale closed really quick because the buyer didn't need financing. Last week." She was talking to fill the awful chasm opening up inside her. Somehow she locked the door to her classroom and, walking beside Clio, started toward the back exit that was closest to the staff parking. "Did you drive by?"

"Yesterday." Clio stole a look at her. "I'm sorry. I shouldn't have said anything."

"No, it's okay. I'd rather be warned." Faith managed a smile and they parted to go to their cars.

She drove home—although she felt more like a guest

in her dad's stucco cottage and knew that she should start looking for somewhere else to live, someplace that would feel like hers. Inside the house she found a note from her father on the kitchen table letting her know he was having dinner with the Friebergs, and she was welcome to join them if she wanted.

"Mary says dinner about 6:00," he'd scrawled.

Mary and Andrew Frieberg had been friends of Faith's mother and father as long as she could remember. They were dairy farmers who were still holding on, determined to pass their operation down to their son, with whom Faith and Char had gone to school. Faith definitely did not feel like chattering over the dinner table with the Friebergs.

She sank down in a chair and wondered if her father knew that the farmland was already being cleared. He'd have said something, wouldn't he?

She hadn't expected to react this way. She'd known that the buyer wanted the land, not a farm; this had been inevitable, and it made no sense to get upset. Faith honestly didn't know which would be worse: driving by the abandoned farm that looked as if it were waiting for them to come home to it, or seeing it all gone.

By sheer determination, she got through the next couple of hours. She made a salad and ate enough to consider it dinner. She worked out the logistics of an art project she was planning for her students to do tomorrow. She watched the local news, although when she turned the TV off she realized she had no idea what the newcasters had said.

She'd be less depressed if only the days would get longer, she thought, glancing at the darkened window.

At this time of year, night had already fallen by the time she got home from school.

She wouldn't be able to see much if she did drive out to the farm.

The sodium lamp outside the barn might still be there; the power company had put it up and would have to come out to take it down. The developer might leave it anyway for now, to discourage trespassers.

Faith was putting on a parka and reaching for her car keys even before she knew she'd made a decision. She would just wonder if she didn't see for herself.

She would be sorry if she missed her last chance to say goodbye before it was gone forever.

THE MINUTE GRAY WALKED IN the front door he said, "Did you know the farm's already being leveled?"

"What?" Charlotte had appeared from the kitchen to greet him. She was playing happy homemaker tonight and enjoying it—a curried chicken dish was ready to come out of the oven and the salad was already on the table. Now, stunned, she let the pot holder she'd been holding drop from her hand. "What do you mean, *leveled?*"

"They bulldozed the house today," her husband said bluntly. "The cornfields are raw land. They'll be a sea of mud the next time it rains. I don't know what the hell they're thinking."

"Faith," Charlotte whispered.

He walked toward her, picked up the pot holder, then wrapped her in his arms.

Burrowing into his warmth and strength, she shook her head. She felt idiotic to realize her eyes burned. She'd spent a good part of her life desperate to escape the farm. The past ten years, she had done her very best to avoid visits home. Now she wanted to cry because the house where she'd grown up was gone?

"What the hell happened between her and Ben?" Gray asked. "All he'll do is shake his head when I ask."

Charlotte stepped back from her husband's embrace. "She says they don't have the same idea of love. She thinks he only liked the idea of rescuing her." Her indignation fired. "Which may be true. He wasn't nearly as interested before."

She loved Gray's face, not exactly handsome but very male, and she especially loved his eyes, calm and clear and somehow able to see the pain she'd once tried to hide from him. Of course, she loved *him*, and the depth of her emotion still surprised her.

He frowned, momentarily lost in thought. "I'm not so sure. I had the impression Ben really had taken a header for her."

"I did, too," Charlotte admitted. "Maybe it's not Ben. Maybe it's Faith." She paused. "I thought she and I had come so far, but nothing's been the same since she shot Rory. This distance has opened up that I don't know how to close."

It hurt, and yet she had long since lost the right to be inside her sister's guard. If Faith truly trusted anyone, it was Dad, who had been there for her all along.

When I wasn't, Charlotte couldn't help thinking, her chest constricted.

She'd tried to be satisfied with the relationship she had with her twin, because they *were* friends now. But the truth was, Faith was still holding a huge part of herself back. Maybe she always would; maybe it was too late to hope for anything else. But...

I can keep trying.

"I need to call her," she said.

Gray nodded, his eyes keen on her face, and she knew that he understood every ounce of her guilt and her grief. "Is there anything I can do to get dinner on while you talk to her?"

THERE WERE A COUPLE of lights on in the small house Don Russell had bought, but neither he nor Faith came to the door when Ben rang and then knocked. Frustrated, he drove around to the alley where he found neither of their vehicles, but one of them might be in the garage. They'd probably gone out to dinner.

His mood restless, he went to Tastee's for a burger and fries. All he could think about was the damn cell phone in his pocket and the ugly message saved in its sent file. How would Faith react? Was he doing the right thing, taking it to her? Maybe it would be the equivalent of trying to return the handgun to her; not a comfort, but a tearing reminder of the worst day of her life.

Ben made an effort to hide his mood and nodded greetings to a few acquaintances, then crumpled the wrappings of his meal, deposited them in the trash can and left before he was forced to actually make conversation with someone.

He'd filled an hour; maybe Faith was home by now. Ben realized he was going through with this, despite his doubts. As it had all along, instinct told him she needed to know that Rory's intentions had been lethal. Yeah, it would remind her of the thunderous crack of the gun firing, of the blood and the way a man's eyes glazed over when he died, of her own terror and relief and horror. But Ben thought her wound still festered, and maybe this bit of knowledge would help it heal cleanly, once and for all.

Don came to the door this time.

"No, I'm sorry, Ben," he said, looking surprised. "Faith isn't home. I was out to dinner, and she didn't leave a note. She might have gone out with a friend, or be at the library."

His restlessness became disquiet. "Did you know your land's already being cleared?"

Don nodded somberly. "I found out this evening."

"Faith?"

"I don't know," he admitted. "She wouldn't have had reason to go by."

"But someone might have told her."

"They might have," he admitted, in his slow, quiet way. "I came home hoping to talk to her." He opened the door wider. "Sorry, didn't mean to keep you standing out there. If you'd like a cup of coffee...?"

"No, thanks." Ben hesitated. "Will you call me when she gets home?"

"I'll do that," her father agreed. "Don't mind telling you I'm a little worried about her."

Ben was a lot worried. Probably for no reason, he tried to convince himself. She did have friends. He doubted she spent every evening sitting at home. She was used to being busy; he couldn't imagine she'd taken to watching hours of TV to fill her time. For all he knew, she was volunteering for some worthy organization by now, or had a school open house she'd forgotten to tell her dad about.

He drove by the elementary school just in case. It was dark and closed.

Seeing no alternative, he went home, where he paced. The minutes crept by. After half an hour, he phoned Charlotte.

"I've been trying to call her," she said, anxiety tight in her voice. "Her cell phone is turned off and Dad says she isn't home."

Ben muttered an expletive and swung around to circle the room again. The sense of urgency wouldn't let up. "Have you tried friends? Is she taking classes? Volunteering?"

"I've tried the couple of friends I know. She hasn't said anything about classes or volunteering."

"Call me if you hear anything."

"Yes. Okay," she said, without asking why he was seeking her sister now, when he'd been absent for weeks. He was grateful for small favors.

Ben set down the phone and tried to focus. Chances were good Faith hadn't heard anything and was up to something innocuous. She knew her father was going out to dinner, so there wasn't any reason to explain her own activities. Why would it occur to her that anyone would worry?

If she *had* heard about the farm—if that's why she wasn't home—where would she have gone?

Where else? he realized, feeling stupid. If the news had hit her hard, there was only one place she'd have gone to mourn.

Home.

Moving fast, Ben grabbed his parka and went out the door.

FAITH DIDN'T KNOW what had made her get out of her Blazer. It wasn't as though she hadn't seen enough when she pulled in off the highway. She'd felt a flash of relief when she saw the solid, enduring bulk of the barn in her headlights. In the next moment, her breath stopped in her lungs. The house. Oh, God. Her house was gone.

No, not gone—it was a pile of rubble.

She pulled in beside the barn, hidden in its shadow from passing traffic. Then she sat there for the longest time, unable to move.

Silly, she kept thinking. Of course the house was a teardown; she'd known that.

But she was rocking slightly, a child trying to comfort herself. Inside, the same child wailed, *Mommy, Daddy. I want to go home.*

What was wrong with her? Why did this matter so much?

Finally, she took the flashlight from the glove compartment, got out and walked slowly to the house. To what had been the house. She turned the flashlight on and moved the beam slowly over the pile, picking out shattered floorboards here, tumbled chunks of the concrete that had made up the foundation, smashed cupboards and windows, crumbled plaster with tattered wallpaper she knew as well as her own face.

That's the living room. She fell to her knees. *Oh, God, there's my bedroom.* A tiny, terrible, torn bit of her bedroom, once shared with Charlotte, always her refuge until the night Rory had invaded it.

Still she didn't cry, although she was in such pain she didn't think she could bear it. It was as if everything that had ever meant anything to her had been smashed along with the house and only shards were left. None fixable, nothing that could be glued together.

She heard a sound, low and agonizing, vibrating through her own throat. Faith pushed herself to her feet and stumbled away. She didn't have the sense to aim the flashlight ahead of her and walked right into a bulldozer that appeared from the dark. She groped her way around it. The blade—*this* blade—had pushed her house down, had been stronger than all the years and the people who'd lived here. Stronger than the memories. She pressed her forehead against the cold metal blade, crusted with dirt and bits of concrete.

From her house.

Perhaps she knew another vehicle had pulled in, that the headlights had swung over her; she must have heard the slam of a door. Because she wasn't altogether surprised when two powerful hands closed on her shoulders and turned her around. When Ben pulled her into his arms and held her tighter than anyone had ever held her in all her life.

"Faith, honey," he murmured. "I'm sorry, love. Let me hold you. At least let me hold you."

Her breath left her lungs in the longest sigh of her life, taking some of the pain with it. She leaned against Ben's tall, powerful body and laid her cheek against his shoulder. What a strange moment to recognize that she didn't just feel safe in his arms, she felt at home. She needed this refuge as she'd never needed anything in her life.

His hands moved up and down her back, soothing, squeezing, loving. His voice, low and gruff, still managed to croon. The words hardly mattered. She pushed herself closer to him.

Abruptly she began to cry. He kept holding her, kept talking to her, and weirdly these tears seemed to be cleansing.

Faith realized they'd sunk down to the raw ground, frozen hard. She was cradled on Ben's lap, his back to the blade of the dozer.

How had he known she was here? Why had he come?

Because he did love her, of course. He must. Anyone else would have lost patience with her long ago. Even Char had; she'd been…wary lately, sneaking quick assessing glances she thought Faith hadn't seen.

They all think I've gone crazy, she thought with a peculiar, tired bubble of amusement. *Maybe I have.*

But Ben was here anyway.

Feeling utterly drained, Faith lay against him. At some point he'd opened his parka and pulled the zippered edges around her, so she was surprisingly warm and the nubby texture of his sweater was under her cheek.

"I'm sorry," she mumbled into his chest. "Here I go again."

His head moved as though he was looking down at her. "Again?"

"Off the deep end."

"Are you?" he said after a moment, quietly.

"Yes." She thought about it. "No. Not the same way. Last time…I hated losing control. But tonight it felt good to cry. I *needed* to cry." Feeling inexplicably shy, considering how little she'd ever succeeded in hiding from Ben, Faith added, "I think I could let myself cry because you were here. So, um, thank you."

He actually chuckled, the warm air of his breath stirring her hair. "You're welcome."

They sat in silence for a long time; several minutes, anyway. She realized they'd both dropped their flashlights to the ground. The weak beam of hers was swallowed by the night. The brighter beam of his more powerful flashlight glanced off the boards of the barn wall.

"How did you find me?" she asked.

"Once I reasoned out that you'd probably heard work had started here, I knew where you'd go."

That made sense. But... "Why were you looking for me?"

It wasn't as if he'd been moving, but she felt his increased stillness. Finally his hands tightened on her. "I found where Rory was hiding."

Faith drew back. "Where?"

"Gold Bar. Did you know a J. P. Hammond?"

He hadn't really been in her circle, and she thought J.P. had been a year or two ahead of her, but... "Yes, from high school."

"His aunt owns a run-down log cabin up the Skykomish. I guess the uncle liked to fish, but he died a couple years back and she hasn't gotten around to selling the place. J.P. let Rory stay there."

She groped at what all this meant. "You were still looking."

"Yes."

"Why?"

"I thought it might help you to know what he intended that night."

She'd believed herself too drained to feel new apprehension, but she did. Faith sat up, her hand flat on

Ben's chest. She strained to see his face and couldn't. "Did you learn anything?"

"Yeah." He exhaled heavily. "I have his cell phone. It retains the last text message he sent. It's ugly, Faith."

He was remembering the way she'd reacted to the gun when he tried to return it. Faith could tell.

"I think," she said carefully, "I'd like to know."

He told her, and she sat there on his lap in the darkness absorbing the straightforward proof that Rory wanted, *needed,* to kill her. She'd already known, in a way, or she wouldn't have been able to shoot him, but a part of her had never wanted to believe that he could really hate her so much. Not that long ago, she would have grieved anew, and wondered what she'd done to deserve a hate so unrelenting. Now...relief blossomed in her chest. Mixed with it, to her surprise, was outrage.

It made her voice shake. "Do you know how mad it makes me, to think of how much guilt and...and *anguish* I wasted on him? I was so afraid..."

"That you didn't have to kill him."

"Yes. But I did." The relief was swelling, filling her with an astonishing feeling that might be peace.

Ben had been right all along. She'd been strong; she'd saved herself from the maniac who had somehow fooled her into marrying him.

"I wish I knew what I ever saw in him," she heard herself say. "Why I married him. No." She frowned. "Not that. Why I stayed with him, when he treated me so badly."

He gathered her firmly into his arms and tucked her again inside the wings of his parka. His hands, bare of gloves, had slipped up inside her coat and were splayed across her back. "You took your vows seriously," Ben suggested.

"Yes, but I think it was more than that." She was silent for a moment, listening to the steady, strong beat of his heart. "I wanted to believe it was because I felt rejected by Char, that somehow I was...damaged. But it's not that simple. I was always the uncertain one, you know. Char would charge ahead, and I'd peer cautiously around corners. I just never had the confidence in myself. What little I did have, he undermined."

She felt Ben's nod. "That's a classic story. The irony is, he was the one who really lacked confidence. He needed you to be everything to him, to the point where he couldn't let you exist if you weren't completely his. It took you a while, honey, because you're loyal and gentle and wanted to believe in him, but you did fight back, and you won."

The words were a balm, even though she didn't like the reminder that Ben saw her as too gentle to be able to hear a single thing from his past that made him heartsick.

The time, she thought, had come to fight for *him*.

Rather fiercely, she said, "You know, I killed him and I'm glad. Tonight I was sad when I saw the house, but I'll survive. I'm not the weakling you think I am."

"I never thought that."

"Yes. You did."

"Not that," he argued. "I thought you deserved a cleaner soul than I have. I should let you go, but I can't." He gave her a little shake. "I can't, Faith. All I can do is try to avoid giving you any more nightmares than you already have."

"Do you think I can't love you if I know too much? Is that it?"

It was his turn to hesitate. "Maybe," he admitted at last, his voice even deeper than usual, rougher textured. "I had a pretty crappy childhood. It left me with a temper I didn't always know how to control and a sense of right and wrong that was more shades of gray than clear-cut black and white. I have to live with things I've done, Faith, but you don't."

"But if I'm to love you, I do." It was that simple.

One big hand came out from beneath her parka to grip the back of her head. "God, I want to know you love me," he said hoarsely. "I don't deserve you, but I need you anyway."

How astonishing that she could feel giddy, exultant, like a helium balloon floating free and rising higher and higher into the sky, leaving behind the murk and misery below. She had been right to come here tonight to say goodbye. It was done. And she was desperately in love with a man who loved her, too. A man as vulnerable as she was, with as many self-doubts. Why hadn't she seen that sooner?

Shaken, she whispered, "I do love you, Ben. If you can trust me, at least a little…"

"More than a little." He sounded as shaken as if he, too, had had to say goodbye to his own rubble of old dreams and regrets. "I love you, honey. So damn much."

He kissed her, his mouth cold. *Her* mouth cold, although they warmed each other quickly. There was nothing skillful about this kiss. It wasn't so much passionate as hopeful, even amazed.

You love me?

I do.

The stroke of a tongue, the graze of teeth, the seal of their lips, could say so much.

She felt the moment his mouth curled into a smile that became a laugh when she lifted her head inquiringly.

"I just lost all feeling in my butt. And, hell, probably some other parts of my anatomy."

Now that he mentioned it, her toes had gone from painfully cold to numb.

"It's freezing out here," she pointed out.

"Yeah. I noticed."

They were laughing and helping each other to their feet when a car pulled in from the highway. The headlights shone on the barn, then Ben's SUV and finally hit the two of them standing in each other's arms in front of the bulldozer. Faith squinted and looked away. Ben did the same.

"Who...?" she started to say, then recognized the silhouette of the Prius.

"Great minds think alike," Ben murmured.

Two people got out of the Prius; two car doors slammed.

"Char?" Faith said in shock. "She came, too?"

"She loves you," Ben said.

"I've never been sure—" She had to swallow. "Never believed..."

His hand caught hers, squeezed. "Believe. You have to believe, Faith."

He'd said that to her once before, and she knew suddenly that he wasn't talking just about her sister any more than he had the other time. He wanted her to believe she could be loved, that he truly loved her.

Her mouth trembled. "I do." Wonder rose in her like

the sun in the morning. "I do," she repeated, and stood on tiptoe to kiss his scratchy cheek.

And then she went running to her sister, stumbling on the uneven ground but meeting her halfway. They fell into each other's arms.

In bursts that made her almost incoherent, Char exclaimed, "I should have known sooner where you were. Should have been here for you, Faith. But I will be from now on. I swear I will. Always."

"I know you are. But I'm okay." It felt so right, hugging her sister like this. "I really am, Char. I love you."

At some point she lifted her head and saw Gray, hanging back by the car, hands in his pockets, waiting. And there was Ben, doing the same, so patient. How could she and Char both have gotten so lucky?

She and her sister pressed their wet cheeks together, laughed and wept and babbled words of healing.

THEIR LOVEMAKING the last time had been rushed, urgent, a tempest too powerful to fight. Tonight's was different, the hunger as strong but seasoned by tenderness. They started with a hot shower and moved, damp, to Ben's large bed.

He said, "I love you," over and over again—against her breasts, and her belly, and her thighs. She said it looking into his eyes, mumbled it into his hair. "I love you."

He was dazed with incredulity, reeling at the miraculous knowledge that, yes, she did love him, that she was here, beneath him, holding him with as much need as he held her.

Afterward, she lay with her head on his shoulder, one

leg draped over his, her hand playing with his chest hair. And she whispered, "Tell me one of your nightmares. Just one."

Ben closed his eyes. How could she ask that tonight, with everything she'd gone through? But he heard her voice.

If you can trust me, at least a little...

He remembered his own promise. *More than a little.*

"I crossed the line sometimes as a cop. I roughed up suspects a couple of times because I was angry," he said. "But one of the hardest things I've had to live with was a simple mistake."

He told her, then, about two women, a mother and her daughter. About the serial killer he'd arrested, about the search warrant he'd carried out and, in his arrogance, violated, finding the evidence he needed in a place he wasn't allowed to look. About having to let the killer go, because he, Ben, had screwed up. About the thirteen-year-old girl who was brutally raped and murdered two weeks later.

"This time he left evidence on her body. The condom tore, or spilled, and there was semen on her legs. She'd scratched him, too. There was blood under her fingernails."

"So you were able to arrest him this time? And convict him?"

Ben shook his head. "Not me. I couldn't be involved, or I'd have been a target in court. I made a mistake. Nothing else I said would have been seen as reliable."

Her hand was no longer playing; as he'd done for her, she was stroking him, using her touch to comfort. She said nothing, waiting for him to go on.

"The girl's mother blamed me, of course. One day she walked into the squad room, asked someone to point me out and laid a picture on my desk. Her daughter—Brianna—had been elected by the student body to be their speaker at the eighth-grade graduation. The picture was taken that day."

Brianna had been almost plain, but looked as if she'd someday grow into prettiness. He remembered her chaste dress, blue sprinkled with white flowers, and her shyness at being the focus of attention. But at the moment that photo had been snapped she had also shone with pride and intelligence and hope.

And because he'd screwed up, she had died horribly, and would never grow into that prettiness, never realize any of her hopes.

"I see their faces." He was shaking. "The way the mother looked at me when she handed me that picture. And Brianna. I saw the crime-scene photos, too. I will never forget…."

He was crying now, the tears hot on his face. He hadn't known he could.

Faith didn't recoil, even though he deserved it. She rose above him and cradled his face in her palms, kissing him, tasting his tears.

"Everybody makes mistakes," she said, so gently. "Everybody, Ben. You didn't kill her. You're not responsible, that monster is."

When he was spent, and able to kiss her back, she whispered against his mouth, "I love you. I will keep loving you."

With a desperate sound, he gripped her hips, lifting her so that he could plunge inside her. Become part of her. Fill her as she filled him.

If you can trust me, at least a little...
With everything I am, he thought, and showed her
the only way he could right now.

* * * * *

COMING NEXT MONTH

Available September 14, 2010

#1656 THE FIRST WIFE
The Chapman Files
Tara Taylor Quinn

#1657 TYLER O'NEILL'S REDEMPTION
The Notorious O'Neills
Molly O'Keefe

#1658 FULLY INVOLVED
The Texas Firefighters
Amy Knupp

#1659 THIS TIME FOR KEEPS
Suddenly a Parent
Jenna Mills

#1660 THAT LAST NIGHT IN TEXAS
A Little Secret
Ann Evans

#1661 ONCE A RANGER
Carrie Weaver

LARGER-PRINT BOOKS!
GET 2 FREE LARGER-PRINT NOVELS PLUS
2 FREE GIFTS!

◆ HARLEQUIN®

Super Romance®

Exciting, emotional, unexpected!

YES! Please send me 2 FREE LARGER-PRINT Harlequin® Superromance® novels and my 2 FREE gifts (gifts are worth about $10). After receiving them, if I don't wish to receive any more books, I can return the shipping statement marked "cancel." If I don't cancel, I will receive 6 brand-new novels every month and be billed just $5.44 per book in the U.S. or $5.99 per book in Canada. That's a saving of at least 13% off the cover price! It's quite a bargain! Shipping and handling is just 50¢ per book.* I understand that accepting the 2 free books and gifts places me under no obligation to buy anything. I can always return a shipment and cancel at any time. Even if I never buy another book from Harlequin, the two free books and gifts are mine to keep forever.

139/339 HDN E5PS

Name _____ (PLEASE PRINT) _____

Address _____ Apt. # _____

City _____ State/Prov. _____ Zip/Postal Code _____

Signature (if under 18, a parent or guardian must sign) _____

Mail to the **Harlequin Reader Service:**
IN U.S.A.: P.O. Box 1867, Buffalo, NY 14240-1867
IN CANADA: P.O. Box 609, Fort Erie, Ontario L2A 5X3

Not valid for current subscribers to Harlequin Superromance Larger-Print books.

Are you a current subscriber to Harlequin Superromance books and want to receive the larger-print edition?
Call 1-800-873-8635 today!

* Terms and prices subject to change without notice. Prices do not include applicable taxes. N.Y. residents add applicable sales tax. Canadian residents will be charged applicable provincial taxes and GST. Offer not valid in Quebec. This offer is limited to one order per household. All orders subject to approval. Credit or debit balances in a customer's account(s) may be offset by any other outstanding balance owed by or to the customer. Please allow 4 to 6 weeks for delivery. Offer available while quantities last.

Your Privacy: Harlequin Books is committed to protecting your privacy. Our Privacy Policy is available online at www.eHarlequin.com or upon request from the Reader Service. From time to time we make our lists of customers available to reputable third parties who may have a product or service of interest to you. If you would prefer we not share your name and address, please check here. ☐

Help us get it right—We strive for accurate, respectful and relevant communications. To clarify or modify your communication preferences, visit us at www.ReaderService.com/consumerschoice.

HSRLP10R

Police chief Juliette Tremblant recognized the shape of the man strolling down the street—in as calm and leisurely fashion as if it were the middle of the day rather than midnight. She slowed her car, convinced her eyes were playing tricks on her. It had been a long time since Tyler O'Neill had been seen in this town.

As she pulled to a stop at the curb, he turned toward her, and her heart about stopped.

"What the hell are you doing here, Tyler?"

"Well, if it isn't Juliette Tremblant." He made his way over to her, then leaned down so he could look her in the eye. He was close enough to touch.

Juliette was not, repeat, *not* going to touch Tyler O'Neill. Not with her fingers. Not with a ten-foot pole. There would be no touching. Which was too bad, since it was the only way she was ever going to convince herself the man standing in front of her—as rumpled and heart-stoppingly handsome now as he'd been at sixteen—was real.

And not a figment of all her furious revenge dreams.

"What are you doing back in Bonne Terre?" she asked.

"The manor is sitting empty," Tyler said and shrugged, as though his arriving out of the blue after ten years was casual. "Seems like someone should be watching over the family home."

"You?" She laughed at the very notion of him being here for any unselfish reason. "Please."

He stared at her for a second, then smiled. Her heart fluttered against her chest—a small mechanical bird powered by that smile.

"You're right." But that cryptic comment was all he offered.

Juliette bit her lip against the other questions.

Why did you go?

Why didn't you write? Call?

What did I do?

But what would be the point? Ten years of silence were all the answer she really needed.

She had sworn off feeling anything for this man long ago. Yet one look at him and all the old hurt and rage resurfaced as though they'd been waiting for the chance. That made her mad.

She put the car in gear, determined not to waste another minute thinking about Tyler O'Neill. "Have a good night, Tyler," she said, liking all the cool "go screw yourself" she managed to fit into those words.

It seems Juliette has an old score to settle with Tyler.
Pick up TYLER O'NEILL'S REDEMPTION
to see how he makes it up to her.
Available September 2010,
only from Harlequin Superromance.

**Watch out
for a whole new look for
Harlequin Superromance,
coming soon!**

*The same great stories you love
with a brand-new look!*

Unexpected, exciting
and emotional stories
about life and falling in love.

Coming soon!